SEVEN PENNIES
and other short stories

SEVEN PENNIES
and other short stories
Zsigmond Móricz

Selected and translated
by George F. Cushing

Corvina

Introduction by G. F. Cushing
Design by Péter Maczó

© Corvina Kiadó, 1988

ISBN 963 13 2714 0

CONTENTS

INTRODUCTION: BY G.F. CUSHING: ZSIGMOND MÓRICZ ... 7
SEVEN PENNIES *(Hét krajcár)* ... 25
JUDITH AND ESTHER *(Judit és Eszter)* ... 31
TRAGEDY *(Tragédia)* ... 39
ZSUZSANNA IN KLAGENFURT *(Zsuzsanna Klagenfurtban)* ... 46
HOW GOOD PEOPLE ARE! *(Milyen jók az emberek)* ... 54
IT WOULD MAKE THE TOWER OF THE BIG CHURCH FALL DOWN *(Amitől a nagytemplom tornya ledőlne)* ... 59
BARBARIANS *(Barbárok)* ... 63
THE SWINEHERD'S FILTHIEST SHIRT *(A kondás legszennyesebb inge)* ... 78
EVENING BY THE FIRE *(Este tűz mellett)* ... 84
THE FLOCK AND ITS SHEPHERD *(A nyáj és pásztora)* ... 88
IT'S INCOMPREHENSIBLE *(Ami megérthetetlen)* ... 99
THE GENTLEMAN ON THE VERANDAH *(Az úr a tornácon)* ... 105
TO EAT ONE'S FILL FOR ONCE *(Egyszer jóllakni)* ... 109
ANGELS OF LITTLE WOOD *(Kiserdei angyalok)* ... 129
THE SCHOLARSHIP *(A stipendium)* ... 151
SULLEN HORSE *(Komor ló)* ... 156
CELESTIAL BIRD *(Égi madár)* ... 178
DIARY OF THE ELECTION AT SZEGHALOM *(Napló a szeghalmi választásról)* ... 181
CHICKEN *(Csibe)* ... 188
LODGERS *(Ágylakók)* ... 199
THE DOCTOR *(Az orvos)* ... 207
THE RAM *(A kos)* ... 210
GEESE *(Libák)* ... 214
LITTLE ORPHAN ANNIE *(Árvácska)* ... 219
THE BREATH OF SPRING ON THE HORTOBÁGY *(A Hortobágy tavaszi lélegzete)* ... 225
ON THE WILLOW-CLAD BANKS OF THE TISZA, WHERE I WAS A CHILD *(Ficfás Tiszaháton, ahol gyermek voltam)* ... 235

ZSIGMOND MÓRICZ

(1879—1942)

"Small nations talk rather defiantly about their great men. They know that the world really has no time to discover them." So wrote the essayist László Németh in an article for German readers at the time of Móricz's death in 1942.[1] For Hungarians, Zsigmond Móricz is one of the outstanding authors of a period rich in good writing, a man with a profound knowledge of his country and its problems, both political and social. He entered into a literary tradition whose main aim was to serve the nation, a *littérature engagée*, in which it was seen as the duty of the writer to criticise and instruct rather than merely to entertain. He continued this tradition admirably, writing for a Hungarian public on themes concerned with the life of the country.

He lived through a period of European history that provided him with abundant material. He grew up during the rapid industrialization and sudden growth of Budapest into the brash new metropolis it had become in 1896, when Hungarians celebrated the first thousand years of their occupation of the Danube basin with great ceremony, including the inauguration of the first underground railway in the continent of Europe. By contrast, the mechanization of farming and the appalling social conditions prevailing in the countryside led to the mass emigration of agricultural workers to the United States as well as a rush to find work in the new factories that ringed the capital, whose suburbs rapidly evolved into slums. There was considerable unrest, and a succession of weak governments did nothing to alleviate the problem. On the surface there was relative

---

[1] László Németh, "*Móricz Zsigmondról, külföldieknek*". In: *Homályból homályba*, Budapest 1977, Vol. II, 420.

prosperity and security, at least for those in power, who saw no reason to tackle a question that had lain unsolved for generations. Then in swift succession came the First World War, the disintegration of the Austro–Hungarian Monarchy, the short-lived Hungarian Republic and the Communist régime of Béla Kun, and finally the Treaty of Trianon, which reduced the territory of Hungary to almost its present area and deprived her of vital raw materials. Then followed the Horthy régime and the clamour for revision of the Trianon frontiers, the financial crises of the inter-war period and the rise of fascism, which led inevitably to the Second World War. Rarely can a profoundly sensitive and critical writer have had so much contemporary material at hand. It was the unsolved and ever more acute social problem to which Móricz kept returning; nowhere in Europe was there such a huge gap between the privileged few and the deprived masses, the rich aristocracy and the poor peasants (and later the urban slum-dwellers), and it was to the accurate portrayal of the society in which he lived that he devoted most of his work.

Móricz was born in Tiszacsécse, a small village in northeast Hungary and a place he recalls with affection in *On the Willow-clad Banks of the Tisza, Where I Was a Child*.[2] His parents, in his words, "came from two different poles": his father was an ambitious peasant, all too ready to risk his money in enterprises that came to nothing, and his mother came from a long line of Calvinist ministers. His father's side of the family was on the way up, his mother's on the way down. 'Peasant' is an all-embracing term; in Hungary it refers to the agricultural population who happened not to be noble and therefore had no electoral rights. Some had land, others had none; some possessed flocks or herds, others lived as day-labourers; some were comparatively well-off, but the majority of them lived in poverty and virtual serfdom. The Móricz family, which eventually included six boys and a girl, seesawed between relative wealth and abject poverty. The ambitions of the father

---

[2] See p. 235.

pushed it up in the world for the first few years of young
Zsigmond's life, but then he overreached himself: he invested in a steam threshing-machine which blew up before
it could be paid for, whereupon the family was forced to
sell up everything and drag out a miserable existence for
some years until the father's industry put it on its feet
again. The atmosphere of this period is well caught in
Judith and Esther,[3] and indeed the ups and downs of his
early life left a lasting impression on Móricz. He wrote an
unusual autobiography entitled *The Novel of My Life*,[4]
which covers only the first ten years of that life, since

> this was really the whole of my life. All that made me what
> I became happened during this period. More occurred to
> me up to the age of ten than during the succeeding fifty
> years.[5]

This is a pardonable exaggeration, but then the book itself
is an unorthodox mixture of family history, local tradition,
folklore and a lyrical evocation of childhood.

Zsigmond received a good education, as indeed did all
his brothers and sister. His father held strong views on the
subject, and even during the worst misfortunes of the
family the education of the children was never neglected.
Zsigmond was a bright boy and went first to the prestigious
Calvinist college in Debrecen, one of the foremost schools
in the country; he revelled in it, despite the handicap of
being a poor pupil who had to earn money by tutoring.
When the family moved to Sárospatak, home of another,
equally famous Calvinist college, he was transferred there,
but failed to settle down in what he felt was too cloistered
an atmosphere. He finished his schooling in yet another
Calvinist school at Kisújszállás on the Great Plain, where
a maternal uncle was headmaster. Here he quickly recovered his spirits and gained a reputation for scholarship.
He had access to the staff library and was able to indulge
his passion for reading, which led him to history and philos-

---

[3] See p. 31.
[4] *Életem regénye*, Budapest, 1939.
[5] *Op. cit.* 372.

ophy in particular. He also enjoyed walking the flat countryside and meeting people; this was something he maintained throughout his life, and helped to develop his sharp eye and keen ear not only for dialects but also for the nuances of expression and behaviour that can be seen throughout his work.

After school he first followed his mother's advice to study theology, and went back to Debrecen. But he soon gave this up in favour of his father's recommendation to study law "to win back all the money those sharks of lawyers have wrung out of me."[6] This did not satisfy him either; he had already decided to become a writer and after moving to Budapest in 1900 he gave up law for literature. His maternal uncle helped him to obtain a post as a clerk and indeed encouraged him considerably in his efforts. It was a lonely and dismal period, relieved briefly by a return to teach temporarily at Kisújszállás. In 1903 he was offered a job with the new daily *Az Újság* (The News), for which he wrote short reports of cultural events in the capital and edited the children's column. It gave him the opportunity to write, but he found it difficult:

> I felt the empty, facile contortions and the superficiality of what I was writing and I simply could not change it...
> I felt compelled to write and neglected my studies for this... but it wouldn't work. I wrote day and night, pouring out words—but I had nothing to write about.[7]

Then his sympathetic uncle died, and he bought a revolver to end his life, convinced that he had come to the end of his resources: he had no qualifications as a scholar and could not fulfil his ambition.

This romantic gesture on the part of a young man in his twenties may appear strange towards the end of a century in which creative artists have often made their mark later in life, as did T. S. Eliot and Ralph Vaughan Williams. But in Móricz's youth the legacy of the nineteenth century

---

[6] Tamás Kiss, *Így élt Móricz Zsigmond*, Budapest, 1979, 58.
[7] Zsigmond Móricz, "*Jókai: Jegyzetek a belső fejlődés történetéhez*". In: *Tanulmányok I*, Budapest, 1978, 436.

was still strong, particularly in Hungary. That had been a time when a vast host "clambered up Olympus in school uniform; throughout the world the poetry of the first half of the century was that of callow youth, almost of child prodigies," as one writer put it.[8] Keats, Shelley, Byron and Petőfi had shown the way, and the pressure to produce a masterpiece early in life was intense. Móricz was not alone in his sense of failure; the novelist Kálmán Mikszáth (1847–1910) had gone through a similar black period, and his contemporary, the poet Ady (1877–1919), always felt that he was old because he did not produce a worthwhile volume of verse until he was in his twenty-ninth year. Fortunately Móricz overcame his impulse. He courted a young teacher he had met and married her in 1905. Eugenia Holics, or Janka as he called her, became the model for several of his female characters as well as an indomitable critic of his work. It was not a happy marriage; they were both demanding personalities, and Janka found it increasingly difficult to accept her husband's frequent absences and flirtations, for what he failed to find in her he sought in other women. They remained together for twenty years, but then she committed suicide. It is no surprise that one of Móricz's recurrent themes is conflict between man and woman, often based on sheer lack of comprehension. And one of his favourite characters is a man who is worn down by two women, one who is happy and the other beautiful. Something of this tension can be seen in such tales as *It would Make the Tower of the Big Church Fall Down*, *The Doctor* and *Geese*.[9] Móricz's second marriage to the actress Mária Simonyi was no more successful and broke up after ten years, by which time the daughters of his first marriage had grown up and he was able to share some of their family life. Between 1903 and 1907 he at last found congenial employment. He was engaged to collect folk tales and verse in the region he knew and loved best, his home county. This he did systematically and thoroughly, tramping from

---

[8] Gyula Illyés, *Petőfi* [English edition], Budapest, 1973, 64.
[9] See pp. 59, 207 and 214.

village to village, visiting some fifty places in all. The collection of folklore material in Hungary had been in progress for over half a century, but there were still gaps to fill. Moreover there was a new interest in it from the musical side: it was in 1906 that Bartók and Kodály produced their pioneer collection of Hungarian folksong settings.[10] Móricz recalls this time as one which restored his confidence in his future: "These four or five years spent in travelling round these districts became my university."[11] More important, he found here the material for his first successful writing. He experienced village life in the raw, a far cry from the idyllic village of the nineteenth-century romantic novel or the operettas then fashionable, and distant enough from his own childhood recollections of Tiszacsécse, where he was protected by the family.[12]

> I was young, and I felt indescribably happy that I was able to walk around this glad and shining world. But one winter day I happened to be sitting in a dark little peasant house. It was stuffy, smelly and gloomy. Outside the snow sparkled like a fairy-tale, while inside people lived like polecats in lairs. Some young girls came over from next door and three or four of them began to dictate song-texts all together so that I could hardly manage to write them down... All of a sudden the door was flung open and in rushed a young man with a knife in his hand; he grasped the throat of an old woman sitting by the stove and screamed at her in a wild, inhuman screech, 'I'll kill you, you old beast, you're not my mother: I disown you, you bitch...' Everyone froze. The man looked at me and, confused at the presence of a stranger, let go of the old woman and slunk out of the room. I was terribly shaken by this scene.[13]

This was when Móricz began to carry a small notebook with him wherever he went, to record what he saw and heard—a conversation, an anecdote, a family scene, a

---

[10] *Magyar népdalok*, Budapest, 1906.
[11] "*Népköltési gyűjtő*". In: *Tanulmányok* I, Budapest, 1978, 756.
[12] See p. 235.
[13] *Op. cit.*, 758.

dialect word—for use in his writing. Thus one of his short stories is little more than a dialogue overheard at a railway junction between trains and another is the result of listening to fellow-travellers talking in the railway carriage. For Móricz was a good listener; he had the ability to make others talk to him. Many photographs of him show him sitting with someone, writing down their words in one of his many notebooks. Here a more extreme English example comes to mind—that of Arnold Bennett sitting beside his father's bed recording the approach of death, a scene he used later in *Clayhanger*. Or there is Ronald Blythe, listening to the villagers who appear in his classic *Akenfield*.

Móricz was able to win the confidence of his informants by his approach. Walking was not only a favourite pastime, but an invaluable asset. In later life one of his slogans was "It's good to walk" *(Gyalogolni jó)*, and it was a practical piece of advice. Gyula Illyés records how some socialist leaders once visited a large estate to investigate the real situation of the farm-workers. They made the fatal mistake of arriving in a carriage, whereupon the labourers immediately classified them as gentry and answered their well-meaning queries with the deference and total lack of frankness appropriate to their betters, so that they never discovered the truth.[14] This recalls the scene in Howard Spring's *Fame is the Spur*, where Pen Muff refuses to go home in a carriage from a socialist meeting. Móricz insisted on walking even in his later years when he was troubled by a bad leg. Shortly before his death in 1942 he visited Transylvania, eager to see how folk lived in the Székely region; to the surprise of his hosts he insisted on walking or at most travelling third class or even on the back of a lorry.[15] And some of his experiences moved him very greatly indeed. Shortly after he had made his name, in 1910, he was invited to tea by a Countess Teleki, who recounted an appalling disaster that had just occurred in Eastern Hungary. A big dance had been held in a barn at the

---

[14] Gyula Illyés, *People of the Puszta*, Budapest, 1967, 228.
[15] György Bözödy, "*Móricz Zsigmond a székelyek között.*" In: *Móricz Zsigmond közöttünk*, ed. L. Kántor, Bucharest, 1979, 122.

village of Ököritó, and the doors had been locked to prevent
intruders. The barn caught fire and 325 young men and
women from 18 villages died in it, while 99 were injured.
Móricz was so distressed that he took down the story in
his notebook as it was related, then forgetting his hostess
and his tea hurried away to write about it in one of his
most powerful reports.[16] Thereafter he often used the theme
of fire as something at once good and bad; one of his most
effective novels is entitled *A fáklya* (The Torch; 1917):
it concerns a young Calvinist minister who arrives in an
East Hungarian village full of plans to improve the lot of
his flock. He is determined to be a torch to light the way
for them, but all he succeeds in doing is to burn himself
out wastefully, unable to achieve anything in the face of
the apathy and ignorance he encounters there. It is, incidentally, an accurate reflection of Móricz's own state of
mind at that stage of the First World War.

He came to fame suddenly, as the result of one short
story, *Seven Pennies*,[17] a simple, unembellished tale of
mother and son who spend a whole afternoon trying to
discover seven pennies to buy a bar of soap. The search
is turned into a game, and when all attempts to find the
final penny have failed, it is a beggar who provides it. This
would have made a dramatic end in itself, but Móricz goes
on: by now the whole exercise is proved fruitless, since it
is dark and there is no oil for the lamp. At this the mother
chokes with laughter and the boy has to support her; as he
does so, her blood drips on to his hand. The story, told
by the boy, is not autobiographical. The evocation of
poverty is certainly true, but Mrs. Móricz did not die of
tuberculosis in Zsigmond's boyhood. *Judith and Esther*,[18]
written at the same time, is much more concerned with real
events and again shows Móricz's love of a startling ending.
He always possessed a strong sense of drama, but in these
early stories he also demonstrated something unusual in

---

[16] "*Ököritó*", Nyugat, 16 April 1910; also in *Erkölcsi sarkantyú
(Tanulmányok II)*, Budapest, 1982, 232—40.
[17] See p. 25.
[18] See p. 31.

Hungarian writers—an ability to treat his readers as adults who can draw their own conclusions from the evidence he supplies. But if this beginning points to the making of yet another East European peasant-writer, Móricz's subsequent career belies it.

Having achieved immediate recognition with *Seven Pennies* and the volume that included it, he became absorbed in writing. He produced altogether 36 novels and novellas, some 600 short stories, a few plays, a large number of so-called reports and literary studies and some poetry. Of these, the novels, novellas and short stories are the most important—and so are some of his reports which are difficult to distinguish from the short stories. His plays can be discounted, despite his fondness for the stage.

> All his life he struggled to write for the stage, and indeed he wrote a great deal from cabaret via opera libretti and adaptations of his novels to major dramas, but he could never produce dramatic form and his works were almost all unsuccessful or else hardly lived beyond the day of their birth—writes his biographer Péter Nagy.[19]

As for his literary studies, they cover a wide range from Greek drama, Shakespeare and Molière to modern Hungarian literary problems and indicate the scope of his reading and scholarship. The reports and short stories show him at his best, and often use the same material. There is little difference in style, and a lyrical note is liable to appear in both; moreover the volcano that smoulders in Móricz can erupt with equal violence in them. Thus *Sullen Horse*[20] has much in common with *The Breath of Spring on the Hortobágy*,[21] and the directness with which he reports the election at Szeghalom[22] is paralleled in many of his stories.

A survey of the whole of Móricz's work reveals first that he wrote almost exclusively about contemporary Hungary.

---

[19] Péter Nagy, *Móricz Zsigmond*, Budapest, 1975, 91.
[20] See p. 156.
[21] See p. 225.
[22] See p. 181.

True, he wrote a vast historical trilogy on Transylvania (*Erdély*, 1922–35), painstakingly researched so that every detail should be historically correct, and started on another about Sándor Rózsa, a swashbuckling bandit who fought in the 1848 revolution (*Rózsa Sándor a lovát ugratja*; 1941, and *Rózsa Sándor összevonja a szemöldökét*; 1942), but these works contain more than a hint of contemporary social attitudes and problems. This does not imply that he was uninterested in the world outside Hungary—indeed he revealed himself as very much a child of his age in some of his comments on the Europe he knew. And though he wrote primarily for Hungarians, it is interesting that he financed the translation of some of his work into German and tried hard to interest North American publishers in his books.[23]

Secondly, it is clear that at some stage in his career he set himself the task of writing about the whole of Hungarian society as he saw it. No other writer gives such a complete picture of it between 1909 and 1942. In the main it is a sombre picture, based on his own observations of life in both country and city, but it is tempered with compassion for his fellow human beings—and not only the peasants and slum-dwellers. There is the occasional glint of humour, as can be seen in *Evening by the Fire*[24] and *The Ram*.[25] After his first success as a short-story writer he produced a long novel. *Sárarany* (Pure Gold), originally written in instalments in the journal *Nyugat* (West), was revised extensively before it appeared in book form in 1911. It concerns the fate of an ambitious peasant who cannot find room for his talents to flourish; he has plans to improve his standard of living, obtain more land and grow better crops, but he is ground down between two women, a faithful wife and an attractive mistress, and is frustrated by the general immobility around him. All his energy—and Móricz firmly believed in the idea of 'primeval strength'—goes to waste and finally he commits murder. It is an extreme picture;

---

[23] *The Torch*, translated by Emil Lengyel, was published in New York in 1931.
[24] See p. 84.
[25] See p. 210.

the language is deliberately coarse and the erotic scenes are overplayed. Yet in the inevitable comparison with Zola and Maupassant Móricz scores with his knowledge of the different castes among peasants and their reactions; moreover the tragedy arises from a genuine desire for improvement, not from innate conservatism or national causes. Nevertheless this is the kind of novel that positively invites a Stella Gibbons to go to work on it—some of the descriptive passages and conversations would not be out of place in *Cold Comfort Farm*. It is not surprising that Frigyes Karinthy, whose parodies exposed the weaknesses of many of his contemporaries, wrote a merciless brief parody of *Pure Gold*.[26]

Móricz moved on to small-town society in his next novel, *Az isten háta mögött* (Behind God's Back; 1911), which contains not a single peasant character. An elderly schoolmaster marries a young wife who tries desperately to find some pleasure and excitement in the utter dullness of the town in which she is forced to live—incidentally the kind of environment from which Janka had come. She is trapped there, and driven mad by frustration attempts to commit suicide by jumping out of a window. But even this fails: she merely lands with a bump in the mud. Her husband is totally uncomprehending, nor can he understand why one of his companions can never seem to get his name right. "He always called me something like Bóvári, though I've told him often enough that my name is Pál Veres, and that's very different."[27] And at the end of the book, unashamedly inspired by *Madame Bovary*, but compressed into a mere 48 hours, nothing at all has changed. *The Torch* introduces the clergy and at the same time continues the idea of the struggling hero already seen in *Pure Gold*. This theme, the fate of a man of ideas whose reforming zeal is quenched by the apathy around him, is often found in the bitter novels of the nineteenth-century author Lajos Tolnai (1837–1902), a writer Móricz much admired. It appears

---

[26] *Így írtok ti !*, Budapest, 1912.
[27] *Az isten háta mögött*, *Móricz Zsigmond regényei* I, Budapest, 1975.

again in *Úri muri* (Gentlemen Having Fun; 1928), whose hero is a progressive landowner and an eccentric; at the height of a huge party he sets fire to his house to provide more light for his guests and then commits suicide. The book is much more subtly written than its predecessors; the anecdotes which appear frequently reveal the characters of the merrymakers and carry the plot forward to its dramatic conclusion. Moreover there is a splendid mixture of gaiety and gloom, mud and paradise, and the gentry in the midst of it all are not condemned outright by the author, as some critics try to make out. For at least until the last decade of his life Móricz believed that the key to the future prosperity of Hungary lay in the hands of the authorities and the gentry. György Bözödy stresses the point that he was an objective observer of the whole of society. Some of his friends,

> who could not see the whole of Zsigmond Móricz but only the side that pleased them, could not reconcile themselves to the fact that he occasionally expressed a good opinion of 'officials'... They would like to have made him belong to a party, in literature and public life alike. But he did not belong to any 'side'; he belonged to Hungariandom as a whole.[28]

Criticism of the gentry does appear very forcefully in the last of his novels on the theme of the struggling hero. In *Rokonok* (Relations; 1932) the nepotism and corruption of small-town society overwhelm the central character, who is driven to attempt suicide. But here he is himself a weak and vacillating person, as grey as his opponents and relatives who weave the web of corruption around him. It is a bleak novel with no dramatic conclusion; we do not even know whether the hero dies or returns to his problems.

If the picture of these novels is sombre and serious, this is explained in a letter Móricz wrote to his eldest daughter, Virág, in 1930. Recalling his early attempts at writing, he states:

---

[28] *Op. cit.*, 125–6.

> I wrote and wrote, but each of my efforts was worse than the last. I did not know what I ought to describe. Here was life, and everyone talked in the same way, in Hungarian: how was it possible to characterize people, to differentiate them? And what was there in a person's life that was worth describing and had to be described?
>
> It took me a very long time to learn this thoroughly. It was very late indeed, after the age of twenty-eight, when I realized that in reality you can only describe what causes you pain. What wounds you. And what is revenge.[29]

This is certainly true of many of the short stories, like *Tragedy*,[30] the tale of a man whose name ('John Little' in translation) is as insignificant as his life and unnoticed death, or *Barbarians*,[31] with its grim depiction of greed and meaningless brutality in peasant society. And at the end of these stories there is no suggestion that anything can or will change. But the letter continues:

> And then at the age of forty-eight I learnt that it was possible to write something else that was not an individual affair—something that can give delight.[32]

This new ingredient is best seen in one of his most unusual books, *A boldog ember* (The Happy Man; 1935), in which a distant relative tells the story of his happy life from childhood through early manhood before the First World War to the present. It is based on a real account, but the hand of the experienced author guides it. The tale is told naturally, with a gentle humour and no trace of complaint or rebellion. All the hero does is to work hard and try not to make any enemies: he is a survivor, and content with his lot.

> I stayed in the village. Now I've got eight acres of land there. I've brought up five children. I've given away two

---

[29] Virág Móricz, *Apám regénye*, Budapest, 1963, 34.
[30] See p. 39.
[31] See p. 63.
[32] Virág Móricz, *loc. cit.*

of my daughters. One of my sons is apprenticed to a master
tailor. And the others are healthy and good children.³³

Here Móricz's technique has altered; instead of leading
the reader into a dark and brutal world that demands
reform, he leaves him to the disturbing realization that
the hero's happiness is based on an absolute minimum of
demands from life and a total lack, indeed ignorance, of
the benefits of modern civilization. *The Happy Man* is a
mixture of novel and report. The naivety of its central
character recalls that of the child-hero of one of Móricz's
most popular works, *Légy jó mindhalálig* (Be Faithful unto
Death; 1921). Móricz relaxes when he writes about children
and young adults; he understands the problems of growing
up and treats them with sympathy and gentleness—characteristics not associated with much of his writing. *Be Faithful unto Death* describes the vicissitudes of a small boy who
arrives from a peasant home to study at the Calvinist
College of Debrecen. Misi has been brought up in a loving
home, and believes that the adult world is good. His faith
is shaken by his experiences in Debrecen, but not broken,
and his character is strengthened as he endures life at
school. Certainly there is much autobiographical material
here, but the book was not intended to be a straightforward
school story. Móricz was surprised at the reaction of a
public that normally read between the lines but totally
failed to do so on this occasion. He later declared:

> In the tragedy of Misi Nyilas it was certainly not his
> sufferings at Debrecen that I was describing, but the things
> I suffered during and after the Commune... At that time
> I was the victim of a terrible storm. I experienced a kind
> of naive and childish suffering that could only be demonstrated through the mysteries of a child's mind; but there,
> the whole world accepted and saw in it the fate of a child.³⁴

---

³³ *A boldog ember, Móricz Zsigmond regényei*, IV, Budapest, 1976. 311.
³⁴ Letter of 12 December 1930 to Olga Kardos, née Magoss, quoted
in Péter Nagy, *op. cit.*, 213.

So Móricz, like many of his contemporaries, had to write out of himself the emotions aroused by the cataclysmic events of 1919 and their aftermath. But he continued the story of his young hero in two other books, *Kamaszok* (Teenagers; 1928) and *Forr a bor* (Wine in Ferment; 1931), though neither of these reached the standard or popularity of *Be Faithful unto Death*. The little boy in *The Ram*[35] demonstrates something of Móricz's lightness of touch when writing about children, but where they are victims of cruelty his anger is uppermost, as in *Little Orphan Annie*.[36]

It was in Budapest that Móricz began to study young folk. The lad and girl in *Angels of Little Wood*[37] are portrayed with sympathy and understanding; both the girl and her father have much in common with the hero of *The Happy Man*, making the most of life and helping neighbours in the shanty-town that did indeed exist on the south side of Pest. Gitka, with her ready tongue and obvious delight in cheating the tram-company, is an example of urban youth encountered later in the orphan heroine of *Chicken*[38] and *Lodgers*.[39] These tales are based on the stories of a slum girl who entertained Móricz with her apparent naivety and fertile imagination, and introduced him to a new section of society. He eventually adopted her, somewhat to his family's consternation, and she took his name.

The blurred distinction between report and story is evinced in many of his shorter pieces. He wrote on all aspects of contemporary Hungarian life, and one of the most pressing problems of the inter-war period was the single-child family, which is the background to *The Flock and its Shepherd*.[40] It was not poverty alone that caused parents to have just one child, but the law of inheritance,

---

[35] See p. 210.
[36] See p. 219.
[37] See p. 129.
[38] See p. 188.
[39] See p. 199.
[40] See p. 88.

according to which inherited land was divided equally among a deceased parent's children. So if the first child was a boy, it was common, particularly in Protestant communities, to have no more children; girls could be married into other families. In Móricz's story the minister, like the teacher in *The Scholarship*,[41] has no answer to the arguments advanced by men who know more of life than he does. Nor does the author; all he does is to pose the problem and show how absurd it is to expect acceptance of a particular solution, however rational it may appear. The same kind of situation occurs in *The Swineherd's Filthiest Shirt*,[42] where there is no 'meeting of cultures', as Móricz puts it; medical science and folk beliefs simply collide and the victim dies.

What Móricz shows throughout his work is that the lowest strata of society are not to be regarded as stupid. They have brains and use them, though their logic may appear strange to the educated. So the old peasant in *The Scholarship*, already suspicious of the young teacher when he arrives at the school, simply regards his proposal as a trick to take away what is his by right. He is not concerned that his grandson is the bright hope of the school and deserves a good education; he is merely a unit of labour, and as such must be replaced if he goes away. The teacher cannot understand this attitude, like the patronizing gentleman in *It's Incomprehensible*,[43] whose offer of help is so decisively rejected, or the kindly sister at the old people's home in *Celestial Bird*.[44] All of them believe that they are doing good to those less fortunate than themselves and they cannot understand why their offers are rebuffed or how they have offended against human dignity.

This does not imply that Móricz has a nostalgic view of the past or believes that society is static. He looks to the future and enjoys the challenge of the new, as can be seen

---

[41] See p. 151.
[42] See p. 78.
[43] See p. 99.
[44] See p. 178.

in his sympathetic portrait of the boy in *Sullen Horse*[45] who is determined to escape from the traditions of the Hortobágy. This is paralleled by his marvellously lyrical account of the arrival of spring in the same region, where the introduction of rice, a totally new crop, offers hope for the future. *The Breath of Spring on the Hortobágy*,[46] one of Móricz's last pieces of writing, is a masterpiece of description. It is to be compared with *Sullen Horse:* in the former the author is the only human being in the scene, listening to bird-song and observing nature in detail, while in the latter all is noise and human life with nature in the background. Both read like filmscripts.

Móricz wrote little about his attitude to writing. In a radio talk of 1930 he declared that he saw himself as a sentry on the watch. "If I do say anything, I feel a sense of responsibility—what is it that I must say to all Hungarians?"[47] That feeling was and is shared by most Hungarian writers, who believe that it is their responsibility to point the way to a better future. He carried this sense with him when he was invited to join the editorial board of *West* after the death of its editor-in-chief in 1929, and he tried hard to widen the horizons of what was already the most influential literary journal in the country. When his efforts failed, he took over another journal *Kelet Népe* (People of the East), in 1939, in order to write as he wanted and to suggest practical ways of ensuring a better future for the country. "Stop playing politics, just build!" was one of his slogans, and one that he himself put into practice at his country cottage at Leányfalu, north of Budapest, though typically he employed labourers who were good talkers and would often entertain him when he went to supervise operations. He also advocated cottage industries, which seemed an intensely practical plan to bring life to the countryside at a time when raw materials were in short supply. And by this time his own observation of Hungarian

---

[45] See p. 156.
[46] See p. 225.
[47] Virág Móricz, *op. cit.*, 406.

society, and more particularly of the situation of the peasants, had been corroborated by the disturbing mass of evidence collected by the so-called 'village researchers'; their statistics and photographs revealed a situation just as grim as Móricz had painted it in his reports and stories. One of his last ventures was concerned with the dissemination of culture. He compiled a cheap paperback anthology of Hungarian literature, mainly poetry, entitled *Magvető* (Sower; 1940) and in a brief foreword emphasized the role of literature in national life, indicating that he had chosen living works that would inspire particularly the youth of the country.

Móricz was a passionate observer of the human scene and a skilful portrayer of its follies. What he saw was bleak and sombre, and he conveyed this with dramatic intensity. But he can be properly accused of merely posing problems and offering no solution; he has no redemptive or reforming message, no glorious future to proclaim, and he rarely probes below the surface. Yet it is precisely his capacity to disturb the conscience of the reader that is his strength. "A real writer," he declared once, "can only discover, communicate and recreate life."[48] This is what he does for Hungarian and foreign readers alike.

George F. Cushing

---

[48] "*Vallomás az íróról*". In: *Tanulmányok I*, Budapest, 1978, 771.

SEVEN PENNIES

What a good thing it was the gods ordained that even the poor should be able to laugh.

In their hovels can be heard not only the sound of weeping and wailing but quite a lot of heartfelt laughter too. Indeed, it is true to say that the poor often laugh when they have more cause to cry.

I know that world well. The generation of Sóses to which my father belonged plumbed the lowest depths of destitution. At that time my father was a day-labourer in a machine-shop. He does not boast about this period, nor does anyone else. But that is the truth.

It is also true that I was never to laugh so much in the rest of my life as I did during that couple of years of my childhood.

How can I laugh, when that merry, rosy-cheeked mother of mine is no longer alive—she who could laugh so sweetly that in the end tears trickled from her eyes and she was seized by such a fit of coughing that it almost choked her...

And even she never laughed so much as when the two of us spent a whole afternoon searching for seven pennies. We searched for them and we found them too. Three in the drawer of the sewing-machine, one in the cupboard—the rest were more difficult to find.

The first three pennies my mother discovered herself. She thought she would find more in the sewing-machine drawer since she took in sewing and always put there whatever money she was paid. For me this drawer was an inexhaustible treasure-hoard; you only had to put your hand inside and there was the fairy-tale table that spread itself.

So I gazed in astonishment when my mother searched through it, scooping everything out, pins, thimble, scissors, pieces of ribbon, braid, buttons, and all of a sudden said with great surprise:

"They've hidden themselves away."

"What have?"

"Those little coins," said my mother with a laugh.

She pulled the drawer right out.

"Come on, sonny; we'll find the naughty things all the same. Wicked, wicked little pennies!"

She crouched down on the floor and put down the drawer as if she were afraid they would fly away; she turned it upside down suddenly, in the way you catch a butterfly with your hat.

It was impossible not to laugh at that.

"Here they are, they're inside," she kept laughing and was in no hurry to lift it up. "Even if there's only one, it must be in here."

I squatted on the ground, watching to see whether a gleaming little coin was peeping out anywhere. There was no sign of movement. As a matter of fact we had no great hope of finding anything inside.

We looked at each other and laughed at the childish joke.

I stretched out my hand towards the upturned drawer.

"Sh!" my mother scared me. "Quiet! It can still slip away. You don't yet know what a sprightly animal a penny is. It runs very fast; it just rolls away. And how it rolls away!"

We rocked from side to side with laughter. We had already had a good deal of experience of the swiftness with which pennies run away.

When we recovered I stretched out my hand again to tip the drawer over.

"Hey!" shouted my mother at me again, and I was so scared that I snatched back my fingers as if they had touched the hot stove.

"Look out, you little prodigal! Why are you in such a hurry to send it on its way? It's ours so long as it's underneath. Just leave it there a little longer. You see, I want to do some washing, and for that I need soap; for soap I need at least seven pence, I can't get it for less. I've got three already and I still need four, and they're here in this little house. They're living here, but they don't like being disturbed, because once they're angry they go away never to be seen again. So be careful: money is very touchy, you've got to treat it gently. With respect. It gets into a huff as easily as young ladies of quality... Look, don't you know some rhyme, some spell that might perhaps charm it out of its snail-shell?"

How many times we laughed during this chatter I don't know. But the snail-charming spell was a very odd one:

> Penny, penny, come outside,
> For your house is all alight...

With that I tipped up the house.

Underneath it were a hundred kinds of rubbish, but no money.

My mother scrabbled around, her lips pursed, but it was no use.

"What a pity," she said, "that we haven't got a table. If we had turned it out on one it would have been more respectable, and the money would have been underneath."

I swept together all the bits and pieces and piled them into the drawer. Meanwhile my mother was thinking. She racked her brains to remember whether some time she had put some money somewhere, but she could not recall it.

But something was pricking my conscience.

"Mother, I know a place where there's a penny."

"Where, son? Let's find it before it melts away like snow."

"It was in the glass-fronted cupboard, in the drawer."

"Oh you wretched child, what a good thing you didn't tell me earlier, or it wouldn't be there now."

We stood up and went to the cupboard, which had long ago lost its glass front, but in the drawer there was the penny I had known about. For three days I'd been preparing to pinch it, but I hadn't dared to. And yet I'd have bought sweets with it if I'd got as far as that.

"Well now, we've got four pennies. Never you mind, sonny, we've got over half. Now we only want three. And if it's taken an hour for us to find this one, we'll discover those three by teatime. Then I can still do one lot of washing before evening. Come along quickly—there may be one in each of the other drawers."

Just suppose there had been one in each drawer! Then there would have been a lot. For the old cupboard in its more youthful days had been in service somewhere where there must have been a lot to stuff away. But in our house it was not overburdened, poor thing; not in vain was it so wheezy, worm-eaten and gap-toothed.

My mother gave a little sermon over each new drawer.

"A rich drawer this one—was. This one never had anything. And this one always lived on credit. So, you wicked, wretched beggar, you haven't got a single penny either. Oh, this one won't have anything; for it preserves our poverty. And as for you, unless you give me something now when I ask you don't ever have anything inside. And this one has the most—look!" she exclaimed, laughing as she pulled out the bottommost drawer, which had no sign of a bottom.

She draped it over my head, and then we sat down on the floor laughing.

"Wait a moment," she said suddenly, "we'll have some money right away. I'll find it in your father's clothes."

There were nails driven into the wall, and on these hung the clothes. And, wonder of wonders, immediately my mother felt in the very first pocket, a penny fell into her hand. She hardly dared to believe her eyes.

"Got it!" she exclaimed. "Here it is! How much have we got now? We shan't be able to count it all. One, two, three, four, five... Five! Now we only need two more. And what's that? Two pennies are nothing. Where there are five, there'll be two more to come."

She searched through all the other pockets with great keenness, but all in vain. She did not find a single one. Even the best joke would not tempt another two pennies out from anywhere.

Now great red roses were burning in my mother's face with all the excitement and labour. She was not allowed to work, because it made her ill immediately. Of course this was exceptional work; nobody can be forbidden to look for money.

Teatime came and went. It would soon be evening. My father had to have a shirt for tomorrow, and it couldn't be washed. Well-water alone would not remove that oily dirt from it.

And then my mother clapped her hand to her forehead.

"Oh, oh! What a donkey I am! Why, I've not looked in my own pocket. But now I've thought of it I'll have a look."

And she did. And there too she discovered a penny, if you please. The sixth.

We became feverish. Now we only needed one more.

"Now you show me your pockets too, in case there's one there."

My pockets! Well, I could certainly show them. There was nothing at all there.

It grew dark, and there we were with our six pennies, which were still not enough. It was just as if we had none at all. The Jew who kept the shop would not give credit, and the neighbours were just as poor as we were, so we couldn't ask for a single penny.

There was nothing else to do but laugh away our penury with a pure heart.

And at that moment a beggar turned up. He launched into a long wailing plea in a sing-song voice.

My mother was almost overwhelmed with laughter.

"Give over, my dear man," she said; "today I've been wasting the whole afternoon because I haven't got one penny—that's all I want for the price of half a pound of soap."

The beggar, a kindly-faced old man, stared at her.

"One penny?" he asked.

"Yes."

"I'll give you that."

"Well, that's all I need—alms from a beggar."

"Don't worry, my dear, I shan't miss it. There's only one thing I'm missing, a patch of land. With that, everything will be all right."

He put the penny into my hand and tottered away with profuse thanks.

"Well, thank God!" said my mother. "Now run along..."

But she stopped for a moment, then burst into a huge peal of laughter.

"A fine time we've got all the money together! Why, I can't do any washing now! It's dark, and I haven't got any oil for the lamp."

Her laughter ended in a fit of choking; painful, devastating choking, and as I went and stood by her to hold her up as she swayed with her face in her two hands, something warm poured on to my hand.

It was blood, her own precious blood. My mother's who could laugh as only few can, even among the poor.

1908

JUDITH AND ESTHER

We were poor. Poorer than beggars, for is there any greater penury than that of gentry who have gone bankrupt?

We hid ourselves away in a little village in the Nyírség, where we possessed not even a square foot of the poor sandy soil, and the sickly-sweet smell of the acacia flowers was torture. Only in our memory did there live on those rich wind-producing rape-fields, herds of cattle and horses, the country house with its pillared veranda, that had once been ours up there on the willow-skirted banks of the Tisza.

We withdrew to the end of the world to conceal ourselves with our shame. At any rate to a place where we had relatives. That relative was good, thought my father, who was warm-hearted and always loved people.

But the relative, the kinsman, was a curse.

The relative lived there in the middle of the village in the largest peasant house, which just sprawled there with its mudbrick pillars and gazed out from its minute windows with a bloated look. What was this compared with our fine country-house? And what a bitter, oppressive air of great haughtiness flooded from it towards us. The relative, Uncle Vince, with his huge double chin, heavy fist and beetling eyebrows, bore the same noble name as we did; all the same, he wanted to put me to work as his servant. He was angry because my father refused to be friendly with him, and was envious because his great grandfather had slipped out of the ranks of the gentry while our branch of the family had managed to hold on for so long. True, when our family fell, it did so with a thump and was squashed flat in the mud like an over-ripe pear.

And what of the womenfolk? My mother was Judith, Judith Simonkay. Her grandmother had been the daughter of a baron, and her relations up there flourished in the world of seven-pointed coronets. Uncle Vince, Vince Szobi Kertész, had a wife called Esther Csitke, and her father was a head horseherd on the Great Plain; it was rumoured that his life had ended at the hands of the gendarmerie.

The two wives were like two sharp knives.

My mother never complained. She became reserved and put up with life without a murmur. But in the village it was rumoured that in the metal-hooped chests she preserved her old velvet skirts with their pattern of tiny flowers, her heavy silks and jewels by the handful. There was a little bit of truth in this, but only very little. My father came and went, cursed, laughed, speculated and hoped; he trusted in everyone, expected something of everyone and was disillusioned every day. Sometimes there were terrible scenes between the two of them.

As for me, I became a quiet little fellow, a timid go-between between my mother and the world. I was frightened of people, I dared not lift a finger. I peered out on the world like a snail, ready to draw in my horns at any moment. And yet it was I who had to go out and about among people. I was the representative of the family vis-à-vis the village. My father was scarcely ever at home; my mother would not even go out into the yard unless it was absolutely necessary. I was the only one who regularly went out of the house to school, to the shop, for milk...

Milk. The thing we missed most of all in our little life. Of all the many little troubles we had to contend with this was the most painful as far as I was concerned. I was very fond of milk and we had no cow. In the village it could not be obtained; even for money it was rarely to be had. Milk was available simply so that there should be something to take to market. Heavens! What a problem it was for me to have to go the rounds of the village almost every day in search of milk. Of course, if my mother had been more ready to talk and had listened to the neighbouring wives' gossip, I should not have had to go for milk. They would have brought it along. But she refused. And I was proud of my mother because she was poor, beautiful and haughty.

One evening at Christmas time milk was the cause of a great event in our house.

I had already been all round the village, timidly proffering the white and red pennies, but not a single glassful could I obtain anywhere. Yet there was plenty of it everywhere. There in my presence they were straining it off into big basins and three-legged pots, yet whenever I asked for some the gaunt, sharp-eyed, money-grubbing peasant women opened wide their two hands and all ten fingers, and with elbows tightly pressed against their hips whimpered, "There isn't any, love. I can't let you have any. We've got to save it. Christmas is coming. We want it for cakes, for pies, for the market. Milk's at a premium these days."

I returned home weary and all ready to whimper.

"There isn't any. They won't give me any."

My mother's large black eyes widened and glinted. She said nothing; she did not sigh, nor did she burst into tears. But I cringed like a little mouse that senses a cataclysm on the way.

My mother also wanted to bake. She said nothing, but fetched the water jug and mixed the dough with water.

And I watched, deep in thought. Outside darkness came quickly, and as the mixing-spoon turned the flour into a lump an idea grew ever more boldly in me.

"Mother..."

She glanced at me, and I came out with it.

"I'll go to Aunt Esther..."

She did not bat an eyelid, though I had made a great pronouncement. I should not have been surprised if the big Bible with its brass clasps that gleamed threateningly on the shelf in the cupboard had suddenly flown at my head of its own accord. We never asked for anything from Aunt Esther, our relative, even if we died of starvation.

But after all she had something like six cows, and for three days we had not seen a spoonful of milk in our house. It was always caraway-seed soup and potato soup... My heart was almost breaking for a drop of milk.

The cold red light of the sun's rays shone in through the window, and my mother just went on stirring and stirring the dough. Then she spoke suddenly.

"Go along."

I thought I was mishearing her. I waited for a moment in case she had second thoughts, but since she did not speak I quickly gathered up the coins from the corner of the table and hurried out. No. I stopped again at the door and looked back at my mother.

"Shall I go?"

"Just get along."

All the way there my heart leapt and pattered.

The dogs nearly pulled me down, and how they made me tremble! And no dogs anywhere were as fierce as those at the Kertész house.

A servant girl appeared and rescued me.

"Where's my Aunt Esther?"

The girl in her finery was grumpy and angry. She seemed to me to be baring her teeth at me more fiercely than their dogs.

"In the stable," she growled at me.

Very innocently, with one eye on the dogs, I slunk off towards the stable. Not even the straw rustled under my feet.

Steam was billowing out of the stable door in clouds.

Suddenly I stopped as if I had turned into a block of ice. Coming from the stable I heard strange cries.

"Leave me alone, will you?" shouted the voice of my Aunt Esther, but it sounded as if she had been pushed.

There was a sound of scuffling. Some plank, the side of the hay-rack creaked as if someone had been pushed against it.

"Villain!" panted Aunt Esther, "filthy villain!"

A man's voice laughed, soft and whinnying.

I recognized it. It was their driver, Feri Pál, the lad with the crane's feather in his hat. Even I knew that he had left his old place of work because of the flashy servant girl and entered service with Aunt Esther and her family.

"What do you want?" hissed my aunt.

"Come on out!" said the lad. "Tonight, come on out!"

There was silence.

And I stood there like a statue. An odd little infant statue of terror. But I did not take in what they were talking about.

"Let me go!" hissed my aunt again.

"Are you coming out? Will you? If you won't come out I'll set fire to the house. Don't keep driving me mad... Once you've woven the spell, come on out... At midnight."

The barred door of the stable crashed open and my aunt dashed out.

As she caught sight of me gaping, scared, lounging just beside the door, she immediately saw that I had heard and understood everything, and at this she was so terrified that she almost dropped the pail.

"What do you want?" she snapped at me with such murder in her eyes that I thought she was going to gobble me up.

"Mother," I stuttered, "sends her respects, Aunt Esther, and would you please give her a bowl of milk?"

"There isn't any!" she roared so loudly that I almost fell over. So saying she turned on her heel and went towards the house. A certain craftiness came over me.

"She'll pay for it," I shouted after her in a voice that astonished me too.

She turned round like someone defending himself against a snapping little dog.

"There isn't any, I tell you!" and on she went. Then she looked towards me once more. "I've got to bake three ovenfuls of cake."

Behind me I heard a nervous guffaw. Feri Pál was standing there. And it was not Aunt Esther I was angry with, but this beast.

I went home crestfallen.

I stood for a long time outside the door before I dared to open it.

My mother had already lit the little night-light. In this part of the country they use lamps with floating wicks in the house as well as in the stables. And I knew very well that there was no oil in our lamp, or in the bottle either.

I put the money down on the edge of the table and whispered,

"She can't give us any. She hasn't got any."

My mother drew herself up and stiffened. I waited for her to shout and curse her.

But she did not speak. She said not a word. She ran her hand over her forehead and said, "All right."

It was a sad, depressing evening. Neither of us said anything. And I just kept looking at the sputtering flame of the night-light as it emitted long wisps of smoke, and thought of all the oil that the big lamp used up, and that there wasn't a drop left in the bottle. And I also thought that it was only two days to Christmas, and if only my father at least would come home for Christmas. Yet it was better for him if he did not come home, because he could not bear even to see this terrible poverty; and when he went away he was always in the company of gentlemen, because only with them was it possible to do business. But it seemed impossible with them too, because he always spent a long time away, yet in the end usually came back on foot without a single penny in his pocket...

I went to bed early, but even then nothing came into my mind except such serious, adult thoughts as these.

It was night-time and quite dark when someone banged on the window.

"Judith! Judith!" we heard.

"Esther!" called my mother. "Is that you?"

"Yes, it is. For the love of God, let me in."

My mother let her in. I was shivering in bed, seized by a cold fit.

There was the sound of a match being struck, but before it could light my Aunt Esther whispered in terror, "No, don't show a light unless you want me to die. Make up a bed; I'm done for."

My mother opened up my father's bed, and my aunt got into it just as she was, with all her clothes on. All of a sudden she gave a scream,

"Oooh, don't touch me. It hurts... He broke my bones!" and she burst into tears. "He gave me a beating. He nearly beat me to death."

I stared into the darkness, but I could see nothing. I listened; my mother might not have been there, I could not hear her make the slightest sound.

The woman wept dully and fitfully.

"Oh what a stupid fool I am! He caught me at it..."

and she ground her teeth, "and he beat me so hard that I fell there in the yard. It's an hour since I was freezing there. Where can I go? He locked me out. I could only come to you. If I went anywhere else, that would be the end of me. Anyone else would tell the whole wide world..."

And she groaned and panted and wept.

"I knew your husband wasn't at home. And in any case you know all about it."

"I?" said my mother.

"Didn't he say anything? The boy?"

I almost fell out of bed.

My mother opened her mouth. She spoke in that terrifyingly calm voice which scared me and almost drove my father mad at times.

"No. My son has said nothing."

And I, "my son," trembled like a poplar-leaf.

My Aunt Esther became silent as a corpse. No more did she speak or weep or utter a sound.

My mother came to bed and I, who slept at the foot of her bed, felt that she was cold as ice.

When I woke up in the morning everything was normal. The stove was already hot and my mother was up and about.

I got dressed and was waiting for breakfast when in came my Aunt Esther's servant.

She was voluble and in good spirits, not as angry and wild as the evening before. She was more inclined to be sarcastic.

"My mistress sends you a bowl of milk. Here's the whole of yesterday evening's milking. She's only skimmed off the cream. She needed the fresh cream for the pies."

"All right, Susie, tell your mistress I'm very grateful... Wait a moment. Take her this pair of earrings as a memento."

And she lifted up the lid of the metal-hooped chest and handed her best pair of earrings to her.

Certainly I did not think the milk expensive. For as Susie went into raptures over the pretty jewels, I was taking stock of the huge, fat earthenware bowl and revelling in it. I was waiting to have milk for breakfast just once more.

But my mother grasped the gigantic bowl and began silently, calmly to tip it into the swill-bucket. For we did have a single piglet as well.

My face turned pale and I was seized by a deadly fear.

My mother looked at me. She started, and her hand poured out the milk in an ever thinner stream.

Finally she gave a great sigh and a tear ran down her painfully beautiful face, whose lines had softened. She spoke.

"All right. Give me your cup, sonny."

1908

TRAGEDY

Everyone was talking about the wedding next day of the Sarudy girl. After their lunch the harvesters lay about in the shade of the stooks or under little improvised shelters made of hayforks and rakes, where a skirt or two provided a little shade for their faces as they lay there. That was enough just to prevent them from getting sunstroke.

These people, who worked as industriously as ants, swarmed merrily over the huge yellow field, and in the midst of all that inhuman labour—which appeared to have no end and no bounds—found pleasure in constantly moving their arms and exercising their lips; the lads and lasses laughed as they pinched and taunted each other, as if this were their chief occupation in life.

János Kis finished eating the apple crumble brought out to him by his freckled, gaping boy, who bore a terrifying resemblance to him. Then he looked round, but he was too lazy to walk as far as a stook and just rolled over where he was in the middle of the stubble. He put his hat over his face and immediately went off to sleep. All he heard was that Pál Sarudy had even killed a calf for the wedding-feast.

With that he went off to sleep.

Nobody bothered about him, not even his own son. He picked up the earthenware pot and looked inside to see whether his father had left a little for him too. He certainly had not. The pot was as empty as if Bodri the dog had already licked it clean. At this he overturned the glazed pot and went off after the dog to look for groundnuts.

When János Kis awoke, his first action was to lick his lips. In his dream he had been at a wedding-feast and had well and truly eaten his fill. It displeased him to realize that he had forgotten all about it, even where he had been and what he had eaten. If only he had not woken up, at the very least!

He was so used to having to give up everything all his life through, that he did not waste much time in self-pity. He turned over and tried to go to sleep again. It was no use. Under his hat, his face turned as red as a boiled lobster. He pushed away the straw hat that was black with dirt and enjoyed the breeze from the field as it cooled his skin.

"Devil take that old Sarudy!" he thought. "I've worked for him quite enough in my lifetime; he might invite me to his daughter's wedding. Let me have a good blow-out just for once!"

He raised his thumb.

"There'll be meat soup. Good, golden, greasy chicken soup. That'll be good. I'll manage a plateful of that."

And now he was gulping it down, sucking at the mass of tiny, yellow-coloured noodles that he shovelled down his throat in handfuls.

"Back to work!" shouted someone.

János Kis moved not a muscle. It occurred to him that in his childhood he had once been at a wedding-feast. It was some relation of his, but all he had of the entire feast was a leg of chicken.

Impotent rage, a wild fit of anger suddenly seized him. He clenched his fist and felt that now he would be able to strike such a heavy blow that everything would be shattered entirely by it.

But the thumb still stuck up stiffly, and when he noticed it he gradually recalled what he had just been thinking about.

"And after that stuffed cabbage... I could eat sixty of those... or if not fifty, then none at all."

"Back to work!" they shouted over there.

He too scrambled to his feet. He felt hungry. He glanced towards the blackened earthenware pot. It was empty... In any case there wouldn't be anything in it but slops.

He gave the pot a kick, a contemptuous and angry kick. That cracked its side. In any case it had been wired together and a piece of wire became caught in his sandal.

"Devil take it!" János Kis swore and kicked off the sandal. "All my life I've always had to struggle along in this poverty and shall always have to. That old scoundrel won't invite me."

All day long he was in a bad temper. Nobody took any notice. János Kis was a kind of invisible man; nobody ever noticed him. That was how he lived all his life. Not for one minute was he ever of any interest. He was neither strong nor weak, neither big nor small. He did not limp and was not haughty. What was there to make anyone notice him? He was just like a human being; he had two eyes and a nose, and he also had a moustache. And never did anything cross his mind. When morning came he got up; at night he went to bed. When the time came, he got married. That was the last time he ate his fill, indeed it made him sick. He had never done military service, and had not been out of the village even ten times, and then only to go to market. As for laughing, he had only had a good laugh once in his life, when his father tried to hit him for having eaten a whole plate of noodles, and as he aimed a blow at him staggered under its weight, fell and hit his head against the wall. He died of it.

And he had only one interest—eating. Because of it he was accustomed to beating his wife, and if ever he thought of anything at all, it was of what would be good to eat. But he was unable to imagine this for long. It was no use: experience did not help him.

That evening as they went home and told the master what they had done—in their village everyone worked on piece-rates—old Sarudy said:

"Men and women, tomorrow evening you can all come to my daughter's wedding-feast. You can eat as much as you can manage."

János Kis almost fainted. He was really scared, scared because he was afraid he would not be able to do justice to the task. The others shouted and cheered, but he remained silent. He stood at the back; night began to fall and nobody bothered about him. Then with the others he too set off for home with heavy steps.

At home he ate his supper, which was sour soup with

bran. He ate it silently, without saying a word. He kicked aside the cat which climbed up his leg and miaowed. He thought of nothing. But he felt very peculiar, as if a great task awaited him, the greatest of his whole life. He was not entirely sure about it, but he thought fearfully of the feast next day.

He was unable to sleep all night long. He kept waking up and tossing and turning, but when he got down to thinking about what was to happen next day, he became very disquieted indeed.

He stretched out his thumb.

"First of all there'll be chicken soup .. I'll have a pailful of that."

He broke into a smile. He thought of all the potato soup, caraway-seed soup, cherry, bran and jam sour soup and all the various mixtures of slops he had ever had in his life; if they were poured into a tub, why, there wouldn't be one anywhere in the world big enough to contain them—even the cellars of the Archbishop of Eger could not produce such a huge barrel. And then if they were to put together all the good food he had ever eaten, perhaps even that old pot he'd kicked over in the field today wouldn't be filled.

Suddenly he seemed to feel his sandals on his feet and the pot with the piece of wire catching in them. He gave a great kick. If he had been in a bed, it would have collapsed straight away, but this straw mattress was not too concerned about such capering. Yet it was a huge kick that János Kis gave. It was poverty that he kicked away from him.

Next morning when he awoke he was grumpy. As he rubbed the bad dream from his eyes, he felt distinctly that his breast was heavy. It seemed to be constricted with iron bands.

"Devil take old Sarudy! Today I'll eat him out of his wealth. I've done quite enough hoeing for him."

He dared not have any breakfast. He did not even taste the food brought out to him for lunch; he was afraid that by evening he would have no appetite.

On other occasions, if he quarrelled with his wife, however often he had to go without eating anything the whole day long, he never noticed it. Now his whole inside trembled, and he became dizzy with hunger.

He clenched his teeth and closed his wide, strong, big-boned jaws and stared stiffly ahead with his grey eyes. He fought himself with the stubborn anger of a wild animal. But he did not eat; he resisted the temptation.

"Fifty stuffed cabbages!" he kept repeating to himself, and with iron determination scythed his way through the field. Rhythmically, like a mechanical harvester.

The world around him ceased to exist. He no longer saw the huge cornfield or the men working around him. He knew nobody, nothing; he had no past and no future, his whole being hardened into one single great desire. It led him on like some superhuman task. And he felt that everything inside him, his stomach had been transformed, and was capable of unbelievable work. As he gazed on the world with fiery eyes, he would have been able to stuff the corn stooks into him like the feeder of a threshing-machine.

At last it grew dark. They finished work and went back. There the feast had been ready since noon. There was no time to prepare for it; they had to sit down at the tables that were already laid.

János Kis got into a corner—so much the better. He sat with his back to the wall, so just let the enemy attack! With just such blind and furious determination one of his distant ancestors must have opposed a Turkish army of some two thousand men.

They brought in the soup.

János did not think anything was too much or too little. He was given a good deep bowl and the cook filled it to the brim for him. The yellow fat floated thick on top of it, not broken up into little pools, but all in one.

János Kis picked up his wooden spoon and set to work, calm and serious. His inside trembled, and he could scarcely control his greed.

At the tenth spoonful he was overwhelmed by a dreadful realization.

He felt he had eaten his fill.

His face turned pale. He sensed that he had undertaken an enormous task. He sensed his human insignificance.

Like a wind, there rushed through his brain the thought that he would not be able to accomplish what he had set out to do.

His features contracted. On his brow vertical lines appeared, his broad firm jaws snapped together and he hurled himself once more into the fray.

Mechanically, just as he wielded his scythe in a curve from right to left, he now lifted his spoon rhythmically to his mouth until he had emptied the bowl.

Then he felt dizzy and horribly nauseated. The food was too greasy for his stomach that was shrivelled and weak and used to slops without fat.

Next came cheese noodles. Tasty, creamy and rich, with bacon fat. His plate was piled high.

And János Kis took out his broken fork with the yellow bonehandle and stowed that away just as composedly as before. He did not notice the flavour of the food. He felt it heavy inside and would have liked to go out for some air. Or at least to give vent to some tremendous, bitter curse. And with unbounded pain and envy he looked round at the people there. Everyone was happy, laughing and wolfing down the food. And he knew already that this was the end for him. He had already eaten as much as he had ever been used to eat at one sitting. But he gritted his teeth and held out his plate for the third course. This was spare-ribs with lentils. Outside among the labourers and servants they were not keeping to the usual order of courses, the one which the best man inside had proclaimed in verse. They were given what was nearest to hand. Some had one course, some another. János Kis had the lot.

So it went on for two whole hours without a stop or a pause.

Then came the stuffed cabbage.

"Fifty!" said János Kis to himself, and a veil came over his eyes.

Among the stuffed cabbage leaves there were big pieces of meat as an extra. And János Kis, wrestling with one of these pieces of tough, uncooked, unchewed meat after three huge stuffed leaves, suddenly stood up in terror. His eyes bulged; they almost leapt out from beneath his eyelids, and the veins in his neck stood out like ropes.

With the last traces of rational thought he dashed out of the house.

He got to the mulberry tree before he had rid himself of the trouble. The piece of meat that had stuck in his throat and almost choked him slid back into his mouth.

Tears welled up in his eyes and he snapped his jaws together so firmly that a wedge could not have been driven between them.

With the drunkenness of passion he said to himself:

"Die then, you dog!"

He swallowed the meat once again.

And this time too he could not manage it. It stuck in his throat and refused to move up or down.

The man's two arms groped in the air, his long lean body twisted round and fell flat on the ground.

He writhed silently on the ground with appalling convulsions until he finally subsided.

Nobody noticed that he had disappeared, just as nobody noticed that he had been there or that he had been alive.

1909

ZSUZSANNA IN KLAGENFURT

Zsuzsanna looked to neither right nor left, but made her way straight ahead beneath the Austrian trees. She was thinking hard and went along almost at a run, like someone hurrying to prevent something being stolen from under her nose... All of a sudden she gave a start of surprise, stopped still and looked around fearfully: would she never be able to find the hussars' barracks?

Terrified, she sniffed around like a little dog who has wandered away from the cart in a strange village. An Austrian in a bowler hat came towards her. Zsuzsanna dared not look at him, but grasped her piece of paper and held it out in front of him. The gentleman read it, looked hard at her and said:

"Well, do you come from Budapest, my dear?"

Zsuzsanna nearly fainted at hearing him speak Hungarian. The blood in her body seemed to drain away and she just stared and stared at the Austrian, blinking at him with her tiny eyes and her wide mouth agape.

"So what's the news in Budapest? I'm Hungarian too!"

"Oh dear sir," said Zsuzsanna, "how ever did you get here? Goodness, what a world it is where they don't understand decent human speech but just croak in their throats—though all the same they understand it among themselves... Please put me on the right road for the hussar barracks."

"Why, have you come to see your husband, my good woman?"

The blood began to rise to Zsuzsanna's cheeks and a lump came into her throat. She found it difficult to blurt out to this man who spoke Hungarian what she had had so much exercise in saying to those foreign speakers:

"Yes," she said, "to see my husband."

And she turned her eyes away, because they had become misty.

"Well, then, my dear, just go straight ahead," said the gentleman, examining the little Hungarian woman with delight. "Go on till you get to a little bridge. There's a little stream there, and you'll see the hussars there rubbing down their horses."

"God bless you, sir," said Zsuzsanna, and set off like a little coloured butterfly above the ground; she ran, because her spirit was anxious and ablaze. Since she had declared in Hungarian to a Hungarian that she was looking for her husband, she did not know where to turn... Suppose the lad wasn't there any longer? Suppose some Austrian girl had pinched him? Men were all rascals. Good God! Why had she followed him here, to this great shame... Why, she had telegraphed to him from Budapest, yet he hadn't come to meet her at the station. Oh dear, if only she hadn't come!

From the bridge she caught sight of the hussars straight away. They were in red trousers and were washing the horses in the stream.

She went down to them and spoke to one of them:

"Can you tell me, love, where Sándor Ember is?"

The hussar looked up from beside his horse, opened his eyes and mouth wide, and then gave a huge shout:

"Come here, you chaps! There's a Hungarian wife here!"

The hussars all rushed up like piglets when they hear the rattle of maize. And in their great joy there was an uproar of laughter and curses. They stared at her, asked questions and sniffed at her, their teeth gleaming white as sugar. And when they had had their fill of the colour and smell of the little Hungarian wife they got down to the main point:

"Sándor Ember? Who knows Sándor Ember?"

The sergeant came along, a man with a big moustache. He too relaxed his sternness and ran his eye over the little Hungarian wife, then shook his head:

"I don't know him. Sándor Ember? Never heard of him."

Zsuzsanna's heart suddenly missed a beat. Then why had she spent all that money? The train alone cost eight forints, and her other expenses came to two forints. The rascal had deceived her. He wasn't here. He'd simply run away from her, because if he were here and were a hussar, then the sergeant must surely know him.

"There's no need to be so upset, love. There's another barracks here, and there are hussars there too. He'll be there, for sure."

"But how am I going to find that place?"

"Trooper Mákos, just show this lady the way to the other barracks."

Trooper Mákos stepped forward, straightening his shirt —for in the warmth of the autumn afternoon he was in shirtsleeves like the other hussars—and they set off with light steps towards the other barracks.

But Zsuzsanna's heart was still troubled. God above! Suppose the lad wasn't there either!... The trooper just blinked at her; he was not a very talkative man, so she just went on thinking about her own troubles. How he had deceived her when he wrote, "Whatever are you thinking of, angel; you can't come here, my dear, the train costs sixteen forints just to get here, that's the fare, dear..." But when she asked a railwayman she knew, it was only sixteen crowns. Of course the rascal had only written that because he was afraid of her; he merely wanted to be free of her, and now here was the trouble, all the lads were in demand, and here some girl would catch him for herself and she could go wherever she pleased... Especially the son of such a well-known rich man, whose father is on speaking terms with the sheriff and had educated all his other sons; only this one was such a rogue even when he was small that he didn't want to study and became a mechanic...

"This is where we go!" said Trooper Mákos.

Zsuzsanna did not say anything; she just went along with him. The whole thing right from the beginning had been nothing but villainy. Even then he had deceived her, when she had been in service at such a good house. He had tempted her away from her place, when once she broke down and declared that she had quarrelled with her mistress (because he kept going to see her, but very grumpily, because she would never let him enjoy himself in the way he wanted...), and then how the young mechanic leapt at her! "Don't you worry, Zsuzsanna, you've worked long enough. I'll tell you what to do: rent a little room and rest there for a couple of weeks. You'll get a better place from the first of October..." How well the swindler knew how to whisper and murmur! He even offered to look for a room since she, the poor little servant, had no time. And she promptly asked for her cards on 15 September and took the little money that was due to her and left her kind mistress. The young mechanic was waiting downstairs and together they walked through the unfamiliar streets to that dreadful strange house, 66, Third Floor, 72 Count Haller Street.

"Indeed we've a lot to put up with here in a foreign land," said Trooper Mákos.

Zsuzsanna stared at him through the tears in her eyes and suddenly wondered what would become of her when she had only one forint and seventeen kreutzers in her little purse; how was she to get home again if Sándor Ember was not here? She wiped her eyes and blew her nose. He deceived me even then, she continued to herself, when we went into that little rented room and I saw a strange chest there. At the time I asked him, "What chest is that, Mr Ember?" But he just hummed and hawed, saying it belonged to the landlady and they'd take it away. And she left it there and they chatted. But the time went on and she was tired then as she was now, and then all of a sudden they locked the outer door and still he hadn't gone away... And she had said to him too, "Look, Sándor, aren't you tired?" Then Sándor Ember had got up, gone to the door and said, "Yes, I'm very tired," and had locked the door. "What are you doing?" "Well, Zsuzsanna, I'm telling you the truth; this room is mine, but never mind!" Then where was she to go for the night, out into the world, and the police would arrest her... whichever way you looked at it, it was a scandal... It was for this that she had had to leave her kind mistress, where she was happy as could be... And he had also deceived her by not telling her that he was to be called up into the army...

"Here we are at the barracks," said Trooper Mákos.

Zsuzsanna poked her head through the bars in the gate, ready to forget all her woes if she could but catch sight of Sándor Ember in the yard. But she could not see him anywhere. There were a lot of hussars all over the place, some in full uniform, others only in shirt and trousers; in the fine autumn sun they were just standing about, walking the horses and so forth. Everyone was there—the only person missing was Sándor Ember.

Trooper Mákos left her there too. He went on ahead, surely to enquire after the villain, and Zsuzsanna, terrified, had a good cry. She might have come up to visit him, just so that he too might realize her condition like everyone else...

"Sándor Ember! Sándor Ember!" she heard them shout. "Has anyone seen where Sándor Ember went?"

Here too a great big sergeant came along, but he was an Austrian, you could tell, his face was red, he had a little moustache, and a long, broad sword hung down from his stomach in front of his legs.

"Sántor Emper," he said, Austrian-fashion, because he did not know much Hungarian. "He's just gone off... Wife... station... telegram..."

Zsuzsanna's mouth trembled. So Sándor Ember was here after all? The good boy, the dear boy!

The whole barracks stirred to life. Everyone knew Sándor Ember. He had only just gone off to the station with Ferenc Sőtér to meet his wife. Well now, it was surprising that they had missed each other... And he'd said that his wife was coming, because she had telegraphed to tell him so.

The little Hungarian girl was thrilled in the great barrack yard; she did not worry now, for after all Sándor Ember was here.

"How did you find your way here, my dear?" That was the kind of question they put to her.

"Oh, heavens!" she replied, "I wouldn't wish such a journey on my worst enemy. I wouldn't have found my way here if it hadn't been for quite a few kind people even among the Austrians. Oh dear, when the train suddenly took me among people who didn't know a single word of Hungarian—neither the conductor nor the passengers, nor women nor children—in a word, nobody! Then there was a gentleman, an old gentleman with such a nice face, and I showed him my piece of paper..."

She pulled it out. The great big sergeant read it through and understood it, because it was written in his language and said, "I am the wife of Sándor Ember. My name is Zsuzsanna Pete, and I am going to my husband in Klagenfurt, where he is serving with the 6th Hussars. I ask kind people to show me where to go."

"Well, that was my good luck, because the old gentleman was also going that way," continued Zsuzsanna. "Bless him, he explained to me with his hands and feet, as if I were deaf, that he was going there too, and I was to go with him and get off where he did... Well, I managed to keep an eye on him all through the long night; I didn't close my eyes even for an instant. Then all of a sudden towards morning at a great big station I saw that the old man was nowhere to be seen. Heavens above! He'd got off! So I jumped out of the train like a madman."

The hussars slapped their thighs with their hands, they laughed so much at the splendid Hungarian tale related by the frightened little wife.

"I was lost, I was really, but the old man noticed that I was lost. Then he ran after me, poor man, telling me to come back. Oh how he dragged me along! I don't know how he found me. He said he'd only got off the train for a glass of beer. And the train started off the moment we'd jumped back on it, though he'd very much have liked to have another glass, poor man, because he got so thirsty on my account... That's how I came here, and those are the woes I had to suffer on the way."

She wiped the perspiration from her face and eyes. The sergeant beckoned to her to come into the office and sit down.

"Now, now, no trouble, not to cry, sh!" he kept on saying to her. "Wife, me, nothing..." and he stuttered and explained to her with the best will in the world that he and his wife would take her in, she could stay with them for three years if necessary while her husband was in the army, she could help in the kitchen.

"Yes, sir," said Zsuzsanna and screwed up her little eyes, looking down at the ground. She'd be a fool to go into service for three years all for nothing! And she wept loudly.

"No, no, sir. Please, I'd rather you let Sándor Ember go. He's a feeble man, a mechanic, and his lungs are full of all that iron-dust and coal-smoke; he's not fit to be a soldier. Please arrange it so that he can come home, Mr. Sergeant, God bless you! And I can't work either, I keep getting fainting fits, and my inside almost turns over when I bend down..."

They explained the little woman's words to the sergeant. The great big Austrian laughed and cried; he raised his right hand and with his thick hand stroked Zsuzsanna's black hair, for by now she had taken the scarf from her head.

"All right, I'll do so... Stop crying, for goodness' sake! *Ein* month, *zwei* month, and that's that... Your husband, I'll do something, you go home."

Zsuzsanna laughed to herself and bent low over the Austrian's big freckled hand and kissed it, however much she hated it.

And at that moment in came Sándor Ember with his mate Ferenc Sőtér. His face was all aflame, Zsuzsanna could see, though her eyes were full of tears. She gave a great cry and leapt into his arms.

"Zsuzsanna Pete!" shouted the lad.

Everyone was glad there, the whole office, the whole barracks—perhaps even the whole town of Klagenfurt trembled just a little with joy.

Zsuzsanna clung to the neck of the long thin hussar.

"You see, I've come to you!"

Sándor Ember saw that everyone shared his joy, and the joke began to please him.

"You don't look at all well, dear," continued Zsuzsanna. "How you must be suffering! But don't worry, it won't last much longer. Here's the sergeant; he's promised he'll make a free man of you in two months... why, I've even kissed his hand for that."

The lad's face stiffened with joy. He hugged the girl with a close and firm grip; he realized what a woman she was!

"Well, Zsuzsanna, you won't regret coming along here... At least you've shown what a good *wife* you are to me!"

Zsuzsanna's eyes filled with tears. At last Sándor Ember had said it...

She drew herself up and smiled a sharp, haughty and proud smile. She was very satisfied with herself.

Ah well, she had known it would be worthwhile coming along... Now those Austrian girls could just look! Now they wouldn't steal her man from under her nose.

1915

HOW GOOD PEOPLE ARE!

"How much are the cherries?"

The fair-haired thin little Jewish woman hurried out with her customary courteous sprightliness and lifted the cover from the finest cherries to be found in the market in Pest.

"Why, finer ones than these even my husband..." and her eyes filled with tears.

I sometimes bought things at this tiny little shop on the corner, where two small wizened gnomes lived. They always had beautiful fruit, and it was cheaper than elsewhere.

I knew nothing about them, but at that moment a thick mist seemed to descend and I felt that I had had a glimpse of a secret and tragic corner of life.

"Where is your husband?"

It was never possible to see these two little people apart, and they were always laughing like happy little gnomes over the baskets full of rich fruit. They were grotesque and kindly.

The little woman looked at me with tear-stained, sunken red eyes.

"He's dead."

For a moment I was struck with terror. This simple declaration of death seemed to come as a personal attack on me.

"Dead?" I repeated.

In this tiny shop full of joyous fruit I had indeed sensed the smell of death before it was really brought to my knowledge. And now I sensed that there were ever deeper and weightier secrets here. How? Why had the happy, courteous little Jew died? His unruffled happiness was almost disagreeable in this heavy world, not to mention the satisfaction that radiated from him. And now all of a sudden he was dead.

"Where did he die?" I asked the woman, almost with hostility.

"In St. Stephen's Hospital."

I was relieved, but I do not know why. A chill, pneumonia... It was no good, he was a little thin chap and could easily have been harmed by anything. I began to feel more at ease and reassured myself by thinking that, after all, everyone has to die, and I too should die. Last autumn a muscle in my leg had snapped as the result of an almost imperceptible and unexpected slip, and that meant that I had spent four months in bed during the winter. One must take note of this and always keep it in view that death is lurking behind our backs; whether one is a huge dromedary of a Russian prize-wrestler or a happy little Jew selling fruit on the corner, it all comes to the same thing: they both run the risk of dying at any moment.

But in the woman's silence, this strained, scared, wan silence that was directed at me, there was something that compelled me not to go off with the kilo of cherries, shrugging off my duty with a commonplace expression of sympathy and protecting myself from the painful realization of the truth.

"What was the matter with him?"

The woman compressed her lips, choked back the tears that were welling, and said simply:

"A chill... Pneumonia..."

I was seized by a new fit of panic; I had received back my own thoughts expressed in words—the same words I had said to myself a minute earlier. The atmosphere grew even heavier; I felt that the woman's grief was reaching out to embrace me, and like an electric light with secret rays, invisible ones like X-rays, was suggesting something to me.

"It was like this," said the little Jewish woman, and her head bent to one side, devoid of strength like a withered flower. "When we got the hundred dollars from Uncle Fuchs in America—we led a difficult life all the time the war was on, my husband was rejected for military service because he was born with one foot twisted inwards—he had an operation when he was a child, but his leg remained as thin as a stick, if you please, and was weak as a fly—yes, well, we kept up our spirits every day by saying that if only we could write to America, all our troubles would be over, Uncle Fuchs would send us money... and that's what happened. In the spring of 1920 the letter came from America with the hundred dollars. Uncle Fuchs wrote that it wasn't the custom in America to make free gifts, and we were not to count on him for a single cent more, but now he was sending a hundred dollars..."

The woman stopped. She felt she had begun her tale a long way off. She collected herself and continued more quickly.

"That was the money we used to buy this little shop here. You remember, it used to be a photographer's, but it went bankrupt because when peace came there was no need to write letters to the front and people didn't have their photographs taken any more. First of all we wanted a sweetshop, but my husband said that was just as much of a luxury as photographs, so we made a greengrocer's out of it. You know, my husband always used to say, 'How good people are, my dear, you must never forget that...' And nobody was nasty to us; I can say that we never got a bad word from anyone... And my husband always bought the finest greens and fruit at the market and sold them at the lowest price, because he hadn't the heart to give the customers rotten apples and maggoty fruit... And thank God, ladies still like to be able to buy good stuff in the shops and, sir, my husband said that the rent of the shop wasn't too much and the overheads weren't too great, so he felt he should sell everything cheaply, and thank God we can't complain; thank God, business is good..."

She told this tale in a quiet, uncertain voice, in self-justification as if she had to clear herself of some charge. She seemed to be talking before a court, and not an earthly one, but something higher, the court of her own conscience.

I listened wearily, as one listens to the explanation of something that is going to depress one savagely and cruelly; it was only the facts I wanted to hear, just the facts.

"Throughout the district the wholesalers were angry—

something we didn't know at the time, sir, we never even imagined it... And a month ago, one Wednesday afternoon, a man stopped by, a gentleman, and bought some Liptauer cheese. A quarter of a kilo of Liptauer, and my husband calculated it at 32 crowns. How did my husband know... And, sir, the gentleman paid for it and said, 'So in your shop one kilo of Liptauer is 128 crowns?' 'Yes, sir,' said my husband. At that the gentleman takes out his notebook and writes down his name, religion, occupation and the price of the cheese, and tells him to report at the police station next day at nine o'clock."

Her voice died away and she clutched nervously at my arm with her thin, freckled fingers.

"Well, sir, my husband went off and, sir, *they didn't lay a finger on him.* No, one can't say that, they didn't so much as touch him, only they sentenced him to a fortnight's imprisonment, a fine of five thousand crowns and the proclamation of the sentence on the posters. And he didn't come home; they kept him there, and it was only two days later that I got to hear about it, when people in the street said that my husband's name was posted there for profiteering, because he had sold Liptauer, which counts as an essential foodstuff, for 128 crowns instead of the maximum permitted price of 84 crowns.

"Well, sir, he came home again last Monday and he didn't say anything, only he was very pale and he dared not show himself in the shop either, because he was so ashamed. And that night he coughed and developed a high fever, and the doctor was good enough to take him immediately to St. Stephen's, and he was in bed there for nine days and all the time he kept saying to me, 'My dear, how good people are! Look, these doctors are treating me so well that you can only bless every step they take.' And on the ninth day he died."

The woman did not weep aloud; but a few tears trickled from her eyes.

"And I didn't know what was wrong with him. He never told me, only he told my brother-in-law that they had made him carry coal up from the cellar."

And she clasped her hands and pressed them to her thin

little breast and looked at me in silence. And I saw the little Jew as with his thin legs that had been operated on and his wizened arm he lugged the coal bucket on his back.

"And since he liked to be clean, he asked them for water to wash in and one of them said to the other, 'Just give him a little water,' and he, sir, threw a pail of water over him..."

She broke off. A customer came, and briskly and courteously she took the cover off the cherries. "Three kilos, Madam? These are the finest cherries, madam, but my husband taught me only to buy the best fruit and sell it at rock-bottom prices..."

And I looked on, watching this strange scene as the little, fair, tousle-haired Jewish woman worked industriously above her basket and scales, while the principle produced by a good soul from his own resources went on working in her.

It was for just such a benevolent little principle that a poor little Jew had to undergo the tribulations of Calvary: just as that other one, the blessed Jesus Christ, had had to suffer it, who carried the Cross and collapsed beneath it like the little fruiterer beneath the coal-basket.

Why, why did they have to die? Was it not because they were indeed right when they said that people were good?

For people are good, but when they are in good health and all is going well for them, their strength does not allow them to realize that this is so.

1923

IT WOULD MAKE THE TOWER
OF THE BIG CHURCH FALL DOWN

There were just the three of them in the room, as usual. She herself, her husband and the Good Friend. They also called him 'Air', because for ten years now they had been unable to breathe without him. It can be imagined what a sensational beauty and in addition what an irreplaceable good fellow he had to be if they never noticed his presence but on the other hand could not exist a single day without him.

The two men, as men will, were talking about something absolutely superficial. With appalling animation and total dedication. They were talking about how to get hold of really good tea today.

She did not hear them; she was incapable of concentrating on this exciting theme. Whether it was via London or Berlin or even Moscow, and what contacts were needed to bring it off. It is odd what preoccupies the male mind.

She was thinking about... Well, what was she thinking about? Quite definitely about when she and her sister... went to say farewell... to her girlfriends... a few days before her wedding... and that was fourteen years ago...

She saw the whole scene in detail, as they walked through the trees, and she was happy, so unspeakably happy... Yet what was that happiness? What had she felt?

And once on the seashore... in Ika, the oleanders were in bloom... like a forest, and the sea was so indescribably beautiful... Big waves, endless water that moved and rolled so happily and regularly, and her own insignificance... A single human being facing the Universe... and she had not felt insignificant, but great and light...

If only she were able just once more to rid herself of the depressing knowledge that *life is serious, infinitely serious*...

Never again had she dismissed the responsibility of Life.

She sought in vain but never found any further moments when she could release herself so much from the burden of the soul. How happy other women are who can take life so lightly!

Now the two men laughed aloud. The Good Friend was telling anecdotes in his own dry style. She laughed with them too, and did not know why and at what she was supposed to be laughing.

"Have I really lost my attraction?" she said to herself with a sudden leap of thought, and closed her eyes. Once upon a time, when she was a girl, she had been able to exercise an attraction for any man if she so wanted... and since she had been married... of course it was a big task to bring up four children and look after them... "But then there's me too!" she said to herself. She too had rights, not only the beings dependent on her—husband, children, friends, company, house and life; everything now seemed to depend on her... and this too was a great burden...

She said something and stood up, and went across the room. It was as if with this movement she wanted to break out of her bonds.

But as she looked out of the window, her heart suddenly missed a beat.

There crossing the road was Someone she had not thought about for such a long time, and who nevertheless continued to live on somewhere right down in the depths of her subconscious mind... And he happened at this very moment... to appear... in person... he looked this way... and her heart missed a beat.

"Oh!" she said, and her throat felt constricted.

And her face slowly began to turn red, and she bit her lips and walked round the armchair and leaned against the banisters with her back to the company. And her heart drummed in her throat and she felt that if Someone were to walk through the door now, she would not be able to take a single step across the room... she believed there were ton weights on her legs, and she would be incapable of saying a single word... What a good thing it was that nobody was coming in!

Slowly and dizzily she made her way to the sofa and

threw herself on it, let herself fall, and lay there with her shapely legs higher than her head. Her head fell back and her mouth remained open. How madly peculiar she felt... no, not that... that was not what she wanted; it was not she who wanted to be a sacrifice. What was missing was that someone else should feel this annihilation when *she* appeared. But she herself? No, that would be no good...

She stretched out her hand and took a cigarette from the little table, and beckoned for a light.

The Good Friend jumped up and brought the tiny flame.

But this was awful... was it two years ago? And worse and worse? She had never thought it could have such an effect on her... such a peril... no, and for two years nothing at all had happened... except that she had grown more stiff, more reserved and more unapproachable... to Someone... to control herself. Was it foolishness? Cowardice? She was the coward.. What a good thing she was wearing white and that Someone happened to have seen her in white.

She felt that her husband was looking at her.

She slowly opened her eyes and turned her gaze on him.

"What are you thinking about now, Marta?" asked her husband.

She simply stared and smiled a stiff, strange smile.

"Come on, tell me the truth, what are you thinking about?"

And she just continued to smile.

"Won't you tell me?"

She slowly shook her head as she lay there and then said, "No."

And strangely, with her eyes closed and looking back into her inner being, she bit her lower lip voluptuously and said once again somewhat defiantly,

"No."

Her husband, hoarsely,

"Why?"

And she, slowly,

"Why?" And she felt that now something was going to happen. She slowly brushed the hair away from her forehead and said:

"If I were to tell you that, perhaps it would make the tower of the big church fall down. And in any case I should die..."

The two men stared at her with such an incredibly stupid expression that she began to laugh aloud... It was so strange and strong and soft that she herself could hear the tinkling sound of her laughter.

Laughter? Was this laughter? Or was this happiness? The third moment of happiness... in life?

1925

BARBARIANS

1

The little dog, the puli, pricked up his ears, sniffed and a moment later began to bark, baring his teeth.

"What are they?" the shepherd said to him.

The dog barked even more.

"Town folk?" asked the shepherd.

The dog was silent for a moment.

"From the puszta?"

The dog began to bark.

"Then what's the matter with you?"

The shepherd lay full length on his sheepskin cloak in the shade of his donkey, and paid no further attention to it all.

A little while later the two big sheepdogs also observed the approach of strangers, and they too struck up with deep, ringing barks. They made such a terrible, rancorous noise that it was as if they were being flayed alive.

But the shepherd knew now that one of his fellow-shepherds was approaching; the puli had left him in no doubt about that.

It was quite a long time before the two shepherds could be made out on their donkeys, approaching over the parched land of the puszta. They came slowly on their donkeys, and there were two dogs too, ambling along just in front of their feet.

The puli came and stood at his master's feet, and never ceased his raucous yelping for an instant.

The big sheepdogs gradually settled down again as they recognized companions in distress. Perhaps they even recognized the dogs too. They would stop for a while, then strike up another stanza or two, but did not really take their barking duties very seriously.

Only the puli refused to give up; he whimpered as if he felt the chopper's knife.

When the two visitors reached the edge of the flock, the big sheepdogs quarrelled with the strange dogs; they all became mixed up and bit each other in a heap on the ground. One of the shepherds roared at them from his donkey and even raised his stick to strike one of them dead at any moment, but then he thought better of it and jogged on towards the sheepskin cloak.

"Hey there!"

"Hey you!"

The shepherd raised himself on his elbow and watched them as they approached.

He let out a roar,

"Lie down and shut up!"

At this the dogs bit each other slightly more amicably.

One of the visitors had already dismounted and was approaching with long, waddling steps.

"Good day to you!"

"And to you!"

He stood up for propriety's sake, although the visitor did not deserve respect, because he was an ill-wisher. Not long ago he had been told at the inn that the visitor had called his flock the bandits of the puszta. Why did he say such a thing? When he had the right to graze his flock wherever his contract permitted?

However, one does not display one's feelings and thoughts immediately. He shook hands with them and said,

"You dismount too."

At this the other shepherd also got off his donkey and the two animals were turned to graze. They simply stayed where they stood and moved not an inch further; only their hides quivered under the bites of the horseflies. Otherwise the most they did was to move their ears; they made not a sound.

The two shepherds took their cloaks from the donkeys, and they too spread them on the parched ground and lay on them. They sat there opposite each other and stared straight ahead. They did not talk.

All three men were permanent shepherds, who spent the

whole year in the open with their flock and never saw the sight of a village unless they went occasionally to a wedding feast or to market. They were hard-bitten puszta folk. Around them was the vast sky and nothing else, for while clouds circled in the sky, there was nothing on the earth except crickets leaping around. And not far away a wild pear tree stood, dejected and gnarled.

The big flock was further afield, and the little boy was with it. The shepherd's little son, a stripling of some twelve years—just a big hat and a little sheepskin cloak, that was all the child was, and a little curiosity too. Enough for him to begin to round up the flock and drive it back to reach his father again at dusk.

The men were still silent even then. A shepherd can spend days without saying a word. When they are together, they are silent together. And even when they are on a visit like this, they do not open their mouths.

"Well now, the wife," said one of the visiting shepherds.

The speaker was a great red-faced man. A freckled, very hard man, with blue eyes and a reddish moustache. What his hair was like could not really be seen, since his hat was pulled right down over his eyebrows.

The other visitor also growled something. He was a smaller man with a tiny nose and gimlets of eyes. He smoked his pipe and looked across, but did not speak.

"She was here."

"When?"

"A week ago."

"When's she coming again?"

"Some time."

"Have you got food?"

"Some."

"Enough for a fortnight?"

"For ten days."

"Ten days."

They fell silent again.

And now the boy was standing there. He just stood, leaning on his gnarled crook and gazed at the visitors without a word. He would have liked to discover what they wanted and why they had come, but he dared not speak.

Nor did he want to. If they did not, neither did he. There was no hurry.

Now the sun slowly went down. That too gazed curiously on the three men; that too was unable to tell who they were and what they wanted. It too was sorry that it had to follow its own flock to the fold. Would the answers be given before then?

Well, they were not, because the three men just stayed there and smoked their pipes. They sat cross-legged.

The host took just one glance around, and even then appeared to be looking towards his flock, but he was really looking to see whether his stick was at hand.

When the sun had gone down, there was a slight stirring of life around them. Birds began to flutter over their heads, tiny birds in a great flock. The midges swirled up in swarms from the grass or from where the birds were hunting them.

"Listen."

"All right."

"Have you a belt?"

"Yes."

"I saw it last year at the wake. It's studded with brass."

"I've got it."

"You should sell it."

"Sell it?"

"Yes."

"It's not for sale."

"No?"

"No."

"Why not?"

"Because it isn't. I made it for myself."

"For yourself?"

"Yes, for myself. And for my boy."

"And for your boy?"

"That's right."

"For the two of you?"

"Yes."

With this they went on sitting there.

Then it became quite dark. The darkness came as suddenly as if someone had blown out a candle.

"So you're not going to sell it?"

"I've told you so."

At this the bigger of the two shepherds took hold of his stick and gently drew it closer to him, as if he was about to stand up. The shepherd who was host moved not a muscle; he lay in wait like a watchdog, but he was ready.

"Is that your last word?"

But now the host leapt up. And the other two fell on him.

One, two, the sticks clashed. First the two sticks on the one, then one stick on the host's head.

He staggered.

"Is that why you've come?"

That was all he could say. The two wild men went for him and in a single minute had beaten him to death. The shepherd lay there on the ground, yet even then they each struck him another blow.

The little boy stood there beside them and looked on. The affair had blown up so suddenly that he had no time to stir.

"Take your father's belt off!" said the red-faced man to him.

The boy just stood there.

"Take it off this minute!"

The child, deathly pale and keeping his eye on the men, went up to his father and undid the belt from his waist.

"Give it to me."

The child lifted the belt and looked to see which of them to give it to. He just looked, and did not observe the stick that was raised high in the air and came down on his head. He received such a blow that he fell to the ground that instant and breathed his last.

The four dogs, who seemed not to have understood what was happening, suddenly recovered their senses. The two sheepdogs fell on the other two, grabbing them by the throat and rolling over and over, covered in blood, snarling and howling.

The puli leapt on the red-faced shepherd and bit him in the leg. He beat him with his stick and kicked him until he could finish him off.

It was impossible to see the four sheepdogs in the darkness. They dealt with each other.

The two men stood there leaning on their sticks, waiting for their dogs to finish their task, and when they came back covered in blood and licking their wounds the red-faced shepherd said,

"Start digging!"

The two dogs began to dig away, making a pit, but it was slow work.

Then the men took short-bladed spades from the donkeys' backs and helped them.

When the pit was ready, the smaller shepherd took hold of the child and laid him in it. But the man was too big for him.

"There's the belt."

He tied it round his neck and dragged him into it.

By the time the moon rose, the host, his son and three dogs were all in their makeshift grave. The men made a fire of dung on the grave and grilled their bacon on it. They enjoyed a tasty supper.

"Well, that's that," said the red-faced shepherd. "Let's get moving."

He set the flock moving. The three hundred sheep started off over the puszta, but with reluctance; they would have liked to settle down for the night. They could not understand why they had to make their way hungry across the magnificent puszta. But since they had no choice, they went. The four donkeys and the two wounded sheepdogs ambled along after them.

The two shepherds walked calmly behind them.

2

Ten days later a tall, dark woman came striding over the great puszta.

She wore a white linen dress and big sandals on her feet, tied firmly with twine, and her head was tied with a linen kerchief.

She had a bundle on her back and went swiftly, though this was the third day she had been walking. The village was a long way off, for her husband, who had his own flock, did not find it easy to obtain grazing-land.

She was delighted when in the distance she caught sight of the gnarled wild pear tree, for it was in this area that her husband usually grazed his sheep.

But now she could not see the man anywhere.

There was no village or farmstead within a day's journey. There were no human beings either, only the vast puszta. If someone is not where he should be, nobody knows how to seek and find him. She discovered the spot where he had had his fire and settled down there for a time.

She spent the whole day walking over that area as she remembered it. But she could not even find traces of the herd. There were no fresh tracks anywhere, or tiny gleaming balls of sheep-dung. The only traces were dried-up and several weeks old. There had been rain and gales, and these had washed them away long before.

She slept under the huge and terrifying sky and could not comprehend what had happened to the man. After dozing all too briefly she set off towards the east to find other shepherds who perhaps might be able to tell her something about him.

She came to a spot where she could see the glad sight of smoke.

It was not her man, she could tell that from the fire. Her man, poor soul, never had any inclination to light a fire unless it was necessary. He liked everything dry and his food cold. He never lit a fire for breakfast; he ate his bread, bacon and onion just as they were. He only made a fire at noon or in the evening in order to have egg-noodles or pastry, and then it was only for the boy's sake.

Huge wild dogs rushed out at her, but she was not afraid of them; she knew how to talk to them—she was a shepherd's daughter herself and the wife of a shepherd. The dogs just yapped, but they did not touch her.

"Good day, good people!" and she came up to the fire.

There was a big red-faced shepherd there and three boys.

"Have you seen where my husband has gone with his flock? He's the one who is over there to the west."

"With three hundred sheep."

"Yes, three hundred. That's him. Bodri, the shepherd. That's his name."

"Come and sit down, mother."

The woman just stood there, but since there was no hurry, she squatted down for a little with the bundle still on her back and rested like a shepherd, on her ankles.

"Well, I don't know where your husband is. He went off to the west."

"Why, wherever would he have gone?"

"He didn't say where he was going. He set off for Transdanubia."

"Transdanubia?"

"It's twelve or thirteen days since he came this way. He said he had to get away from this place for a while because he was in trouble with the cops."

"In trouble?"

"Yes."

"With the cops?"

"With the law."

"He never said anything. It's exactly two weeks since I was out here with him. He said nothing about it."

"He was a silent sort of man."

"He was, but that's what he said."

The red-faced shepherd handed her the fork with which he was stirring the pot.

"Have something to eat."

"I've already eaten."

"Go on, eat as if it were your own food. I'd like you to."

But the woman shook her head. She did not take the fork or dip into the pot, though the meat in it was good, with corn-meal. These shepherds do well for themselves even in the morning.

She looked at the sheep. They were a mixture of ewes and Hungarian long-haired sheep. She just gazed at them, rigidly, as if she were looking at something belonging to her. If her husband had gone off, she would never have any ewes or sheep again.

"I even remember," said the red-faced shepherd, "that when he came this way he had a belt. It was studded with brass."

"That was him," said the woman. "He loved that belt and always wore it round his waist."

"I asked him to give it to me, but he wouldn't."

"No. He wouldn't have given that to anyone in the world."

"I promised him everything, but he wouldn't budge an inch."

"Oh, my dear, my husband!" The woman started up and clasped her hands.

"That's when he said he had to go away."

"Did he mention me?"

"No. I only asked him, but he didn't answer."

"Not a word?"

"All he said was, 'She was here.' I asked when. 'About a week ago,' that's what he said."

"About a week ago? Is that what he said?"

"Yes."

"So it was only a week since he was in these parts."

"Would it be only a week?"

The woman looked round at the lads, but they did not know.

"They didn't see him, because they hadn't arrived here yet."

"Where were they?"

"Some here, some there."

"Are they new?"

"New or not, they weren't with me."

"But all the same, why did he come?"

"He just came along. He came this way with his flock and rested for a while here. There must have been something on his mind, because he was very silent."

"That was him," said the woman.

She stared ahead with dry eyes, but her heart grew increasingly restless.

"He left no sign?"

"Sign? What for? He wasn't one to do that."

"Well then..."

She stood up.

"Wasn't the boy with him?"

"The boy? I saw him once. There were two of them by the flock, he and a slip of a boy."

"Yes."

"And he had two sheepdogs and a puli."

"That's right."

"Well, just wait for him, perhaps he'll come back by autumn."

"I'm going after him."

"All right, go along then. You can stay here too, if you like. We're only human. You can stay here for a day."

"Transdanubia, was it he said?"

"Yes, Transdanubia."

"Then I'm going to follow him to Transdanubia."

"Just keep going towards the west."

"I'll ask my way."

With this the woman stood up, gave the bundle on her shoulders a shake, then nodded and went off.

The shepherds watched her for a long time. They ate and drank. Wine from the wooden flagon. Then they rose and looked after the flock.

As for the woman, she went on and on, right away. She was lost in the vast wilderness. The sun rose higher and higher in the sky and watched the dark woman dressed in white linen as she trudged along over the puszta. And she simply went on and on. She did not look in at home. She went steadily on her way until the puszta swallowed her up. And she continued until she reached the Danube. She crossed that too. She found a man with a boat, and he put her on the far side. And she went on.

She went where she heard that shepherds usually grazed their flocks.

She went on throughout the summer; she went on till the snow began to fall. She visited every flock in every part of the countryside; she sat down with every shepherd and asked him if he had seen such and such a sturdy little silent man with his three hundred sheep.

She reached her home in the village again by winter. She opened up the house with the key she had hidden in the eaves and saw the winter through. By then her piglet had grown, her hens and chickens had increased because the neighbours looked after them while she was away.

When spring arrived she could not bear to stay there any

longer. The puli had a puppy, and that too was a clever little black dog. She said to it,

"Come on, puli, let's get on the track of your master."

She went once more to the puszta. She took what she could on her back and tramped to where she had left the shepherd last year.

Once more she found her way to the big pear tree. She settled there as if she intended to spend the summer there.

And she stayed there for two or three weeks—she did not count the days. She watched over the dog. When her food ran out she went home again, packed things up once more and went out. Out into the great puszta, where now another shepherd was driving his flock.

The days passed by, hot ones and wet ones. But she was unable to break free from the place; she just wandered around in the great barren waste.

Suddenly, in August, the puli discovered something. It brought along a hat.

"It's my husband's," said the woman. "Where did you get it, puli?"

The dog led her to the place.

The dog scratched at a small patch of smooth sand, angrily yelping, barking and snarling. It dug away.

Then it dug out a hand.

The woman went at the sand with her ten fingernails and soon uncovered her husband. Rotting and disgusting. The brass-studded belt was round his neck.

She also found her son. The child lay on his stomach with the big hat on his head. When she lifted it, there was the great slit in his little head. His mother looked at it with dry eyes. Just one blow, and it had been all over. He had not suffered long.

All day long she sat out there by the grave. In the evening she scraped the sand back into place. She made a little hillock above it and stuck into this two dry stalks in the shape of a cross; then she went away eastwards.

By morning she caught up with a flock of sheep.

"Where's that red-faced shepherd?" she asked. "The one who was grazing his flock here last year."

"In Szeged," said shepherds she did not know.

"Is he?"

"The police traced all sorts of nasty things to him and took him away for questioning."

The woman did not stay; she set off and went to Szeged.

She arrived there two days later. She went to the police commissioner and told him everything.

The police went to the spot; they took her with them in a horse-drawn cart.

They dug up the grave and noted down what they had seen. They removed the belt from the dead shepherd and took it back to Szeged.

3

The examining commissioner questioned them.

One prisoner after another. Word was added to word, leading one to another, and gradually a whole host of thefts and murders was proved to have been committed by the red-faced shepherd. The hangman's rope was ready and waiting when the examining officer said,

"And what about the shepherd Bodri?"

The red-faced man did not bat an eyelid.

"Shepherd Bodri?"

"Yes, that's what they called him while he was alive."

"While he was alive?"

"While he was alive, Bodri was the shepherd's name. What's happened to him, then?"

"I don't know him, sir."

"He had his flock next to you at Csobor puszta. He had his little boy with him."

"That's possible."

"Well, do you know him?"

"If that's him. The one that went to Transdanubia."

"You should know where he went. Was it to Transdanubia or somewhere else?"

"He was with me before he went off, yes. He said he was in trouble with the law and was off to the west for a time."

"Temporarily or permanently?"

"Permanently, I think."

"So do I. It was you who made it permanent."

"Me, sir?"

"Together with his son."

"Never, sir."

"Look, shepherd, as far as you are concerned the case is complete anyway. There's only one thing you still have to admit. What harm did shepherd Bodri do to you?"

"None, sir."

"He did nothing?"

"He never put so much as a straw in my way."

"Then why did you say in the inn at Csür that Bodri was grazing his flock where he ought not to be?"

The red-faced shepherd twitched his eyebrows.

"I never said that."

"You were heard saying it."

"Nobody ever heard me say that."

"You know very well they heard you say that. To whom did you say it?"

"If I did say it, it wasn't for that reason."

"Then why?"

"It wasn't on his account that I said it. A shepherd is free to pasture his sheep where his contract allows him."

"He had three hundred sheep. What's become of him and them? They couldn't just have disappeared from the face of the earth. Isn't that so?"

"Yes."

"But if he's disappeared the sheep must be somewhere. Were they sheep or ewes?"

"They were sheep rather than ewes, if they were anything at all."

"They were, they were. Were they his, or did they belong to an estate?"

"He'd be able to tell you that."

"What did he tell you?"

"I never spoke to him."

"Then how do you know?"

"They said so. I saw them. He grazed his flock next to mine. He wasn't a talkative man. He was a silent sort."

"He didn't say anything?"

"Well... he didn't talk."

"Was he silent even then?"

"When?"

"When you beat him to death with your stick. Him and his boy too."

"Did he have a boy as well?"

"He did. He had one son. You only struck him once on the head, and that was the end of him."

"Please don't say things like that to me. I never spoke to him, neither to him nor to his son."

"If he didn't speak, at that moment he couldn't have spoken. He was a silent sort of man."

"What is it you want of me, sir?"

"For you to get it off your conscience. One more or less."

"I can't undertake something that has nothing to do with me."

"Just think about it."

"There's nothing for me to think about."

"Did you take spades with you too?"

"Spades?"

"On the donkey?"

"The donkey?"

"Because it was a clean piece of work."

"Not mine, sir."

"Did you drive the sheep away?"

"I had sheep of my own, sir. I wasn't interested in anyone else's."

"And they were fine sheep. Three hundred. Shepherd Bodri was a fine man. He acquired them himself and looked after them."

"Maybe. I don't know about that."

"Are the sheep still with your flock or have you sold them?"

"Please don't say things like that to me."

"Will you listen? You're not an infant! A man who has confessed to all his crimes has no need to play the cheat over three hundred sheep. What are they to you? Now when you may go unsullied into the presence of God, is shepherd Bodri to be a stain on your conscience?"

"I can't help it."

"I'll spit in your face as if you were a snivelling brat!

You went there, struck them on the head after sunset, killed the dogs too and buried them in the sand."

The red-faced shepherd turned stubborn. His eyes blazed and he looked straight at the examining magistrate.

"That's not right, sir."

"Get out, you rogue! I don't want to see anything more of you."

The shepherd faltered.

"Out of my sight! You a shepherd? You're a scoundrel and a rascal! Know for certain that there'll be no peace for you even on the scaffold!"

"I can't take on myself what isn't mine."

"Get out!"

The shepherd turned round and set out with big firm steps towards the door. When he reached it and was about to put his hand on the latch, he staggered back.

He was unable to touch the latch. He could not move an inch. He merely stared, stared fixedly and began to foam at the mouth.

There hanging from the latch was the brass-studded belt.

The shepherd slowly raised his hand to his head and turned back.

"Sir... I admit it..."

The examining magistrate did not say a word but merely looked at the man with fire in his eyes—his eyes simply blazed.

"It was we who killed shepherd Bodri for his three hundred sheep and for his two donkeys."

So saying, he bowed his head.

The examining magistrate looked at him, then rang.

Two policemen came in.

"Take him away. Give him twenty-five strokes."

The shepherd hung his head and went out of the door a broken man.

"Thank you, sir."

The magistrate gazed after him and pondered.

"Barbarians!"

1931

THE SWINEHERD'S FILTHIEST SHIRT

The landowner's manor-house stood there in the middle of the estate. In front of it there was a very beautiful garden, tended by the lady of the manor herself. The roses had been released from their winter protection and had survived its stuffiness; their buds waved, stretching towards the lovely sun. The daffodils stood up in a long line, their flowers beginning to burst into bloom. The camellia buds waxed fat in the beautiful spring and began to open. Everything was alive, rejoicing and happy, all ready to flower.

The lady stood there, kind and energetic among the labourers, and gave her orders. She too was like a wonderful spring plant, fresh and alive. Her beauty seemed to flourish; the fresh breeze plucked at her cheeks and the rays of the sun warmed her through her short spring coat.

Her little boy hung around her. That morning she had not let him go to school because the school was three kilometres away from the house and the child had not felt well. The horses were all fully occupied at the moment, and though she was not opposed to the child's going to school on foot on a fine sunny day, this morning she had looked at him when he was ready to set out and asked him worriedly what was the matter with him. She took his temperature; there was no trace of fever. All the same she thought he might be sickening for something, so he had better stay at home—in any case he was well advanced compared with the others. Why sit there in the stuffy atmosphere of the classroom when he could run around at home and live like the chickens and piglets? That was better than breathing in the smell of the other children.

But the little boy did not feel well. He did not run about; he was out of sorts and kept hanging around her all the time.

What a lot of trouble there is with children! How mysterious is the small life of a child! She watched him anxiously, wondering what was wrong with him. A colder wind suddenly swept through the garden. It shook the bushes, and she said:

"Go into the room and play with your gramophone."

After a little show of reluctance, the child went inside.

She watched him go and worried about him. He was the only one of her children left at home. The others were all at boarding-school in Pest, so she felt all the more anxious about him.

Now her husband came across the park and said,

"Dearest, you might go out into the fields for a little. Take a look round, dear, and see whether those lazy louts are working. I can't go, because I've got to stay with the Yorkshires."

There too there was trouble. They were constructing new ponds, and two of the pigs were out of sorts; the vet was coming to give them an injection.

The little carriage was all ready, so she went out into the yard, got into it and drove out to the field.

They were sowing maize, and the potatoes were also being planted. She went all the way through the fine fields and saw how the corn was turning green, its short stalks waving in the wind. The labourers were hard at work. Here and there women were hoeing in large groups.

Suddenly she was struck by a peculiar thing. She saw a dwarf of a child on the earth that had been hoed, and could not understand what was the matter with him. He was like a little manikin. He seemed to have nothing but tiny arms and they were flapping as if blown by the wind.

It roused her curiosity, and she got out of the carriage to have a better look.

As she went up to the little infant, who could scarcely be eighteen months old, she saw that he was dug into the earth.

She stopped beside him and looked. Yes, indeed he was dug into the soft, dusty spring soil.

"What have you done to this child?"

A woman broke away from the line and ran up.

"Is this child yours?"

"Yes, madam."

"What have you done to this child?"

"It's so that he won't crawl away, madam."

She had buried the child in the ground up to his waist, and only the upper part of his body stood out of the earth. The little infant looked up with shining eyes and stretched out his little arms towards his mother.

"Take that child out immediately!"

The woman lifted the child out of the ground.

"Just look! The lower part of his body is all wasted away. How can you be so cruel?"

"Oh dear, madam! There's nobody at home to leave him with, so I've got to bring him out to work with me."

"Well?"

"Well, that's our custom."

"And a fine custom it is! Why, the child will catch cold."

"Of course he won't, madam. The earth is nice and warm."

"Don't say such silly things! That child will die if you don't look after him."

"The good God looks after him."

"The good God does, but you don't. I never want to see a child buried in the ground again."

Very angry indeed, she gave the mother a good dressing-down, and even when she went home she was tormented by the thought that she had never seen anything so terrible as this. She told the vet, who laughed and said there was still so much superstition in this part of the world that it was impossible to talk sense to the people.

A few days later she went down to the labourers' dwellings where the woman who had planted the child lived. She caught sight of her, called to her and asked,

"Well now, how's your child?"

"Oh, madam, he's got a fever! A spell's been put on him."

"Who's put a spell on him?"

"We don't know yet, but he's been struck down."

"Struck down? How?"

"With the evil eye."

"Show me the child."

She went with the woman farm-worker into the house and started in horror.

On the polished cold earth floor of the house there lay the child in a grubby little shirt on top of a dreadful pile of rags. His whole body was on fire.

She bent down and looked at him.

"This child has got meningitis."

She measured the mother with her glance. There was also a girl there, Piros, who had been in service with her in the house for two years, but had left her now because she was engaged to be married at Whitsun.

"Piros!" she called. "You haven't any sense either. Is that the way to treat a child? Didn't you see in my house what we do with a child if there's something the matter with him?"

The girl hung her head with hate in her eyes and was silent.

The mother of the little infant intervened.

"This isn't a gentleman's child, madam. He's of peasant stock."

"So what? Isn't it all the same to the child, the house in which he's born into the world? Sickness is sickness. It's meningitis, I tell you. You're killing that child."

"Oh, the good God will look after him."

"Don't throw all the responsibility on to the good God. Pick him up this instant and put him in the bed."

"No, no! The child mustn't be touched or he'll die."

"Why should he die?"

The woman said nothing.

"Throw out all that filthy stuff! Whatever do you mean by putting that poor little innocent in such a disgusting filthy mess on the bare floor? Open up that bed!"

The woman reluctantly opened up the bed. It had neither pillow nor eiderdown, just rags, old clothes and a threadbare shepherd's cloak.

"Haven't you got any bedclothes?"

"No."

"That's dreadful! Piros, go straight to the manor-house and tell the housekeeper to give you a pillow and little Ivan's old eiderdown, this instant!"

When the girl had run off, she shouted at the mother.

"And as for you, take that child on your lap this very moment and keep him there until they bring the bedclothes. How is it possible that you haven't any bedlinen? Let's just see."

But the mother did not stir. She just wept and stared straight ahead with hatred.

"Didn't you hear what I said?"

"Oh, madam, please don't interfere, or my poor little darling will die."

"What nonsensical talk is this?"

She now began to suspect that she had come up against some superstition, and tried to find out what it was.

"Have some sense, you stupid woman! What are those disgusting rags on which the child is lying?"

"They're what will cure him."

"Whatever are you saying?"

"The old lady said we had to lay him on that."

"On what?"

The woman confessed with great reluctance.

"He had to be laid on the swineherd's filthiest shirt, and she said a prayer over him, and cast coal[1] for him. If you break the spell now, the child will die."

"I'll telephone the magistrate this instant if you won't pick up the child. I'll teach you a lesson. You're condemning your own child to death."

She kept raging and fuming until Piros arrived with the bedclothes, but even then the mother did not want to touch the child.

They made the bed, and it was Piros who lifted the child from the ground. It was only too obvious that the child, tortured by fever, had a grateful look as he rested on the soft pillow.

---

[1] The reference is to a folk cure. An elderly woman would say a brief prayer as she sat by the fire; during the prayer she would take a few small pieces of cinder with a knife and drop them into water, one by one. If the coal went to the bottom, the sick person was bewitched; if it stayed on top, he was suffering from some other illness. Drops of the water were then given to the patient, and he might also be washed with it.

But the mother wrung her hands and wept and wailed that now that meant the end for her child.

The lady of the manor left them and went home. She hurried to her little son and was glad to see that the child was full of life, playing happily in the warm room.

Four hours later Piros appeared and said,

"Madam, the boy is dead."

The landowner's wife was dismayed.

She went out to have a look at the child. There he lay, poor little thing, stretched out lifeless on the white pillow.

"You see, you poor unfortunate things... To give that sort of medicine to a child!... Well, of course he died! You dig him into the cold spring earth and when he catches cold you lay him on the bare floor in the swineherd's dirtiest rags. And you believe that will cure him. Oh, what boundless stupidity!"

The mother gazed at her with anger and hatred.

"You are the cause, madam. It will be on your conscience! Three days ago the child was as full of life as could be. He was so lively, yet now he had to die, because you, madam, went against the divine will!"

"I don't want to hear that wicked talk again," shouted the lady, beside herself with rage. "You kill a child with trickery and then you even make me responsible for it! You should be ashamed of yourself."

She went out of the little labourers' dwelling with tears in her eyes and returned to her own life.

The sun shone brilliantly and there was no hint of a breeze. The whole of nature was happy and gay, but the tiny child was a poor little corpse. He lay there stretched out on the aristocratic pillow like a sad relic at the point where cultures meet.

1931

EVENING BY THE FIRE

The house was in a good position in the little town. A little side street, an alleyway so narrow that anyone walking along it had to draw in his elbows so that one of them at least should not become covered in lime, yet only a couple of steps to the market and the fence at the back of the church came up to it—in a word it might be regarded as being in the heart of the town.

And if two neighbours were able to live here from the time they were born, why should they not know this?

The little house had a small garden too. It was very small, but the soil in it is good, very good. It produces everything. And the church wall protects it from the north winds; in spring the earliest flowers bloom here. In a word it is a little paradise and its greatest merit is that nobody can ever look into it. Only the birds can do that.

This is where Mr Mánkay and Veron Polnisch settled when they were married.

Rarely had an odder couple come together.

Mr Mánkay had once belonged to a landowning family; then he was a clerk and a photographer—he took up photography as his hobby and with the changing times made a living of sorts out of it for a long time.

Veron Polnisch was a widow, but she had lived for such a short time with her first husband that she had never had time to get used to her new name and really stayed an old maid.

They were somehow recommended to each other and Mr Mánkay went to visit her.

In the first quarter of an hour they discussed the exact details of what each possessed and what their income was—but with such hostility that each of them was scared that it might be to the detriment of the other.

As they faced each other, each of them had a hooked nose and each of them was over sixty. They looked like reflected images of each other. Joyless, reserved and hard.

"My proposal, madam, would be that we should unite our affairs on a proper basis. The Malveczky house in Church Alley is for sale now, and we could buy that by pooling our resources. I cannot raise the whole sum to buy it, nor do I wish to tie up my last farthing in it, so you would undertake to pay half the price of it, half the tax and half the conveyance-fee, in other words a proper division. My principle is to divide each item exactly in half. I would not desire of you, even after that, a farthing more or less than my proper share. We shall even share lunch, madam, in this way. If we buy a kilo of cherries, each of us will pay for the amount consumed."

Veron Polnisch considered the matter and simply said, "I find that fair."

They came to an understanding on this basis, and now the marriage was in its third year.

It would have been a good thing to get hold of their house-keeping journal. Every day they entered every farthing and divided every item in two.

Sometimes suspicion crept in. In particular old Veron often suspected Mánkay of such villainy as being unfair in the matter of cherries. He puts one in his mouth, then swallows it... She watched his mouth; it moved far more than one would imagine necessary for just one cherry... and he only spat out one stone. Other items proved easier to divide; butter was weighed out into two exactly equal pieces—for this they had a precision-balance that Mánkay had used in his photographing days to measure out chemicals. Bread, salt and vinegar (which they used with onions) and sugar were all divided exactly by weight, and so that there should be no misunderstanding there were two dressers in the room where they each kept their own things separately under lock and key.

There was only one thing about which they failed to agree, and that was oil. They had tried everything. First Mánkay bought a litre, then Veron the next. One litre lasted half as long as the next. They also tried each having oil, and every evening they poured enough for that evening into the lamp. But every evening they went to bed angry because some injustice had occurred. Without exception every day there was some commotion because the lamp went out five minutes earlier than it had done the previous evening.

Now this was a big item, since both of them shared one and the same passion—reading. They shared the lending-library subscription exactly. And this was not altogether a straightforward affair either, because there were always books which one or the other of them had already read. Yes, indeed, but they still wanted to read them, except that the one who had read the book first went on reading it. And the one who already knew the book did not read everything in Xavier Montépin, but only the exciting bits. Now how was it possible to divide this properly? There are some books which one reads in vain; once one has started on them, they have to be read again as if for the first time. For such books it would be fair if the other partner paid as much for the second reading as the one who reads it for the first time.

There was a lot to make mother Veron suspicious here. She froze when she brought home a book from the lending-library and mentioned the title. Mánkay would nod,

"Yes, I know it... I know it... I know that one too."

Who really believes that anybody knows every book? All this was simply so that he should pay a smaller share of the six pence which was the cost of reading one volume.

At this she had recently got into the habit, when she brought back a book, of sitting down first in the churchyard, looking at it and learning the names of the main characters. The names which appear most frequently in the book. Then when Mánkay began saying, "I know it, I know it," she would say,

"Well, then, what's the name of..."

She had caught Mánkay out once or twice like this.

All the same, everyday troubles and perils reach their peak now when the days are growing shorter, all because of the oil.

It is dreadful how even nature cheats one; every day she steals a couple of minutes of daylight. So every day someone has to light the lamp earlier. And this means that it goes out earlier. Mother Veron recalls clearly that in August her oil lasted till midnight, while now in October Mánkay's lamp goes out at nine o'clock.

However, they help things a little by lighting it later each evening.

There they sit by the fire. Mánkay stares at the fire with red eyelids. He does not smoke, since he is an educated man and has banished tobacco from his life. He never did smoke. So he just gazes and gazes, and envies his wife that she can work even by firelight. She is knitting stockings. He cannot do a thing; he just waits for the lamp to be lit, irritated, ruffled and champing with his toothless mouth. He watches the wood as it burns. There is enough—but how much money wood costs! Sometimes he calculates how long it takes a hundredweight of wood to burn, and how much that costs per hour... And it pains him to see that good, expensive hard wood really burning away; all that is left of it is useless ash. It is as if his bones are burning... In any case he considers it a tremendous injustice that a man eats and then grows hungry again, eats again and grows hungry again, and so on and so on for ever and ever. Everything exists simply to use up money...

Then all of a sudden his pent-up emotions burst out.

"Well, aren't we going to light the lamp yet?"

But he tends to say this only when it is mother Veron's turn to light it. Because if it is his turn, mother Veron's patience usually runs out and she sighs,

"This fire is ruining my eyes..."

1931

THE FLOCK AND ITS SHEPHERD

The minister stood up in the pulpit, cleared his throat and began his sermon:

"So the text for my sermon today is taken from the words of Jesus, 'Suffer the little children to come unto me.'"

He stopped, took a deep breath and surveyed the congregation.

There was a slight stir. But it was not the same movement as at other times, when they settle themselves more comfortably to listen, or when the girls take another sniff, in the approved fashion, at the little bouquet of flowers they are holding in their hands, though they catch nothing of the perfume; they only do it because that movement is permitted.

This movement, the minister suspected correctly, betrayed a certain disquiet.

"What's the new minister up to this time?" some of the old peasants wondered as they scratched their chins.

And the minister really had it in mind to give them a lecture about the birthrate in this village of one-child families. He had received official instructions to preach about this problem on the first Sunday after Easter. The reason was that the society which concerns itself in salons with the welfare of the people and has the princess as its president had invited the Bishop of Pest to tea, and had made him promise to have sermons preached that day throughout the whole diocese about the blessing of children.

The minister was still new to this parish and to the diocese too. He was uncertain whose demands he should satisfy—the people's, who did not wish to hear, or the bishop's, who wished to be heard.

So he tried to preach a fine poetic sermon. First he pictured Jesus surrounded by children, then the mother of a family living a sweet and happy life in a host of children just like a bird among her fledglings. He declared that for parents the best investment was children, for the love of children makes their old age sweet and light.

All the same, he had to come to the theme—the life of the family from which God had withdrawn his blessing, whose good mother had only once been blessed with a child. A child, if he is alone, lives an empty life; he becomes spoilt and turns into a little tyrant. When he grows up, he carries all this over into adult life. He will not be a whole person—and this applies to man and woman alike. He bears the burden of the things he has lacked from birth, and his life remains empty, like the nest from which he has come.

But at this point the whole congregation was restless. Everyone was fidgeting, then sitting still again, holding their hands up and then down; the women kept wiping their mouths with their handkerchiefs and the men stared grimly ahead.

In other words there was no sign of that good Calvinist church atmosphere, in which there is no need to pay attention to those beautiful long sentences rolling off the minister's tongue—ordinary mortals cannot understand them anyway—and the adults can take a gentle little nap to the music of the minister's voice.

No, here everyone waited on tenterhooks, expecting an approaching thunderbolt to strike.

And it did.

The restless atmosphere swept the minister into talking about something he had not intended to mention: the life of those families to whom God had sent his angel of blessing, but whose doors had been locked and the angel with his blessing rejected. Indeed there were mothers who resorted to sin to drive away God's greatest blessing.

However cautious he was, everyone understood what he wanted them to understand. The thunderbolt had fallen. The minister had made some kind of allusion to abortion.

The congregation was in such a state that it was on the point of getting up and walking out, so one would have thought.

But they were kept in check by the sense of order that had grown up through the centuries, and the minister too digressed; hurrying back again to the flowery meadows, he told tales of his own childhood, when he danced about on the smooth grass of the field with his childhood friends in the joys of Paradise...

Well, at last he finished his address, which in the end turned into a kind of apology. The minister even indicated that it was not of his own free will that he had delivered this sermon, but on instructions from above, for the highest authorities in the country had decided to appeal to the whole Hungarian people, addressing to them words of warning and inspiration, using newspapers, books and sermons, to put an end to this national misfortune. So he, the humble servant of God and country, had simply bowed to this command..., so for this reason he hoped that none of his beloved flock would cast stones at him...

When he descended from the pulpit and took his place in the old canopied minister's seat, he glanced round and saw that every face was turned away from him; nobody was looking at him, or if they did, it was with a reproachful glance.

During the last hymn the congregation went out in the prescribed order, led first by the schoolgirls, then by the old women; he was the last to leave together with the teachers.

As usual, a few big farmers were standing in front of the church.

The minister walked up to them, and was at a loss what to say to them.

"A nice spring we've got," he said. "It looks as though the good Lord will give us a good crop this year."

The churchwarden hummed and hawed.

The minister shook hands with them in turn. They all took his hand, but only with the tips of their fingers, he felt.

There was silence. Then the churchwarden said, "Minister..., I fought at the front..."

"So did I," said the minister.

"Then you've also seen what I went through. In the Doberdó. Did you see how they moved us down in the

Doberdó? Men fell there like leaves when the wind shakes the trees in autumn. The slaughter there was so great, you know, that only five or six of our men survived in each company. Bodies just burst. Grenades sliced men up so that their heads, arms and legs were sent flying separately into the sky... At that time I said only fools send children here... Sir, one boy is sufficient in a family. For that single boy gets exemption as a breadwinner, but the others have to go. Is a parent to have all the trouble of bringing up his children so that in the end they are drafted off to war, to die?"

The minister said nothing.

"We're all at the beck and call of our country," he said after a while.

"Our country," repeated the churchwarden. "What does our country give us, minister? Look, we too shot down the Italians. Where we were successful, they too fell like rabbits and like caterpillars in spring when you crush them with your fingers... We hadn't done them any wrong, nor they us... But that's where they had to die... So don't preach to me about children. Let the unborn child be glad that he hasn't got to go through that experience."

"You're not right," said the minister gently. "There's not war all the time. Your father and grandfather never went to war. They lived happily on their land in their village.. Now lots of people are needed so that life can be lived in times of peace. Many children mean much help. Much help, much joy."

The magistrate spoke up.

"Minister, my family grew rich through only ever having one child. My grandfather had a single child, a boy. He had twenty acres, and he married a girl with twenty acres too, so he left forty to this son. His son married a girl with sixty acres, so he left a hundred acres to his son. I inherited a hundred acres from my father. My parents made me marry my present wife—she had eighty acres—and I'm leaving a hundred and eighty acres to my only child."

The farmers nodded their approval.

"But what would I do if I had four children, and each one were to inherit only forty-five acres? They'd become smallholders. That way my descendants will always be big farmers."

The minister shook his head.

"Look, I've got four children, but I wouldn't let one of them go."

"It's easy for you, minister. Because you get your children educated at the parish's expense, even if there are a dozen of them. And they'll become gentry. They'll make a living. But peasants can't, sir."

"Anyway, ministers don't all think like that," said another big farmer, buttoning up his brand-new leather coat. "Take the old minister we had here. When we appointed him he was a bachelor, and he too began by scolding us for not having children. At that time the teacher—one of them—married a peasant girl, and he only had two children. This teacher said to the minister, 'We'll just see when you get married how many children you'll have.' Well, the minister did get married, and he had two. There weren't any more. Yet even at that time the manse was quite large; there'd have been room for more. But all the same he never had more than two. And the teacher told him so too: 'There you are, minister. You also stopped at two...' And the minister had no reply to that."

The minister surveyed the men. They all had only one child, or at most two. If the first was a boy, there were no more to come, but if the first was a girl, then they tried for a son, but if that turned out to be a girl too, they made do with her. There was, however, a day-labourer standing some distance away from the big farmers, and he knew he had a host of children, so he beckoned to him and said, "Well, my friend, and what is it you want to say?"

The poor man came up to him.

"I only came, minister," he said, taking off his hat respectfully, "to ask you to christen my sixth boy."

"Well done! You're not afraid of the blessing of children, at any rate. See what a fine thing it is, and how right you are. The country's only hope is here in the poor folk who still have no fear of the blessings of the good Lord. And it will be good for you too; when you grow old, even if you have no money there will be someone to look after you in your old age."

The poor man shook his head.

"Minister, I'm not counting on that, because I know it's easier for one father to keep ten children than for ten children to keep one father."

At this the big farmers laughed complacently and were just about to disperse and stroll home for the Sunday chicken soup, when a woman came hurrying up to them.

"Please ring the bell, minister. Pista Bocskor's dead."

This caused a sensation. Pista Bocskor was one of the biggest farmers in the village and the churchwarden's nephew.

"He's dead then," they said, "dead. Well, he didn't last long."

"Twenty-seven years old he was, and died of drink."

"He couldn't take it, poor fellow."

"It was certainly a big thing to take on."

The minister already knew the man and his story. Once upon a time Pista Bocskor and two others, all three big farmers' sons, had a huge Palm Sunday spree. They became dead drunk and said, "That was fine; from now on we'll keep on doing it."

They shook hands and vowed that from then on they would drink themselves silly every day. All three of them happened to be newly married, and they kept their vow so well that none of them had a single sober day thenceforward.

They had kept it up for six years, and now Pista Bocskor was the first of them to die.

"There you are," said the minister, "that's what single-child families lead to. They were only children, all three of them, and that's why they were so haughty and touchy. Nobody could say a word to them, neither father, mother, magistrate, relatives—nobody. From the time they were small they got used to the idea that they could get away with anything. And now their leader has died at the age of twenty-seven. The turn of the others will come too."

The farmers were silent. This was true. They gave the minister a sly glance.

"We'll see, minister, what your funeral sermon is going to say."

With this they parted, and the whole village spent the two days before the burial wondering what the minister was going to say at the funeral.

The minister sent for the dead man's nearest relative and said to him, "Just tell me about this man's life."

The man looked at the minister and simply said, "Clergymen are the biggest liars."

"Indeed!" exclaimed the minister. "Why do you say that to me? To the best of my knowledge I've never told a lie in my life."

"Well you will now. For that man was the biggest scoundrel in the village, but you're going to praise him at his funeral."

"No, I shan't."

The minister thought for a long time about the text. In the end he found a good saying in the Book of Ecclesiastes: 'Be not foolish and wicked, that you may not die before your time.'

The whole village came to the funeral. The greatest and the least in the community, for the family was the most important, and everyone cultivated its acquaintance. Beside the coffin the dead young farmer's mother and wife stood weeping. With them was his little daughter who was obviously degenerate, an expensively-dressed little wreck like the gaudy coffin.

When the minister announced his text the whole village once again became restless. They did not like the words from the Bible: 'Be not foolish and wicked, that you may not die before your time.'

The minister began by saying that life was God's greatest gift. Only on this basis can the rest be received, accepted and understood. Without life there is no world... Then he began to talk of how strange it was that there were fools who did not understand this chief good and did not respect it. Examples of such foolishness can be seen in the man who works himself to death, living for nothing except his work and making money... Others regard life as a game, and he instanced a villager who swam across the icy river and died of it... Or there are those here who eat and drink themselves to death...

"This newly-dug grave warns us, Christian brethren, that..."

At this the crowd began to murmur.

"This young man is neither the first nor the last to be the victim of the sin of intemperance... Must this really happen in today's world, when our country is in ruins and surrounded by enemies on every side? Be not foolish and wicked..."

Next day the churchwarden turned up at the manse. He stood grimly before the minister.

"What was the point," he said, "of denouncing my nephew?"

The minister behaved like those bold men who give offence easily, then, scared, try to make up for it.

"Look here, churchwarden," he said, "it is my duty. Here's my address; I'll send it to the Dean, you go and see him. If I was unjust, if I've done something I ought not to have done, I'll submit myself to the judgement of the church tribunal."

The churchwarden muttered:

"Just as expected! Dog doesn't eat dog."

And the Dean did indeed support the minister, and the village was up in arms, waiting for the hour of revenge.

When the atmosphere was at breaking-point, the richest man in the village died, a big farmer with three hundred acres. The minister received the death certificate; on it the cause of death was 'chronicle alcoholism.' (Later he asked the doctor where he had learnt his Latin.)

What was he to do now? He had died in exactly the same way as the previous young man. As the peasants put it, 'the brandy caught fire inside him.'

The family came to see him.

"Minister, we'd like to ask you not to preach at the funeral. We'll get the minister from another village."

"Very well," said the minister, "but you'll have to pay me the fees."

But the minister from another village would not take on the funeral. Such matters are rather delicate, and he was not going to meddle in his colleague's affairs just for those few shillings. The family made its shamefaced way back to the minister.

The minister kept the big farmer's son-in-law behind.

"Well, my friend, tell me something about your father-in-law. What sort of a man he was. But say something good about him. Only something good. If you can. Praise your father-in-law to me."

The son-in-law thought hard.

"All I can say is that he was a very good man. He gave to everybody. Nobody could go to him, rich or poor, and ask him for money without him giving it. He's got so many debtors, we don't even know who owes what. He didn't even ask for a receipt; he just gave away his money."

The minister was afraid that he would spoil the effect, because the paean of praise was getting dangerously close to improvidence, and praise of improvidence in the peasant's view is worse than the charge of miserliness, so he broke in:

"That's enough. No need to tell me any more. I know now what I'm going to say."

He chose the text from the Bible which runs, 'Be ye merciful as your Father is also merciful.'

He built his oration on this, saying that Christ our Lord has many commands, so many that feeble mortals would hardly be able to keep all of them. But if a man keeps one of them, that is a good thing. For when at the Last Judgement the angel asks, 'What have you done?', this our brother can answer 'Good!', and his other sins will be forgiven.

Well, the village was not at all pleased. On the way back from the cemetery Pista Bocskor's mother detached herself from one group of mourners, seething with rage, and shrieked:

"So you can close your eyes in one case and not in another, can you?"

They tried to silence her, but it was no use.

"I shan't be silent! The minister denounced my only son! A hundred acres he possessed, did my son; he drank away thirty, but I'll devote the remaining seventy to ridding the village of this minister!"

The minister's life in the village became difficult.

He looked out over the beautiful Hungarian village, so fair that few in the country could match it. After the great fire a hundred years before it had been methodically rebuilt, and everywhere stood big houses with tiled roofs, splendid mansions. The earth in the fields was good; even in this year of drought the average yield was sixteen quintals of wheat. It was a rich village, a haughty village, a proud Hungarian village.

The following Sunday there were few people in church. It came out that Pista Bocskor's relatives were standing in the porch, turning the folk away, so that they should not listen to this minister who dared to preach against single-child families.

The second of the three drunken young farmers died too.

The minister preached about the transience of life.

He did not mention how the three farmers used to derive entertainment from competing with each other to see who would give most to the gypsy band. When Pista Bocskor gave them money the next one declared, "I'll give them ten pengős more than you." There was one night when they gave five thousand two hundred pengős to the band. Next day the leader bought a house with it. Now here was the second member of the group.

So he spoke about the transience of life, but even now he could not refrain from declaring this at least: "Live so that if you die your conscience will not trouble your last hours."

The church became even emptier after this. Now there were two families standing in the church porch.

The clerk said, "Report them and have them punished."

As if the minister would dare to do that.

But to put an end to the affair, he called the leading men of the village together on day and held forth to them.

"Men! It is something the country commands and the law ordains. Let us discuss whether you have something sensible to say. Who knows, you may be right. So declare openly what you think of the problem of the single child."

"Minister," they said, "don't ask us such questions. What's it got to do with you? It's really only our affair."

"The people are dying out. Look around. The family where there's only one child is a feeble one."

"Minister, we don't think there should be lots of hungry mouths in the home, but we are concerned that we educate the one there is properly. I'm a respectable man, sir. I think carefully what I'm doing. I love my child. I want to give him everything. I'd die of shame and grief if I couldn't give that only child what he needs. If he wants a hussar's cap, I buy it for him; if he wants a new suit, I buy that—whatever he wants I wish to give him. But I couldn't do that for six. I'd die of humiliation if I were compelled to deprive my child of anything. And then there's schooling, I'm sending this one boy of mine to school. And I'll give him four years at grammar-school too. But how on earth could I do that for six? I don't want one to become another's slave."

"Minister," said another of them, "do they want a beggarly country or a rich one? Every family could increase the number of children to ten or twelve if necessary. But what shall we do with them? We're overrun with hungry people. So how can the gentry have the conscience to want an unlimited increase in the population? After all, every town is full of unemployed already. And look at the villages: there are thousands of idle hands—can they give them bread?"

"Minister," said the third speaker, "does the country really want children? If it does, then let it buy them... Establish hospitals and institutions, and proclaim far and wide that if anyone will take their child there they will be responsible for them and give their mothers money for them. Don't disgrace girls who get into trouble, but reward them... For a fine healthy child let them pay not more, say, than ten pengős, and the state will get as many children as it wants. In any case there's nothing else for the poor man to do all the winter long; come the spring, there'll be so many children to bring in that the state won't know what to do with them."

The minister hung his head. Here he had come up against such wisdom, knowledge of life and determination that he felt too weak even to start arguing with them.

1932

IT'S INCOMPREHENSIBLE

Valika and Pannika went along the street hand in hand. They were on the way home from school. Usually they parted at the corner of the side street; here Pannika went along the side street while Valika continued on the main one.

But this time Valika refused to let go of Pannika's hand and dragged her along behind her.

"Come on, come on! You're going to have lunch with us!"

"No-o..."

"Teacher said you must."

"But... no-o-o..."

Valika took no notice of Pannika, but just pulled her along. She was stronger, fatter and bolder. Pannika knew that teacher had told Valika to ask her father to give a meal to one of the poorer little children in the class. Pannika would do, since they were good friends anyway. All the same, Pannika didn't really care about going off to lunch with Valika. She didn't know why; she just didn't want to go.

But Valika knew that Pannika was hers today, and she would not have allowed her to escape for the world. She held her tightly, pulled her and carried her along. She was proud and could scarcely wait to get through the big iron gate, after which Pannika would not be able to escape.

"Mummy, mummy!" she rushed ahead and shouted to her mother. "Pannika's going to have lunch with us from now till Easter. Teacher said so."

Mother laughed and kissed her little daughter. She was very glad that Valika was so pretty, sweet and healthy. And she could chatter so divinely.

"Teacher said so? Well, that teacher..."

She kissed her little daughter once more, then had a good look at the other little girl she had brought with her.

"Is that true, little girl?"

But the little girl said not a word; she just looked at the floor and fiddled with the hem of her dress.

Valika however went on noisily:

"Because she's a poor child, and every poor child has to go somewhere for lunch. Teacher said so."

And she unstrapped the little satchel on her back and pulled out of it a letter sent by the teacher to mother.

Mother took it from her, read it through and said,

"All right then, little girl, just put your things outside in the hall, then both of you go to the bathroom and give your hands a good wash. And you too, wash those sticky little paws!"—and she tapped her little girl's hand and then kissed her sticky little hands.

She sent them to the bathroom and turned on the tap. The water gushed out of the gleaming pipe, and mother poured some of the water into a bowl and stood it on a very beautiful little white chair. First she gave Valika's hands a good wash and kissed her little hands that were now rose-coloured, and then she said to the little girl,

"Now you wash your hands too, but mind you wash them well!"

And she went off to the dining room to tell the parlour-maid to lay another place at the table. Then she said to the girl,

"Oh, and Rózsi, go into the bathroom and wash that little girl's hands—thoroughly. The master's very particular about children sitting down to table with clean hands."

Rózsi went into the bathroom. It was just as well, because Pannika had not put her hands in the bowl even now. She took hold of the little girl and washed her hands well and hard; she also gave her face a good wash and then took her own comb out of her hair and combed her hair with it.

"There!" she said, pleased with the result.

Now Valika and Pannika went back to the dining-room. They were just in time, for the master arrived and immediately asked,

"Who is this little girl?"

Valika ran and hugged her father and said,

"She's going to have lunch with us every day till Easter."

"Oho!"

"Teacher said so."

Mother explained the situation briefly and showed him the letter. Meanwhile Pannika stood hanging her head, just waiting.

"Well now, what's your name, little girl?" said father gently.

"Pannika!" shouted Valika.

"I wasn't asking you," said father.

"Just say it, will you?"

"Pannika," said Pannika in reply.

"Very good. And what do they call your father?"

"Father," said Pannika.

"That's what you call him, but what do other people call him?"

"You there," said Pannika.

"Don't you know his other name? János Varga? or Mihály Kovács? He must have some name. Well now, what's his other name?"

"I don't know."

"Dear, dear! Your father hasn't been able to teach you even that! Well, what do they call you?" he turned to his little daughter.

"Valika," replied Valika.

"All right, all right. And what do they call me?"

"Daddy."

"Oh, what a silly billy you are, little donkey! What do other people call me?"

"Sir."

"Oh dear, you're taking a leaf from her book now... I tell you, this general school isn't a good idea. It makes silly little children like her stupid. Come on, let's go and have lunch, because I'm hungry."

They sat down at the table. Valika sat in her place. The parlourmaid put a cushion on a chair for Pannika and sat her on it and laughed at her.

There was a white tablecloth on the table, and white plates and a white dish in the middle. Every plate had a gold band round it on the inside, though there was no gold band round Pannika's plate; all the same it was a nice one.

Mother served Valika, then father, then herself and then Pannika too.

"Do you like soup?" she asked her, but Pannika did not reply.

When Daddy had finished his soup, he asked Valika, "Don't you really know my name?"

"Doctor Antal Vadkerti," said Valika.

"There you are, you see. Everyone has a name. Every person has one, but this girlfriend of yours, she doesn't even know her father's name."

Pannika hung her head.

After the soup there was meat with sauce. Mother cut up the meat into small pieces. She cut up Pannika's too, and said to her,

"You have to eat it with a fork."

Pannika looked at the fork and tried to eat with it, but the meat would not stay on it.

"Oh well, let her eat it with a spoon as that's what she's used to," said father.

Pannika found it easier to eat the meat and the sauce this way. She also crumbled bread into it, but when Valika laughed out loud at this, she blushed and hung her head again.

Then they were given noodles. Lovely white noodles with fat curd cheese on them. They allowed Pannika to eat these with a spoon too.

"All the same, you'll have to learn how to eat properly. See how nicely Valika eats!"

When they got up from lunch, father said,

"Well now, little girl, just go straight back home and tell your father to come along here, because I want to speak to him."

Pannika instantly looked for her coat, put it on and started off.

"Stop! You must say thank you too! You must say thank-you for the lunch, and then when you are leaving a place you say good-bye to everyone."

But Pannika just stood and said nothing.

"Oh well, she'll learn," said father. She'll have time to learn by Easter."

Father said this very kindly and laughed too; he was not angry, but all the same Pannika just hung her head once again and went away.

They would not let Valika go outside in case she caught cold.

"And don't forget to tell your father to come along immediately, because I want to give him some work."

Father then lay down and slept for an hour. When he woke up, the man had arrived. He went out to meet him on the verandah.

One of those poor day-labouring kind of men was standing on the verandah in very ragged clothes, just waiting. When the gentleman stepped out on to the verandah he took off his hat and stood here in front of him. The gentleman was a large fat man; the other was small, thin and coarse-looking.

"You there, what's your name?"

"János Takaró."

"Good... Well, your little daughter is going to have lunch here with us every day till Easter. Do you understand?"

The man said nothing, but merely nodded his head.

"If she behaves properly, she will be given my little girl's left-off clothes and shoes. She'll get everything she needs if only she behaves herself. What do you do for a living?"

"I'm out of work."

"Since when?"

"Since harvest."

The gentleman looked at him and said nothing. The man did not say anything either, and held his hat in his hand.

"Then what do you live on?"

The man shrugged his shoulders and still did not speak.

"How many children have you?"

"Six."

"Six? Hm... How dare you take on six children if you can't provide for them? Oh, well, never mind... Anyway look here, my friend, I'll make myself responsible for your daughter. She'll come home with my little girl every day till Easter, and there's no need to pay anything for that, understand? But I don't want you to feel that I'm keeping her for nothing, so you're going to do something towards it. There's the woodshed," and he pointed to the shed at the end of the courtyard. "Go over there and chop some wood. You'll chop a little wood and then we're all square."

So saying he turned round and went into the house.

The man also turned round, put on his hat and went out across the yard where the snow had been cleared to the shed and found the axe. He started chopping wood. He chopped wood for two hours and then went away. He did not speak to anyone. Rózsi the parlourmaid came in towards dusk and said that the man had left already.

"Never mind," said the gentleman. "If he's gone, he's gone, though I wanted to give him a glass of brandy."

Next day the little girl did not go to school and did not turn up for lunch with Valika.

Valika cried because Pannika was not there.

"She'll come along tomorrow."

But Pannika did not come again.

A couple of days later they had forgotten all about her.

But one day the gentleman caught sight of the man outside the town hall and recognized him. He was standing among the unemployed, looking gloomy.

"You there, are you János Takaró?"

"Yes."

"Well, where's your little daughter? Why doesn't she come to lunch?"

The man made no reply; he remained silent. Then after much prodding he said angrily and sullenly,

"I don't like people trying to find out what poor folk live on."

The gentleman looked at him in astonishment, and simply said,

"It's incomprehensible! Aren't you sorry that your little girl is famished and starving? What sort of folk are you? It's incomprehensible!"

The man made no reply. He just turned away and gazed sullenly ahead.

1932

THE GENTLEMAN ON THE VERANDAH

"They're like enemies. If you're not there at their side, they'll rob us of everything we possess," said the gentleman on the verandah wrathfully, as his wife came out of the room.

"What's that, dear?" said the lady, startled. She was not accustomed to hearing her placid, stout husband talking so loudly. She was afraid something was very wrong.

"All that was wanted was one stake, and he cut it out of a piece six metres long! He could easily have done it with a stake one and a half metres long!..."

He made his complaint with all the bitterness of a landowner whose employees are causing him damage.

His wife calmed him down, telling him not to get so upset about it; he would have to get used to it, because things had always been like this and would go on being so.

"Oh, look!" the man shouted now, and looked from the verandah towards the garden. The gardener's wife was working in it. She was hoeing the young strawberry beds and now two little children had come up to her and she left her work to go off with them.

"What does she want? Where's she going?"

He watched the gardener's wife as she went, slovenly and terribly slowly, up towards the walnut tree.

He just could not imagine what she wanted. She had annoyed him all day long by working so slowly that the shadows raced with the speed of an express train compared with her; but now the blood rushed to his head—why had she abandoned her work?

He had his watch in his hand; now he intended to calculate how long it took her to get back to her hoe.

His wife went off to fetch the breakfast. She herself brought out the coffee and she put a good helping of cream on the top, because that was how her husband liked it. She could not drink it with all that froth, but if that was how he liked it, well, she would humour him, and she piled on all that she had in the pot.

When she returned, her husband was still sitting there, and his watch was in his hand.

"Wherever has she gone now?"

"God alone knows. All day long she's been giving me a fit, just standing and moving as if she deliberately wanted to annoy me... She stands more than she bends down. She wields the hoe ten or fifteen times, then she straightens up. I've just been counting the seconds she works and the seconds she spends lounging about."

"Oh, don't upset yourself. She always does that. You've got to get used to it."

"I can't. I can't get used to this sort of thing. She's doing no work at all. I can't call in a different day-labourer, because her husband will take offence that it's not his wife who's getting paid, and as it is they're simply stealing the money out of my pocket... I can't comprehend this scoundrelly behaviour—how has she the effrontery to spend the whole day, whole days, the whole summer, without making the slightest effort for a single minute!"

"You really are making a chase of it, my dear. You're standing there like a hunting dog on the watch."

"That's just what I am. But today I'm timing her. Today I'm noting things down, recording exactly how many seconds she is at work in an hour. And just when I've been recording her for half an hour, she abandons her place of work and goes off with the children, and I don't know what she's doing there behind the walnut tree... In the first half hour she worked for sixteen minutes and slacked for fourteen... And now she's been over there for seven whole minutes. And I don't know what the devil she's doing..."

"Why don't you go over there, dear, and take a look?"

"What I want to do now is to determine how much work she's doing and how much she is stealing."

"Go over there and speak to her."

"First I want to work out her rate of productivity so that I can have something to refer to. Because I want to find out what these folk can do when I'm not here. If I go out now and shout at her, I'm certain she'll start working, but I've got to be quite clear about her character, so that I can find out what to reckon on if there's nobody to keep an eye on her... Now it's nine minutes and I still don't know what's become of her."

"She's picking gooseberries," said his wife.

"Gooseberries?"

"The cobbler's children from next door must have come round and asked her to pick them enough to make soup."

"There you are, you see! She wastes half a day for the sake of one lot of gooseberries to make soup. It's fourteen minutes now, and she still hasn't picked those few gooseberries."

"Here she comes now."

The gentleman on the verandah counted the seconds it took for the woman to get back to the hoe.

However, she did not go to the spot where she was working, but went towards the gardener's house with the two children. With increasing exasperation, almost feverishly he watched the woman's comfortable pace and the racing of the minute-hand.

At last the gardener's wife emerged from the house and went back to the hoe.

"Seventeen and a half minutes," said the gentleman on the verandah. "She's been wasting the day for seventeen minutes. Náncsi! Náncsi!" he now shouted to the gardener's wife.

The gardener's wife did not understand all the shouting at first. She turned slowly round, looking in all directions, and this too with calmness fit to give one an apoplectic fit, so that the gentleman on the verandah huffed and puffed and went purple with rage.

"Náncsi!..."

And he went and stood on the steps of the verandah. "What are you doing?"

The gardener's wife began to come towards the villa, because she dared not call out to the master. She came obediently and humbly.

"Tell me, what have you been doing?" shouted her

master, on the verge of a dizzy fit at the thought that this was wasting more seconds.

"Hoeing the new strawberry bed."

"But you're not hoeing now... You're walking about... Where have you been?"

The gardener's wife could not understand the gentleman's hoarse and agitated tones.

"The cobbler's boy came for gooseberries."

"How many gooseberries?"

"Half a litre."

"So, for half a litre of gooseberries, you... How much do they cost?"

"Six fillérs."

"Six fillérs. Your daily rate for ten hours is three pengős, that's thirty fillérs an hour. So far that has taken you twenty-four minutes... For half an hour's work you are paid fifteen fillérs, and you've sold six fillér's worth... I'm deducting nine fillérs from your pay..."

The gardener's wife went back to her hoe mortally offended. Then she raised the corner of her kerchief to her eye and from that time onwards till noon did nothing but keep dabbing at her eyes. As for the gentleman on the verandah, he drank up his coffee and then, somewhat calmer, read the newspaper.

1932

TO EAT ONE'S FILL FOR ONCE

1

In the Jurassic age the great Hungarian plain was a sea. But today, in the age of Famine, it is still like a sea.

It is an endlessly flat land in all directions beneath the sky. No hillocks, no slopes anywhere: it is as flat as if it were the surface of the sea, if the sea were capable of freezing into this form. The wheat grows there as evenly as if God's draughtsmen had measured it with a ruler to determine how high each young stalk of wheat might be permitted to grow so that not one might spoil the evenness of the mirror-smooth surface.

The sky covers it like a glass dome on which playful angels project clouds and marvellous blue and white colours.

It looks as if the count's farm is right in the centre of the world, for if you look around from it you see the rim of the sky in every direction, all three hundred and sixty-five degrees of it, whichever way you turn.

The young count also believes that he himself is the centre of the universe, for wherever he goes on his Arab stead, the labourers greet him as if a young god were passing through their midst.

Now he arrives at a three-hundred acre field of beet. Sugar beet, and an area so enormous and flat that anyone looking at it for a long time grows dizzy. They grow sugar beet here, and the little plants stand there like dainty little schoolgirls drawn up in regular rows by the physical training mistress: wherever you look they are in dead straight lines.

From his horse the count can see a long way, since there are no trees either in the region, and the saddle seems to be a gigantic height above the minuscule world of plants.

The count looks around, searching for the gang of labourers he visited yesterday and the day before, in fact every day this week—and today is Friday and the time noon.

The labourers are divided into gangs of seventy. Seventy men armed with hoes, and they bend double over the little sugar-beet plants and carefully hoe the weeds and make a little inverted funnel of a mound round each single seedling.

At last he makes out the gang he is looking for and rides towards them along the road.

By the time he reaches them it is just twelve o'clock.

At the gang-leader's sign the workmen straighten up and stop hoeing. It is lunch-time; they break ranks and go off to the edge of the field where the wives and children are already waiting with their lunch.

They bring the food in pots from the village, but they all arrive there punctually as the bells begin to toll in the distant church-towers.

The young count dismounts from his horse and throws the reins to a young lad who leaps forward; he himself goes up to the gangmaster and asks,

"When will you be finished with this little job?"

The count is a tough young sportsman of thirty, the gangmaster sixty-five, old and surly. The count is happy and easy-going, the old man is crook-backed and sullen.

He answers with deep humility,

"Don't be angry, your excellency, but the soil's very hard. We haven't had rain for a long time. We're making slow progress because the only thing that's growing is grass. Certainly we could only get the job done by Saturday evening if we hoed all night long."

The count is not really interested in all this. He merely asked the question about the end of the job in order to justify his presence out here on the puszta.

He nods and says,

"All right, then go on hoeing all through the night."

The gangmaster scratches his head and replies,

"Your excellency, you couldn't persuade the men to do that, whatever rates you offered them."

The count laughs, looks round and catches sight of the reason for his trip, a slender, tall, pretty young wife who is just handing her husband the bowl of food.

2

The woman also looked across at the young count, blushed a little and nodded rather coquettishly, then pretended that she was not aware of the count.

She turns towards her husband, who has now settled himself on the ground, and says, "Eat!"

"What have you brought?" asks the man.

"What should I have brought? The same as yesterday, a little soup."

The man knows very well that there is nothing at all back at home. The little pantry is empty. He takes the bowl sullenly and sets it between his knees.

He lifts it out of the string bag in which it was brought and takes the lid off. He looks inside.

Yes, there is nothing inside but some kind of brown liquid. On top of it floats a little congealed fat. As he dips his spoon into it, the cold fat sticks to the thin spoon.

He says nothing, because there is nothing he can say. There is severe famine in the villages now. The winter was a very hard one. There was nothing to eat, because last year there was a bad harvest owing to the drought and they were unable to put anything into store for the winter, and now they are up to their ears in debt. Now that work has begun the daily rate is very low—one pengő per day. Labourers in distant, happier countries would not even begin to understand how it is possible to exist on that. They, however, even pay their debts out of it and starve like famished dogs. The man cannot blame his wife for not bringing something more and something better, because it is a good point to the wife if she does not complain... The price of corn is very low and the estates cannot pay either.

So he heaves a sigh and spoons out a little soup. He is even pleased to find one or two dumplings in the liquid; his wife has made them of flour and they float in the dark brown slops like primeval, soft-bodied animals.

The man is called Kis, János Kis. He has the shortest name and the longest record of poverty. His poverty floats after him like a shadow at evening when it disappears into the landscape in the east.

He grinds his teeth and resolutely settles down to the meal.

Always this soup. Soup in the morning and soup again when he gets home in the evening.

"When I consider how much soup I've had in my life," he says, "if it were all poured into one tub, why, it would be bigger than any of those huge barrels in the cellars of the Archbishop of Eger!"

The woman makes no reply. Absent-mindedly, as if it were by accident, she looks across to where the young count is standing talking to the men.

The labourers meanwhile sit down all over the place, one here, another there. Each one of them hides the pot that has been brought out to him. Each one of them has something paltry to eat, something not worth boasting about. They bend over the earthenware pots and ply their spoons in the same way.

"Have you brought water?" asks János Kis.

"No."

"Why not?"

"Why, you brought some out this morning."

"One litre. I brought one litre, but it's all gone now."

"Why did you drink it all?"

"Why did I drink it? Have I got to go short of water too?"

The woman pondered a little.

"All right, then I'll go and get some."

"Be quick."

The woman takes the litre bottle out of the haversack. There is nothing else in it but a little bread. She takes that out too and hands it to her husband.

"Eat this up."

"Eat it up... If I eat it up, then there won't be any."

"All the same, you can't die of starvation."

"I can't die of starvation? It's easy for a woman to say that... One can tell you've never been a soldier...

Because when I was a soldier, anyone who ate his last tin of food was court-martialled. And if we were in battle, they shot him... So I'm not going to eat the last slice of bread in case there is even greater famine on the count's estate..."

The woman does not say anything. She sets out towards the well with the bottle.

Her husband does not even watch her go; he just goes on spooning out the soup slowly, very slowly.

The well is quite a distance away. Next to the sugar-beet field there is a gigantic cattle pasture, ten thousand acres of it. On the near side of it there is a cattle-trough. Once the beet-field was also pasture land, but it was ploughed up, thus leaving the trough on the edge of the pasture.

The woman walked swiftly on and on, and her skirt fluttered in the breeze. The young count watched her until she disappeared in the distance.

Then he suddenly said,

"I've got to water my horse... Is there any water in that well?"

The old gangmaster was silent for a long time. Finally he spoke.

"There is, your excellency. There's still water in the well."

"Right then, I'll go and water the horse."

So saying he leapt on his horse. There was a fine yellow saddle on the horse, and smart buckskin trousers on the young count. As he sat high up on horseback he was a very handsome young man, and he began to gallop towards the well to get water for his horse.

3

The woman had just drawn up the bucket of water when the count arrived.

She seemed to be startled when the young count appeared at the well.

"Is there any water in the well?" asked the young man.

"Yes, your excellency, there is," answered the woman.

"Well, in that case I'll water my little horse."

With that he jumped from the horse and led the animal to the well.

The woman forgot about filling the bottle. Obligingly she poured the water into the trough, but the trough was very large and totally dry. The bucket of water was a mere trickle in it. So she let the bucket down into the well again and brought up another bucketful, then a third one.

The horse buried its nose in the water and noisily drank a little of it, but it did not want to drink; it was not thirsty.

The woman laughed.

"The horse isn't thirsty."

"But I am," said the count.

At this the woman let the bucket down into the well again without a word and drew it up carefully when it was full. She filled the bottle, slopped a little of the water into the well and offered it to the count.

But he just gazed at her with eyes ablaze and said,

"It's not water that I'm thirsty for."

"Then what is it, your excellency?"

"A kiss."

At this the woman glanced at him saucily, as only pretty young women know how to look.

"That's nothing you'll die of, your excellency."

"I don't want to die of it."

So saying he stepped closer to the woman.

She blushed to the roots of her hair.

"Your excellency, we're in the puszta!"

"So?"

"I'm only telling you."

"Why are you telling me?"

"You know why, your excellency."

"I certainly don't."

"Of course you know why... They'll see us."

"Let them go blind if they want to see us."

But the woman did not take it as a joke; she went and stood on the other side of the well.

"Don't come so close, your excellency. People see with their eyes in such a way that they can even catch sight of what you are thinking."

The count had wanted to follow her, but at this he stopped.

"Listen, this is the fifth day I've come out to the puszta on your account... But you don't want to understand..."

"No."

"But you won't escape until I've kissed you."

The woman said with all seriousness,

"I've got a husband."

The count was silent.

"What do you mean by that?"

"I leave the explanation to you, your excellency."

"And I'm certainly not going to explain it..."

But his eyes blazed like fire and this gave the woman a very good explanation of what he wanted.

"Do you love your husband?" asked the count.

"I stood with him in front of the priest," said the woman.

"I'm asking you whether you love him."

"It's not right to ask such questions of a wife."

"But I'm the one who's got to know."

"Perhaps you'd better ask my husband. He knows."

"Listen! Don't try to be funny with me... I want you."

"People want lots of things that can't happen."

"Except that I'm not used to this sort of thing. What I want usually happens."

"And this time too what must happen is going to happen."

"What's that?"

"Your excellency is going to get on your horse and leave me in peace."

"Look, I don't want to upset you... I only wanted to speak to you this once."

"We've nothing whatsoever to talk about."

"We have... Last night I couldn't sleep because of you."

"The gentry have enough medicine to make them dream."

"You're the only one who could make me dream."

"I'm not a witch."

"But I think you are, because on Monday you looked me straight in the eye and bewitched me. Since then you've always run away when I approach."

"Your excellency has plenty of countesses to console you."

The count said hoarsely,

"Now I'm going to kiss you."

He made a movement as if to vault over to the other side of the well.

The woman shouted in terror,

"Don't you dare move, or I'll jump down the well!"

The young man stopped. He wiped his forehead.

"You're an evil cat! You're playing with me."

"How should I dare to do that with a count?"

"Look at me! My eyes are almost jumping from their sockets. I haven't slept for five days. Aren't you sorry for me?"

"Oh dear, your excellency, tell me honestly, what have you eaten today?"

The count was astonished. For breakfast he had eaten cold roast meat. A good big slice. With it he had drunk two glasses of brandy too, good strong brandy. Because he had wanted to screw up his courage to dare to speak to the woman today. But this he did not want to admit, so he said,

"I haven't eaten or drunk anything for five days. I've been pining for you all the time."

"There you are, your excellency. For five days my husband hasn't eaten anything else but brown soup for breakfast, brown soup for lunch and just brown soup for supper too... Haven't you any pity for that poor man, your excellency?"

"Why don't you cook him something else? Cold roast meat. Jam for his bread. Meat soup for lunch... fried chicken..."

"Please don't joke about poor folk... I can't even fry anything for him, poor wretch, because there isn't enough fat in the house to add to a scrap of flour... I cook for him with salt and water, and I haven't got any potatoes either to give him."

"There you are, you see. That's where you should have started. If you'll only listen to me, I'll give you everything. You can cook what you like."

"Leave me alone, your excellency. I'm a decent woman."

"And I'm a decent man too. I won't abandon you if you'll love me."

The woman gave him a hostile look.

"Your excellency, get on your horse and go away. That is the only decent thing you can do to me. We've already been talking for a long time... I shan't be able to explain to my husband what we've been talking about..."

"Invent something that we've been talking about."

"I could suggest something, but I don't know whether you will do it."

"Anything."

The woman closed her eyes and threw back her head.

"I'll tell you something. The men will soon finish hoeing. To celebrate that, sir, give them a good supper."

"Of course, I'll be glad to..."

"That's all I wanted to say."

"I'll get a gipsy band too... But then you'll be there as well!"

"If all the wives are going to be there, I will be there too."

"And you'll dance with me!"

"If you dance with everyone, then I shall have to as well."

"And you'll kiss me!"

"If you kiss all the wives, then you can kiss me too."

"You're a witch, but I don't mind. I'll even kiss the old women just to get at you!"

"Well then, now get on your horse and go away."

"No. I'll take the reins and lead my horse and go back with you."

"That's impossible, sir. You are not permitted to accompany me. Even now there's going to be a lot of gossip about the time you've been talking to me, your excellency."

"What's your name?"

"Eve."

"Then I'm Adam."

"No, your excellency's name is Victor."

"There, you see! Victor means 'Conqueror'—and I'm going to conquer you."

"Oh what a lot of time you must have on your hands, sir, if you don't regret chattering so much to a poor woman."

"See here, little Eve, I shouldn't regret it if I could spend all my life chatting to you."

"That's a very long time for a count."

"For me it's going to be a long time till tomorrow evening."

"Then get on your horse and gallop; perhaps you'll get there faster on horseback."

The count looked with glowing eyes into the eyes of the woman. He felt that never before in his life had he met such a lovable woman. He felt dizzy when he mounted his horse, then he waved once more to the little wife and galloped off.

As for the woman, she picked up the bottle and set off towards her husband, deep in thought.

4

"What the devil were you talking about to the young count?" János Kis asked his wife angrily when she arrived with the litre of water.

"Something very good."

The man stared straight ahead. He had finished all the soup, but he was still dizzy with hunger. They had an hour's break now, and he would have liked to sleep a little. He was furious that his wife had taken half an hour of his sleep away and now instead of closing his eyes he had to go on questioning her.

"Tell me what it was, you wretch, or I'll strike you dead this instant!"

The woman sat down beside him on the ground. She saw that the men, all seventy of them, had their eyes on her, and everyone would like to know what she had said to the count. But the women and children too, who had brought out food to the seventy men, were looking at her as if they would have given half their lives to find out what had kept her talking so long with the count. On the puszta people see everything, however far off a woman is when she has been courted by a man.

"He said... He asked..."

"And don't you dare tell lies!" growled her husband as she began.

"He wanted to know what there should be for supper... Because he wants to give you all supper when you've finished hoeing the beet..."

The man blinked in surprise. All of a sudden he forgot all his anger.

"Supper?"

"Yes."

The man listened to his stomach. It was so thin now, so wasted...

"So what does he want to give us for supper? Brown soup?"

"Meat!"

"So! Because you've feasted me well enough on soup..."

He would have liked to ask why she was the one he asked what he should give them for supper. But his head was so weary that he did not feel like saying a word.

They looked over to where the count was having a discussion with the gangmaster. There was a big crowd there. They saw the count get on his horse and gallop away. The men who were standing round him all took off their hats and cheered him, then threw up their hats and shouted at the tops of their voices.

A young lad ran towards them and said,

"If we finish the hoeing by tomorrow evening, his excellency the count is going to throw such a banquet that everyone will be able to eat as much as he likes."

János Kis hung his head.

"By tomorrow evening?" he said. "That means we shall have to work all night..."

The woman kept silent. She did not look into her husband's eyes. She looked straight ahead. She thought of how the gipsies would come with their violins and play tunes to make the feet itch... She shivered, because she seemed to hear the gipsy music already... She felt the count coming up, clasping her round the waist and going to dance with her...

Another thin man crawled across to them.

"Have you heard?"

"Yes," said János Kis dully.

"He's a gentleman," said the man.

"A gentleman? A scoundrel..."

"Why?"

"He wants us to work all night long."

"There's moonlight... Full moon... It's possible."

"It's possible for the moon, but for us..."

"For every ten men there'll be a fat sheep... Mutton stew can be made of that... And he's giving a couple of hundredweight of flour... And everything to go with it... Twenty kilos of fat and twenty kilos of curd cheese... That'll make cheese noodles and five hectolitres of wine..."

"Too little," said János Kis.

"Too little?" said the other man in astonishment.

"It's too little just for me," said János Kis.

"Everyone will get a kilo of meat, or two kilos... And some dumplings, about two kilos... Good fat cheese noodles... and seven litres of wine... per head... Isn't that enough?"

"It's too little..."

"You won't be able to eat three kilos of food and seven litres of wine—that's ten kilos!"

"It's too little," said János Kis obstinately.

"Well how much ought there to be?"

"All the lot! All the lot isn't enough!"

"There'll be rams, big rams... Big old rams... Great fattened beasts... Would you be able to eat all seven of them?"

"Yes!"

"And noodles from two hundredweight of flour, with twenty kilos of curd cheese..."

"Yes!"

"And the five hectolitres of wine?"

"That too!"

"Well, how much should there be?"

"All the lot... Everything the count possesses, all the lot... His thirty thousand acres of land and his mansion, his farms, his cattle, his horses and pigs..."

"You'd swallow the lot?"

"Yes, and him too, for good measure."

"You've got a good appetite."

"Yes, I have. An appetite, that's something I have got... For I'm thirty-six years old, but all my life I've lived on watery, wishy-washy soup... Even my mother kept me on it, on water. When I come out into the fields to work, what do I bring with me? I bring a litre of water in my haversack so that there's no need to go to the well, so that I can go on working during the time it would take me to fetch water... If I feel faint with the work I just take a swig and get rid of the dizziness that way. I can wait until my wife brings out lunch... Boiled water... I drink it up... Then back again to work... Well, to me that's too little..."

"Maybe it's too little... for life," said the other labourer, "for it's true, however much a man eats, next day he's so hungry again; it's as if there hasn't been a feast at all."

"There's not too little work to do... There's still some of that left over for tomorrow," grumbled János Kis. "I've worked for nobody else but this count all my life... from spring till autumn..."

"That's good!" said the other man. "It's a good thing we've got this estate. It's a good thing that at least here you can get work."

"All I do from morning till night is hack the soil. I dig it over. It can bring me to the grave... And now for the sake of a little supper I've got to work all night long... Well, why? Just for a bite of meat? A few noodles? A glass of wine?"

"He's fetching gipsies too, music! A band!"

"Isn't he fetching the police? The gendarmerie?"

The other man said thoughtfully and slowly,

"Don't you want to come with us? Do you want to go home? Don't you want to take part in the feast tomorrow night?"

"Of course I do... But for me it's too little."

"Then what do you want?"

"What do I want? Tomorrow I'll eat that dog of a count out of all he possesses. That's what I want..."

The woman listened with downcast head to what her husband was saying. She sat there crushed... She was afraid of tomorrow.

5

The seventy men worked all night long. They were beyond looking to see whether they were cutting through the beet seedlings; they just went on hoeing.

After midnight the moon disappeared. It went down in

the west, following the sun. Then they were in darkness and lay down where they happened to be standing at the time.

The night was chilly. They were cold. Nobody had thought they would have to spend the night outside.

When dawn came the gangmaster woke up and gave a great shout.

"Back to work, men!"

The men stumbled to their feet. They gave themselves a shake. They went off in a long line to the cattle-trough and washed their heads to freshen themselves up. They cursed the count who was resting at home in his comfortable bed while they were suffering out here in the field. Just for one supper. They cursed him, because that was the custom. But then they thought of the supper, the mutton stew and the cheese noodles, and they laughed.

The young men in particular laughed and called out like blackbirds at dawn.

The old men kept a bear-like silence; they belched from time to time, and that was all.

On the great flat puszta seventy men got down to their daily work earlier than the sun.

The women brought out breakfast. Every one of them collected whatever morsels of good food were left at home, because they knew that the men had suffered all night and they were sorry for them. They too were getting ready for the evening feast. Their feet were itching and they were already dancing and laughing.

János Kis's wife too came out to him with a big pot of food. It was not soup that she brought, but cooked food. There were a lot of noodles in it and a lot of potatoes.

"What's this?" asked János Kis.

"I borrowed it," said the woman, "because I knew that you'd had a hard night and would have a hard day... You've got to have something to eat, or you won't last out till evening."

János Kis gazed into the pot for a long time. Then he said,

"What was it the count said to you yesterday?"

"What would he have said? He said nothing."

"Nothing?"

"No. Nothing at all."

"Because I dreamt that he did say something."

The woman blushed.

"What did you dream? What did he say?"

"You know very well."

"Well, I've forgotten."

"Why, did he say something you had to forget?"

The woman hesitated.

"No, it wasn't anything like that."

"Well, what sort of things did he say?"

"Nothing at all... He only asked whether fifty kilos of flour would be enough for the noodles."

"So what did you say?"

"That it wouldn't be enough, because there'd be a lot of us. Because we're coming along too, the wives."

"You said that you were all coming?"

The woman pulled her head-scarf over her eyes.

"Why do you keep on asking me questions? I didn't say anything of that kind to the count."

"What kind?"

"The sort of thing you have to ask questions about... I said that he had to reckon on one sheep for ten men because you would all be with your families."

"Wives?"

"Well, you'll be by yourself, since you haven't any children."

The woman sighed.

János Kis pushed the pot away.

"It was a pity to borrow," he said, "because if a man borrows, he's got to pay it back."

"We'll pay it back sometime."

"Out of what?" I can't earn any more than six pengős a week. And it'll be just the same in future."

"All the same, eat it up. It's a long day, and you won't have the strength."

"Of course I shall. For this day I shall have enough strength, Eve."

The woman gave a shudder at the sound of her name. That was how the count had said it yesterday—"Eve".

"Come on, have something to eat," she urged her husband gently.

"I'm not going to eat, because then I shan't be able to eat the count out of his fortune tonight."

"Of course you won't. Whatever are you thinking of?"

"Will we have a fortune tomorrow?" asked János Kis. "However much I eat, do you think he'll still have something to eat tomorrow and the day after? For ever?"

"I don't think anything at all."

"All right, then just go back home. Take the food home with you too. I shan't eat today anyway. And don't come out at lunchtime either. It'll be enough for you to come out to the dance this evening."

The woman shouted furiously.

"What is it you want?"

"And don't come out at midday... And make sure you come along this evening. Or else I'll fetch you..."

"My dear husband, you're ill!"

János Kis smiled quietly like a man who knows what he is smiling at.

"Well now, go home," he said, "and don't have to be told twice..."

The woman's eyes filled with tears.

"Oh, my dear, dear husband..."

She clasped her hands and began to cry.

At this János Kis had another thought. He thought he wasn't making a very good job of this... The woman was cunning, she suspected something...

"All right then," he said gently, "I'll have a bite."

So saying he settled down and ate. He did not eat very much, but he did have something. And he slapped his wife on the back as if she were a fine horse, and did not even want her to take the pot away. He watched the woman cover it with a cloth and some grass, then dig it into the ground to keep it a little cooler.

6

They made good progress up to midday. They saw that they would be finished early with the hoeing. They even let two of the men go and start building the fire.

At noon all the women came out. Seventy women, all of them dressed in their Sunday clothes, as if they had discussed the matter, even the old women too. There was to be a dance, and it was for this that they had got ready.

Only János Kis's wife was not dressed in her best clothes. János Kis smiled at her and said,

"Are you beautiful enough as you are?"

"If to you I'm beautiful, then I'm always beautiful," said the woman.

After lunch the women did not go home, but stayed there out in the field.

By teatime the hoeing was finished. Three hundred acres lay behind the seventy men. It was a good piece of work. The huge tract of land was fresh and black as far as the eye could see, and in it the little seedlings fluttered their tiny leaves, refreshed in the gentle breeze.

The sheep had already arrived. Nor was it seven that the count had sent, but fourteen. They were not all chopped up to put in the big cauldron; what was not needed they simply divided up among themselves.

Everyone was in thoroughly good spirits. They shouted and sang. The great puszta carried the sound into the distance and it faded far away on the wind.

Towards dusk the count also came out on horseback.

The young count was dressed for the occasion too. He was wearing shining patent-leather boots and a brand-new suit. He looked as if he had just been taken out of a bandbox. There was a Tyrolese hat on his head and a rifle over his shoulder.

They welcomed him with cheers, and the count went the rounds, shaking hands with them all, every man and every woman. With János Kis and Mrs János Kis as well.

"How are you, Eve?" he said to the woman, and held her hand in his a fraction longer than he did the rest.

János Kis said with a laugh,

"Today we're going to eat you out of your fortune, your excellency."

"Just eat as much as you can put away!" said the young count, who addressed them all in familiar terms, the very old and the young children alike. As counts generally do.

He even slapped János Kis on the shoulder.

"The labourer is worthy of his... supper..." he said, as Jesus Christ said in the Bible—except that Jesus Christ put it that 'The labourer is worthy of his hire'. But the young count did not dare to say it in those words, because the peasants might then have demanded a rise in wages. He regarded it sufficient to say 'of his supper'.

János Kis smiled.

"We've got an appetite... Such an appetite that we would be capable of eating up all the fields, soil and all, like the worms."

"Ah well, don't eat them all up," said the young count, "or you'll overburden your stomachs."

So saying, he pinched the woman's cheek, as if he expected her to protect his estate.

János Kis laughed.

When the count had moved on, he said to his wife,

"All the same, it was a pity you didn't dress up a bit. You've got a nice dress; I bought it for you."

"I'm all right as I am," said the woman, and felt disturbed.

They settled down to supper.

The cooks had even made soup. The soup was like oil, rich and thick.

"Are you having some?" asked the woman.

"Is it good?"

"Very good."

"Then I'll have some. For, you know, I've had quite enough soup in my life, but that was all such nasty, thin washing-up water that it wouldn't even have made good slops for the pigs... But as for good food, if all that I had been given in my life were piled together, it wouldn't even fill that pot you brought out to me this morning..."

The woman filled his plate full, spilling a little over the rim, and he began to eat... His whole body trembled with hunger, yet after the tenth spoonful he felt he could not eat any more.

A terrible dread and anger broke out in him. What was going to happen here today? How was he going to fulfil his promise?

He swallowed down the soup and drank wine with it. A big glass of wine.

Then he felt he was ready for real work.

He was given a big dish of meat, with a big piece of bread. He looked at it.

"Why don't you eat?" asked his wife.

"I'm in no hurry. I want to eat till morning... And that was only the soup!"

The sun had gone down now and the moon, which had long been in the sky, began to grow bright.

The count was everywhere and talked to everyone and embraced everyone; but every minute he was at their side and said some pleasant things to them.

By then the wine was beginning to take effect, and the feast became noisier and noisier. János Kis saw the count kissing all the women in turn.

He was just waiting for Eve's turn to come.

Eve too was waiting, and her body trembled like that of a mare in season.

And at this moment there appeared out of the blue a posse of police.

They were fine, merry lads, who had not come with any evil design; they turned up by accident. They said so. They wore plumes of cocks' feathers in their hats. They greeted everyone politely. János Kis laughed.

And he firmly grasped the knife with which he was eating.

Then the count reached them in his round of kissing.

He stepped up to Eve, bowed and—did not kiss her.

Two policemen sat down by him when the count asked Eve to dance.

Eve looked at her husband.

"Off with you, then," said János Kis. "Dance! The supper's a good one; you've got to dance it away, or it will upset your stomach..."

The dancers were whirling round now, fifty or sixty couples. The count was in front of the gipsies.

János Kis settled down to eat.

He swallowed one mouthful. He could not take it. He brought it up and spat it out.

"Mr Policeman," he said, "you see, that's the trouble..."

"What is, my friend?" said the policeman.

"Here's this good supper, and a chap can't even make a bargain to eat his fill for once, because he simply can't eat."

"Why can't he?"

János Kis looked for his knife on the ground and wiped it carefully.

"A poor man can't eat. Why? Because he's poor... The poor man can only swallow his anger, true? He has his fill of the soup. By the time the meat comes along, it's all up with him... Others wolf that down."

"Go on eating, just eat," said the policeman and looked hard at János Kis.

But János Kis was not watching him, he was looking elsewhere. He was looking towards the gipsies.

"A man hasn't got two stomachs to take everything in... A poor man hasn't even got a belly."

At that moment the count kissed the woman.

János Kis smiled. He turned white, but he smiled. His hand stiffened on the knife, and he plunged it into the policeman up to its handle.

1933

ANGELS OF LITTLE WOOD

1

Two hundred and forty women in the great ballroom.

Blondes, brunettes, short, tall, young and old. Every kind can be found among two hundred and forty women. In the other room, the mirror-room, there are another hundred women.

And for all these women there are only ten or twelve partners altogether.

"All the same, they know how to make us dance, devil take their ankles!" grumbles Mrs Kátai, who does not join in the chatter of her neighbours unless she can say something spiteful and unpleasant.

"Folk from Little Wood aren't scared of their shadows!" shouts Gitka, one of the girls, in her direction.

"No, they're not," grumbles Mrs Kátai, "not even if there were twelve lads to each one of them."

The women suddenly grow silent, because the director is approaching. And the director, who is a pink-faced, pleasant little young man, is held in great respect: he is the one who pays them.

With the director come two gentlemen, visitors who just watch this strange ball.

The women scarcely glance up; their eyes are bewitched. Not one of them ever glances to left or right. They look at one place, and as far as they are concerned anything may happen, they are not interested, they only watch the place where their fingers are at play.

One of the visitors plucks up courage and begins to say such things as,

"All those angels in a row!"

And:

"It must be a good place to show off a bit here... That little blonde... This little brunette."

The women however do not even smile. With deadly seriousness they watch their fingers which work industriously, never stopping for an instant.

They are shelling peas.

2

A word or two of the director's explanation reaches their ears too, otherwise they hardly know anything about the nature of this business in which they are engaged.

"The Dutch company realized that Hungary had the best soil for growing seeds. In particular the quality of the peas produced here is incomparable. Five hundred wagons of peas are exported from the country, and all of them are produced here. The flat region of Borsod is particularly good soil for peas. The germination rate is over ninety per cent, and that figure cannot be reached anywhere else in the world."

"Nor the fact that so many pretty girls are assembled to select them," said one of the visitors.

The director takes matters as seriously as the women; he does not react to the facetious interruptions, but continues his expert exposition.

"This is where we select them and prepare them for distribution to all parts of the world. They will be used for planting. They will be divided into small sachets and paper bags and sold like that in China, India and Africa and Australia—in other words all over the world. All we do here is sort them; we pick out the imperfect, underdeveloped, brown and bad seeds and export the healthy ones, all of uniformly prime quality, to the firm abroad. This means profit to the Hungarian farmer too, because one and a half acres produce two hundredweight: for this he receives sixteen pengős per quintal, which means 192 pengős from that acreage, whereas if he grows wheat, he produces eight quintals for seven pengős per quintal, in other words 56 pengős."

"And what do these beauties get?"

So saying the stranger puts his hand in his pocket and brings out a large bag of cough-sweets.

"Are any of you here from Little Wood?"

"Indeed there are, we're here," answers Gitka.

"Well, this is for the folk from Little Wood."

The girl catches the bag of sweets and looks round.

"Those from Little Wood..."

Every second or third woman glances up. Gitka throws the sweets one by one and they catch them.

Mrs Kátai does not look in that direction. The sweet bounces on to the table and bounds off. She does not bat an eyelid. She works on.

3

The work comes to an end at a quarter to seven in the evening. Then they put on their coats swift as lightning, because the shops are only open till seven, and most of them have still to go and buy something to take home for supper.

When Mrs Kátai reaches Boráros Square with her bag made out of ends of baize, it is a fine autumn evening. The sun has still left a red glow in the sky, but the yellow electric lights devour the colour out of the sky and cover the street in a mosaic of semi-darkness.

The trams come and go clanking on their way. A host of routes runs into this square. Most of them terminate here, and passengers change to go in all directions.

Gitka stands at the shop outside the Széchenyi Café. On her head she is wearing a little beret, from beneath which her short golden-brown locks spill out. She stands there gravely and like an inspector examines the tickets brought to her by little girls in their teens.

The young girls are lively as sparrows as they pick the thrown-away tram tickets from the ground.

This requires a good deal of cunning, because there is a policeman standing there in the middle of the road and the tickets can only be snatched up when a tram hides him. Some of the teenage girls are so reckless that they even jump on the trams when they are still moving and fetch the used tickets from the floor.

Mrs Kátai watches all this going on with loathing. She does not belong to their secret organization. She just keeps a stealthy watch on Gitka's movements as she takes a quick look at each ticket and says where it comes from, how far it is valid, whether it can be used to transfer to the tram going to Ferencváros station, and immediately distributes the valid ones. With that the fortunate ones fly across to the right tram and with untroubled conscience save the fare out to Little Wood.

"One day they'll lock you up, and you'll deserve it," hisses Mrs Kátai with hatred.

"Oh, don't be so jealous!" says Gitka seriously. "You'll be eaten up with spite."

"Yes," pants the woman, bobbing her head with its cheap knitted woolly cap, just like those worn by children, with a pompom on the top, "a fine thing you're teaching the young folk! You're always the ringleader in it all!"

"Do go home now; the children are hungry."

"I'll tell the policeman, I will so!"

"And you would, too." And the girl examines more tickets and distributes them.

But the woman rattles on wildly; she foams at the mouth with rage and jealousy. Here everyone is given a ticket except her, because she's not in the plot, because she's always honest and wouldn't ever do anything that was against the law, not for the world.

But the folk from Little Wood have only one law: it is that of the sparrows which swarm down on thrown-out food wherever it has come from into the street, and pick up whatever they find good for them.

All of a sudden the sparrows fly off in a swarm; they disappear in an instant and nobody is left at the tram stop except the woman, the girl and two young boys who watch Gitka with hungry eyes.

The policeman comes over to them with dignified steps.

"Why are you lounging about here?"

The boys look at him pugnaciously. They are bold, because they are not holding a trace of a ticket in their hand.

"You picked a ticket up from the ground too!" says the

policeman and grows red with excitement in the effort to prove his point.

"I certainly didn't. I don't need one," says the boy and takes out his pass with its photograph and holds it out in front of the policeman's face.

"Do you live in Little Wood?"

"Of course I don't. I live in Lónyay Street."

"Then why are you lounging about here? I'll take you along to the station!"

"You can, constable; but in any case you'll let me go, so why bother?"

The policeman looks round helplessly. The whole area is empty now, but he knows that the minute he leaves, the street corner will fill up again. He can't be everywhere at once. He can't have a hundred eyes and two hundred hands to catch all these fly-by-nights. He looks at the girl who stands there like an angel.

For a brief moment his eyes seem to fasten on to the pretty girl, whose girlhood radiates from her, though this does not worry him. If once he catches her out, he will take her inside just like the rest of the rabble.

Now a tall, strong young man appears, steps up to Gitka; they turn and walk along Mester Street.

They disappear.

Mrs Kátai also crosses to the other stop and goes home on the first 22.

4

At Ferencváros station she clambers down from the tram and at the terminus turns into Little Wood estate. She drags herself along heavily and in a very bad temper. Beside her little girls jump down and disappear like little animals or flitting birds. She envies them their youth and merriment. How can anyone in this estate of death be young and merry?

She shuffles her way along the narrow alleyways of the shanty town. This is the route she has to follow all the way every day, because she lives at the furthest corner of the settlement.

The estate is the most astonishing world anywhere to be found. It is nothing but shanty after shanty, hovels made of planks and about as large as the outside lavatory behind a village house. Each of them has a box-hedge round it, so there is a modicum of order in the estate. The little streets and alleyways between the box-hedges twist and turn in right-angles. The shanties stand there in lines, by the hundred, by the thousand. In some of them there is light; through the tiny windows filter the rays of an oil-lamp. These are the wealthy ones. For in most of the windows there is no light; at most a fire still glimmers here and there. The mothers arrive back from work late and only now knock up a little supper for the children who have stayed at home. For there are children here, plenty of them, two or three in each house and in quite a lot of them six or eight.

Mrs Kátai does not even have a shanty-home. She has been taken in by a widow who is very old; her old husband died not long ago, and since they both come from the same part of the country, she has taken her in as a lodger to keep her company.

She goes past the church.

The church too is like the shanties, built of old planks that have been collected together. God's house is like those of his believers. And that is right and proper.

When she reaches shanty no. 1000, she notices that the girl has got there too. Of course they came by a shorter route and their legs are young. They got there before her—and she paid sixteen fillérs on the tram, too.

As she reaches her shanty, her two little children are standing there in the open air, playing.

"Mother!" they screech and cling to her skirt. "Have you brought something for supper?"

Bad-temperedly she shakes the little ones off.

"Don't keep pulling at me! You'll get something to eat if there is anything."

The old woman stands in the doorway of the shanty. She is a wizened little creature. She has no teeth and lisps with old age.

She just gives her a nod in greeting. She goes into the

darkness inside. There is no lamp and no fire; no oil and no wood. She opens her bag in the dark and takes out some bread. She tears off pieces for the children and gives each of them a saveloy, putting it into their little hands.

The children shriek with happiness.

"Saveloy! Saveloy!"

She too sits down. Even in the dark she knows her way around. She too settles down to chew her portion with tears in her eyes.

The old woman totters to her bed. She sees that Mrs Kátai has not brought her anything. She does not take her to task or complain, but begins to make ready for bed. There are two beds in the room; their eyes gradually get used to the darkness, and the little window lets in a faint glimmer of light.

"The little hen isn't laying," mumbles the old woman. "They say she won't lay this winter."

She is in no mood to reply. The sausage in her hand begins to burn and scorch.

"They didn't give me a food voucher for next week," says the little old woman. "They wouldn't give me one. From now on they're only going to give me one for two weeks each month. There's nothing else to be got now but slops at the church. Slops morning, noon and night."

Suddenly no more food will go down her throat. Angrily, as if she is trying to tame a raging dog, she presses the quarter of a saveloy still left and a little bit of bread into the old lady's hand and says,

"Eat it up!"

The old lady is stunned to silence for a moment. Then she sets to immediately, nibbling like the children, who have already learnt that good meat, good horsemeat sausage must take a long time to eat in order to enjoy the delectable flavour for as long as possible.

Only when she has sucked away at it for a long time in her toothless mouth does she say,

"Mrs Kátai, you're beginning to learn too..."

"What am I beginning to learn?" the woman bursts out.

"The kindness of Little Wood," says the old woman, and in the darkness tears begin to trickle from her eyes.

Gitka has still not gone into the shack. In theirs a lamp is alight; in theirs they have a fire. They are cooking. They have food ready for her.

She merely knocked on the door, saying that she was back. Then she goes back and waits outside with the young man, leaning against a slender acacia in the box-hedge.

"Tell me Gitka," says the young man, "Are you capable of loving someone?"

The girl gives a laugh.

"Why do you ask?"

"I'd like to know."

The lad chokes over his words.

"First get a job, then ask me."

"If only I had a job," mutters the lad.

"You wouldn't take any further notice of us, isn't that so?"

The lad grabs hold of the girl. He seizes her arm and almost jerks it out of her shoulder. But the girl does not wince.

"You've got a doggy sort of nature."

The girl laughs.

"Doggy?"

"Yes."

"What sort of dog?"

"A spotted dog."

"Is that different?"

"It's the doggiest of the lot."

"That's all right then." And the girl laughs even more. "Are you saying that because I'm faithful?"

The boy is silent. This puts a new twist in his thoughts. Perhaps she is faithful. It's impossible to tell. He only knows that as they were on the way here every boy in the street turned to look at the girl, because in her movements there is something that stirs young men and even older ones to curiosity. That canine curiosity with which a dog sniffs after a bitch.

But he would very much prefer it not to be like this. He has been on her trail for quite a long time and sometimes believes he has won the girl and committed her to him, but all the same she will not give up this hip-wriggling, swaying, titillating walk or this flirtatiousness, and he grows increasingly black with rage that nothing succeeds for him and that he cannot lay his hands on any income of any kind. Today, like yesterday and the day before that, he just loiters around in the world; he comes and goes, talks, offers his services and cannot put his hands on a couple of farthings. For a fortnight now he has not seen the sight of a farthing. Last week he borrowed three pengős, and he ought to repay it, so he is compelled to avoid being seen in Józsefváros where the friend lives who lent him the money. He spent all that money on the girl too; he told her that he had earned it.

And now he dare not follow the girl, because she has a job. And anyone who has a job knows very well what it is to have an income and keep up a certain style.

And soon the cold weather will be coming. That is the worst of all. When the snow falls and the wind blows and it freezes hard. That is even worse than hunger.

So what is he to do with the girl? She has eaten into his blood and he cannot take her away, yet all he need say would be "Come along!"—but where to?

So they just scrap with each other. He with wild and brutal words and clutches, because he would like to eat her up so that she might no longer live or a single thought of hers belong to anyone else, she with feline softness and fawning, as if she wanted to escape from his clutches.

They stood there for a long time. He grasped the girl's hand and she let him. That was all. That is all he gets out of it.

He cannot even open his mouth; he merely thinks, thinks terribly hard and thinks appalling thoughts. If his thoughts were to become reality, first of all the whole of Little Wood, then the whole city and then the whole world would go up in smoke and flames.

Gitka's mother called from inside the house, "Gitka!"

For a while they did not answer.

"Gitka, dear, are you there?"

"Yes. What do you want?"

"Come and eat."

"I'm coming. We're coming."

"I'm not coming," grumbled the boy.

"Of course you are!" laughed the girl.

"I'm not!"

"Then I'm not either."

The woman realized what was the matter. She called to him,

"Come on, Jani. There's plenty."

"All right then," muttered the lad. "Then you'll have a good meal."

Gitka laughed.

"When you've got a job, you can help too."

So saying she grasped the boy's hand and pulled him along as children pull each other.

The lad was terribly hungry, and thought that what Gitka had said was right; if ever he got a job, then there would be a feast to end all feasts. Of the three pengős the only money he had spent on himself was for a glass of mulled wine because it happened to be bitterly cold and he did not want to approach the girl freezing and shivering. Then he had brought her everything that could possibly be bought for three pengős. And since then he had not been inside the house in case her parents might perhaps think that he was not in such dire straits... Because there is only one really bad thing, and that is if folk know that you are a beggar. If they have a good opinion of you, then it is possible to make further demands...

So the girl won the day and took the lad into the shanty.

The little room was heated as fiercely as an oven. A couple of minutes inside, and one began to perspire.

"Good evening."

There was Gitka's father, the upholsterer, and her mother who even now was by no means bad-looking, and her two younger sisters. Four of them. Now with their arrival there were six of them in the tiny space.

"Never mind, we'll make room," said the upholsterer, who had only one leg; the other he had left on the battlefield.

He sat down on the edge of the bed. Next to him sat

Gitka. Opposite him were the father and mother. The father sat in a large armchair he had fetched from where he was working; it had been thrown out. He had repaired it, and it was a very elegant armchair that would not have been out of place in any aristocratic salon.

"Father sits in that armchair like a king."

"I'll sell it to you for twelve pengős. And if you can sell it for more, my lad, you can keep the difference."

They laughed at this. Father believed they thought the chair expensive, so with great good humour he began to explain that it had horsehair stuffing and the brocade covering, now that he had cleaned, washed and mended it, was more valuable than when new, because true gentlemen called it an antique. And it was so strong that it wouldn't fall to pieces for another thirty years, not even in this place, where these naughty little infants were always wanting to bounce about on it when he wasn't at home. In short, it was worth seventy or eighty pengős at the very least, but of course there was nobody to buy it. One antique dealer had already offered him eight pengős for it, but he would rather sit on it than sell it for such a price. He would sell it for twelve, but not go any lower, not even for Jani, however much he liked him.

Mother brought in the food. The whole room was filled with a wonderfully good smell of stew. The young man did not say a single word because this smell awoke in him a truly heathen hunger, and his only thought was that if he had to leave now without eating he would hang himself.

Plates, knives, forks and spoons appeared. Mother sliced bread into splendidly big pieces, and he felt faint with dizziness, because hunger reaches its peak when the morsel, the tasty morsel is in front of one's mouth but has not yet got to the point of entering it.

This time came. He did not notice when he gulped down the magnificent stew. There were potatoes with it too, and the gravy tasted so good that he could have died of it. In general everything reminded him of death, and he did not speak but just ate. He merely took a little care not to let these people observe his appalling ravenousness. But however slowly he ate, he was still ten times faster than the others. He could not make himself chew the meat; he simply gulped it down like a heron, then waited a couple of seconds before swallowing another great mouthful. He looked neither to right nor to left and dared not look at anyone until he had tamed the wild animal in him a little, because he was afraid they envied him his portion and if he caught sight of that he would throw away the spoon and rush out, for even if a man has been living for the last fortnight on any kind of garbage he still retains his sense of honour.

Nor did he say anything when Gitka piled his plate high yet again, though when it was full he said quietly,

"I'm not hungry anyway."

That much he owed to the girl; if she had brought him in and offered him food, at least he could play the gentleman.

6

After supper a good atmosphere prevailed. Everything had been eaten. The children have a good meal every day, but all the same a child is someone who knows how to eat! They even brought the saucepan to the table and those growing girls cleaned it out.

Gitka was the only one who was not as hungry as the rest. And her mother. In general mothers are never hungry. Their good meal is to see the children eat. But the father with his one leg ate without saying a word as long as there was something for him to eat. He ate a tremendous amount, though he had one leg less to provide for.

At last everything was eaten to the last bite and the last crumb, then they breathed freely again.

"When the field-kitchen was delayed on the battlefield," said the upholsterer, "there were times when we got no rations for three days. And we were not allowed to eat our iron rations, because they shot my best friend for forcing the tin open with his bayonet and wolfing it all. Well, if a chap manages to escape the Russian cannon, he doesn't want to be hit by a bullet from his own officer," he said laughing, "so we starved, and that was that."

The upholsterer was most fond of talking about the battlefield, especially when he had fed well. Then everyone had to listen, and the children were not allowed to make the slightest noise, because the upholsterer always had his crutch in his hand. He also liked to say that he was due to have an artificial leg, but they always kept doing him out of it.

After that he talked about where he got today's supper.

"I repaired all his chairs for him and his settee; the job was worth a hundred and twenty pengős and I got four for it. Because if he goes to any big firm they'll strip off the material and he's got to buy new; to show that it isn't worth anything they'll simply rip it before his very eyes. 'Look at it! It just comes to pieces, it's no good.' Now the new material costs thirty to forty pengős per metre, so altogether it would have cost him not a hundred and twenty but three hundred pengős. And I said, 'Look, Mr Solicitor, I'll repair it in such a way that it will be an antique.' There mustn't be a single tear in it. I took it off and undid it all. Then I did it all up again and his wife deducted one pengő from the five we had agreed on because she said I finished early."

The upholsterer laughed.

"That was good too. I bought two kilos of meat and mother made a good stew, and that went down well too."

Now that he had got a good meal inside him the young man laughed with him, but he said,

"It's not a good thing to spoil business like that. You should have taken at least thirty pengős off that scoundrel."

"It's easy to say that," said the upholsterer, "but you've got to take into consideration that nobody's got any money now, my friend. If I ask thirty pengős, then he won't have the repairs done, because his wife even made a great fuss over the five pengős, saying that a solicitor doesn't make anything these days, but only loses on his clients. Well, I thought to myself, I've got even less of an income, so let him live and let me live too. In any case there was some deceit in the affair, because that material is so poor that in any event it'll fall to pieces within a year if they sit on it—and now they will sit on it, and so a year hence another upholsterer will make some money again. That's how you have to think these days, my friend. We here in Little Wood can't give ourselves airs, because truth to tell we're not allowed to undertake such work; it's regarded as non-professional—though why should I be an amateur, when all my life I've dealt with nothing but artistic work like this? The only thing is, I haven't got a licence to trade. Let's help each other! I help the solicitor, and he perhaps helps others, because he said how many poor people's affairs he took on for nothing. And when I was there poor folk came one after another to him to ask him to stop them from being evicted. In today's world you only live by not being another man's enemy, but by helping where you can."

On the spur of the moment the young man could not think of any counter-argument, because charity, he thought to himself, is man's greatest ailment, but nevertheless it's the kind of ailment which doesn't need a doctor.

"But I did even worse," said the woman, "because I was sent for by the teacher who's just got a new flat in the city, and I took Walter the house painter to see him as well. He told me to bring along a cheap painter from Little Wood, so I took Mr Walter because he's got six children. He painted the two rooms and kitchen so beautifully that you had to admire them, all for sixteen pengős. He worked there for three days, because the flat was like a pigsty and now it's sheer paradise. And I cleaned up the whole place and he gave me eighty fillérs. So I said to him, 'Sir, whatever makes you think I'd accept eighty fillérs? For all this work—after all you saw me at it—I carted out so much rubbish and my hands nearly dropped off with all that scrubbing.' Look, the backs of may hands are still full of bloodstains with that caustic soda, because he kept on saying, 'Please don't be stingy with the caustic soda...'"

The young man grew even more gloomy.

"And eighty fillérs? That scoundrel ought to be hanged!"

"Nobody ought to be hanged," said the upholsterer. "What point is there in hanging? If they hang him, he won't even pay eighty fillérs."

So they went on talking. Gitka simply listened to them and did not join in. She sat there quietly on the edge of the bed and held the young man's hand so that he should not talk either but keep quiet; the old folk must not be upset.

But the young man could not bear to listen to all this, so seeing that everyone there would like to go to bed soon after supper, so that the lamp should not be kept alight for too long, he said,

"Gitka, please will you come out for a little? There's a beautiful moon and the weather's fine and mild."

At this they got up and went out of the house. Inside mother immediately began to make the beds ready for the night.

7

It was a fine evening, with lots of stars in the sky, but there was no moon.

"Wouldn't you like to go for a little walk?" said the young man, and led the way, because he felt ill at ease among these little houses. He thought it was impossible to talk there; the shanties were so close to each other that even the tiniest whisper could be overheard.

"I don't mind," said Gitka. "I'll come out a little way; at least we shan't disturb those who are asleep."

They walked until they arrived on the bank by the high wooden fence of St. Stephen's Hospital.

From here it was possible to look right over the whole of Little Wood in the dim evening light. On the left there were still standing the trees from which this estate got its name of Little Wood. At their feet below them was the endless area of tiny shacks, the tranquil above of all those poor folk. The whole world was asleep now. Only in one or two places was there a glimmer of light. Here most probably they had arrived home late from work and were now eating their evening meal, if there was anything to eat. There was silence everywhere, no sound of altercation anywhere.

The young man, Jani, embraced the girl and asked her,

"Gitka, are you capable of loving?"

The girl gave a laugh.

"You've already asked me that today. Why? Is it perhaps because you've got a job?"

The boy was silent for a long time.

"No. And that's just why I'm asking you, because I want to know whether you can love, even if there isn't any job."

"How is it that you just can't find any sort of work?"

"That's what I'd like to know too," muttered Jani. "But winter's coming and now I hardly think I'll be able to get myself any sort of job till spring. I'm a mechanic and I've a driver's licence. In our trade there's nothing but lay-offs. Elegant porters sit in glass boxes at the factory entrances and you can't even get within sight of an engineer because the porters won't let you in. And how lovely the factories are inside! They've got fine smooth roads, green lawns between the factory buildings, and anyone who gets employment has a wonderful life because they get very good flats and as much fuel as they need, food, clothes and everything. Cheap shopping, a good salary and a casino, baths, general interest lectures—those in the factory have got everything... But those who are left outside have nothing!"

They remained silent for a long time.

"Why, if I could get a flat like those I wouldn't ask you whether you are capable of loving me. In that case I'd say, 'Gitka, come along with me. There's my flat, inside one of those factories; come and share my life with me!'"

He fell into such a bitter silence that the girl raised her arm and put it on his shoulder.

This filled the boy with the bitterness of happiness and he said,

"But as things are, what am I to say to you, Gitka? Shall I say 'Love me?' when I'm just like a stray dog? I can't even give you encouragement by talking about America, because there too the unemployed march in their tens of thousands on the streets and in any case, how can one get to America? If I had enough money for the boat ticket, I'd be able to set up a little repair shop immediately in a basement somewhere, and I shouldn't be frightened of life, because your father's right—a poor man works cheaply, but somehow he manages to get his evening meal. But I'm not even a poor man, I'm only a vagabond beggar.

Though so far I don't know how to beg. But I often feel when I'm walking along the street and see how everyone here in Pest has a sheepskin coat and elegant shoes that I'll trip one of them up and pinch them!"

The girl trembled.

"Just don't do anything stupid, Jani dear."

"That's just the trouble! I don't know how to do anything, either stupid or wise. I'm just one of many. I'm like mould; I live somehow and I don't even know how to die or to help myself, yet I exist."

The weather was so mild that they grew weary of standing and sat down, each of them on one of the stones that had not yet been carted away by the folk of Little Wood to help them build their shanties.

In front of them there were empty lots where there had been shacks.

"There are fewer shacks here than there were last week," said Jani.

"Yes, because they've moved them away. By spring the whole of Little Wood will cease to exist. They've just given notice to everyone who has a regular job. Only those can stay on till spring who are so destitute that they've nothing in view. They've given us a warning too, telling us to pull down the shanty because I've got a permanent job at the pea-factory."

The lad ground his teeth and hugged the girl as if he were afraid that the powers that be would tear them apart.

The girl allowed him to hug her, because she too was afraid and because she was inexpressibly sorry for this honest, handsome lad who was so full of despair.

"What shall I do, Gitka? You're a sensible girl; give me some advice. I don't want to be bad, I don't want to be a scoundrel or a thief or a deceiver. I want to work and I want to provide for you and for my children out of my own hard work. But what am I to do when there isn't any work, or if there is, I can't got any?"

And from the lad's despairing heart there welled up tears that streamed on to the girl's face.

The girl was very scared on his account, for she realized that this was true and that there was no way of helping.

Nor could she tell him to come and live with them, because there was scarcely room for them in the little shack and it was only theirs till spring anyway. She could do nothing but embrace the lad impetuously and cover his face with kisses.

The lad misinterpreted this and hugged the girl with ever-increasing feverishness there in the dry autumn grass.

8

When they came to themselves again, both of them were very ashamed of themselves.

The girl regained her composure and moved away from the boy. He sensed this and infinite anger blazed suddenly up in him.

"What do you want?" he said harshly. "Are you going to escape now?"

"Don't say silly things."

"What shall I say?... A girl—you can never tell what she wants... So now you'll run away from me and tomorrow, if we meet in the street, you won't even recognize me."

"What's the point of all this talk?"

The boy grabbed the girl's shoulder and shook her hard.

"You're just as much of a bad lot as the rest of them!"

"Have you said that to so many before?"

The boy gave a start. Did the girl know something?

"Gitka... Let's die..."

The girl tried to jump up, but the boy would not release her.

"Let me go, or I'll shout for help."

The boy said, panting,

"I see now, I can see you're just playing with me, but you don't love me."

"You say that now? It's a good joke."

"Tell me, what use is this life? True, your life isn't so much of a curse, because you've got parents; your father is a clever man and can do something with his craft, but I can't even do that, I can't repair upholstery for solicitors... And the factory is closed to me... Oh well, if you won't come, I'll go myself."

"Where to?"

"I'll see. I'll find a place somewhere on a river bank where there isn't a policeman. Or a rescue boat."

"You're mad."

"Maybe I am, but I'm not the one who's driven me mad. I too have parents; they educated me and apprenticed me, they thought to make a man of me... I'd be happy now if I were at home in the village and had some maize-bread to eat..."

"They're dreadful things you're saying. God will look after you too."

"Yes. I only trust in the fact that God has given me enough brains to be able to finish myself off."

"That wasn't what God gave you brains for. It was to find a bit of bread to eat even in the worst time of trouble. Birds can find some, and men have got to find some too."

"God looked after the birds better than men. And if a bird falls from a tree because it is frozen, its heart doesn't ache as much as mine, because the only thing that'll kill me is that I've got to leave you here."

They were silent.

Once again the boy embraced the girl with ever greater passion. He clung to her as a drowning man clutches at the last straw: this girl was all that bound him to life.

"Are you capable of loving?" he asked again, stubbornly. He did not know himself why he stuck to this question. It was as if this would save him, this would throw light on the meaning of life for him.

"How do you mean?"

"Love."

"Love," said the girl. "What's the use of that to poor folk?"

"Yes, what's the use? You're a whore... If there's no love in you, then why did you give yourself to me?"

"I didn't give!" panted the girl and wrestled to free herself.

"You didn't?" snarled the boy. "Then what did you do?"

"I took!" shouted the girl through clenched teeth.

The lad was so astonished that he relaxed his hold on her.

"You took?" he panted. "You took?... Was that why you gave me supper, to put me in the right mood? You bitch!"

And he grabbed the girl by the throat and with great strength squeezed her windpipe with his hand.

The girl choked and went limp; at this the lad became scared and let her go.

Once more they just lay there, exhausted and despairing.

The boy stared in silence, then gazed into the terrifying jungle of poverty.

"You're right... Take all that's good... Leave the rest to someone else..."

The girl remained silent for a long time, then recovered her composure and said slowly,

"I was sorry for you."

The boy gave a start as if the whole earth had turned over beneath him. A girl was sorry for him. Who was he to have reached such a pitch that a girl was sorry for him? And that was why he had been given what he should have had from joy and happiness.

9

If he had a cigarette now and could smoke, perhaps he would feel better. But all he can do is to sit parched and with burning mouth on the top of a rubbish-heap in the night, where a little while ago the greatest desire and happiness in life had reached fulfilment and gone up in smoke.

Now he was totally drained of energy. As far as he was concerned the girl could go wherever she liked. He knew he would never again look in her direction or think of her. Everything was over between them.

The girl made an unfamiliar and peculiar movement. Creaking and crackling sounds came from beneath her hand. He looked across and saw that she was tearing at the dry weeds. He could not understand what she was doing.

The girl worked with increasing industry. She went down on one knee and crawled around after the weeds. She tore and pulled up the waist-high growths.

At least he broke out,

"What's that?"

The girl answered quietly, gently,

"It's to make a fire."

He understood. Even at this dreadful moment the girl's thoughts were turning to work. She was working. Getting money. Dry weeds were worth something, and that's what she was pulling up. But how much money? Only an infinitesimal fraction of the smallest coin. Still, it had some value. It was profit.

A new fit of anger burst out of him. Now when he could see nothing else before him to do except to destroy himself as quickly as possible and as completely as he could, this girl was thinking about preparing breakfast. She was stealing weeds—someone else's, anybody else's—and was providing firing for it.

Once again there flared up in him the blind rage that he must kill her. He must kill her because she was not doing this for love; he was not the one who was going to eat that breakfast, it was not for him that she was tearing up weeds to cook whatever there was to eat; and yet he stopped, because he sensed that this was a woman who worked up to the very last moment and took thought for others.

In an offensive and badgering tone he growled at her,

"I'll tell the policeman and have you locked up."

"You know, Jani, there's a poor woman here with a lot of children and she's nothing in the world to make a fire with. You'd do better to set to work and collect a few twigs for her. We'll put them outside the door."

The boy gave a shudder of horror.

He could never have imagined that this too was possible. And he didn't even know who it was to whom the girl intended to give the kindling...

He was silent for a time, then he too began to tear the dry stalks on the bank. The weeds were thin, spiky and full of thorns, but it was true enough that they were good stuff for making a fire. Even they would burn well.

"Just as we shall burn in hell," he growled.

"In hell?" said the girl." That's not a place I want to get to!" and she laughed.

Her laughter was tiny and tinkling. Then she said,

"But if I do get there, it won't be me who has to collect the firewood — it's all ready and waiting there."

The boy jumped up and went for the hospital fence.

He worked at a plank and tore it out.

He kicked it with his foot and tore it and broke it up with his hands.

The girl was terrified when she saw what he was doing and kept watch in case they heard the creaking and cracking inside. Nothing happened.

Jani split the plank neatly and threw it on to the girl's pile of twigs.

Gitka laughed.

"And now come along, let's take it to her."

With that they gathered it up and carried it away. They tiptoed to Mrs Kátai's and laid it outside the door. The girl was careful to put the twigs on top of the bits of plank, so that if anyone happened to look in that direction they would not see the plank.

1933

THE SCHOLARSHIP

The old peasant came to a halt in the school porch. He had already taken his hat off outside and in order to make his presence known he began to shuffle his feet as if he were knocking the mud off his boots. There was no mud; it was the height of summer and there was a drought. It was time to be at work, but if the teacher had done him the honour of summoning him to the school during his working-hours he wanted to behave as his father had taught him: he must give expression to his respect for the gentry.

So he shuffled once more and cleared his throat too. Perhaps they might hear him inside.

The teacher, who was expecting him, did hear him and came out to meet him.

"There you are, Uncle János! Welcome! Come inside, come in, come in!"

He talked to him as a young teacher trying to make himself agreeable to peasants has to talk. He smiled, made welcoming gesture and demonstrated very clearly how welcome a guest the old man was. He had never yet been in the house since it had been rebuilt.

"Thank you kindly, sir," said the old man and crossed the threshold uneasily, as if something unpleasant were awaiting him. You can never tell what these gentry want.

The teacher's room was just as new as the house itself. The old man did not really have a look round, but he was not pleased that in this little village they had built such a damned great palace for the school and that a skinny little teacher had such bloody aristocratic furniture. It hadn't been like that in his time, when the school had a thatched roof and the teacher too was old and very poor.

"Well now, Uncle János, do you know why I've asked you to come here?"

"You'll tell me soon enough, sir," said the old man cautiously.

"Well the reason I've asked you to come, Uncle János, is because I want you to do something very big."

The seventy-year-old man looked at the teacher stiffly and solemnly. He didn't like this tone. In his young days they hadn't talked like that to the peasants; they'd said, "Listen, you!" and "Not so fast!" There was something behind it all if they talked in such a sugary way.

"Well, Uncle János, the point is that I want to educate your grandson to be a gentleman."

Not a muscle stirred in the old man's face. Not a nerve quivered. He waited. He waited to see what would come out of all this.

"This little grandson of yours, Janika, has got a good head on his shoulders... For six years he's been the pride of the school. He's the best pupil, the most diligent and the cleverest... Well, I've long been getting ready to send a poor child to upper school, to grammar school. Do you know what a grammar school is? It's where the children of the gentry go... It's an expensive school, but I've already arranged for them to take your Janika in free and teach him and put him through school. He can become anything he likes—a priest, teacher, lawyer or judge or whatever he turns out to be. Do you understand?"

"I hear what you're saying, sir," said the old man thoughtfully.

"Well, will you agree?"

This one phrase the teacher put over badly, because when he heard it the old man immediately realized that here was something that depended on him. If he was asked for something, then he must think the matter over.

"Well, as far as that's concerned," he said, "he's mine."

"Of course he's yours."

"He's mine, sir, because his father died of the illness he got during the war. My son. Then, when he died, the three children were left to me. Especially when my daughter-in-law died too; then all three children remained entirely my own property. I feed them, I keep them, I pay the fines for them when they can't go to school because we live a long way out and in winter if there aren't any good boots they can't get to school and then they make me pay the fine for them."

"All right, all right; that's nothing to worry about. They've never fined you on Janika's account. He's had new boots every Christmas, isn't that so?"

The old man said nothing. Now they wanted to trick him out of what belonged to him.

"Well, that doesn't mean they've settled his account yet."

"Now don't let's haggle over that," said the teacher. "The child is going to have such a chance that he will never be able to thank us enough. We're going to take the child to college."

"Well that's not certain yet," said the old man.

"Why isn't it certain?"

"That boy hasn't got the right sort of clothes for that."

"Never mind," said the teacher, "I'm so fond of that boy that I'll undertake to make a collection among the well-to-do folk in the village and we'll clothe him and give him his fare. I myself will take him there and make all the arrangements. I'm glad to be able to take such a genius of a little boy to the college."

"But why do you want the boy to be a gentleman, sir?"

"Because he's the right sort for that. God has blessed him with an exceptional brain. Such a bright little star must not be allowed to perish in the mud. Well now. Do we understand each other?"

The old man was silent.

"The child is mine," he said gravely. "He's a clever boy. I can already make good use of him on the farm. He's a very useful little boy, sir. He already knows how to drive horses like a true farmer. Why, in spring he did the ploughing and he turned the plough so well, you should have seen him! And in any case he doesn't need to go to school any more now, he can work."

"What are you getting at?" said the teacher, getting hot under the collar. "Why, aren't you pleased that your grandson is going to become a gentleman?"

"I'm pleased, sir, but all I'd like to know is: what am I going to get for him?"

"What do you mean, what are you going to get for him?"

"Well, the gentry are going to do very well out of him. He's a very fine boy. And if I agree, the gentry will get a child who'll suit them down to the ground. Hand over such a diligent little worker, such a clever child? That's a big thing, sir."

"Well, how do you see it?"

"Now, sir, the child is mine. Nobody can take him away from me, not even the law... If he's taken away from me at a time when I could get the most profit out of him, then what will become of me?"

The teacher listened aghast to the old peasant. But he went on:

"Because up to now I've had no profit out of him. He was small and he had to go to school too, but now, sir, my heart will break if he's taken away when he's just becoming worth something."

"Then what do you want?"

"He's being apprenticed to someone else... to be a gentleman... Who's going to cover my losses?"

And stubbornly certain of his own just claim, he looked the teacher in the eye—the teacher who as the representative of the gentry wanted to steal his property for his own gain.

"I'm not handing him over for nothing, sir... But if you pay for my loss, I won't say no."

Just like a barbarian slave-trader who is selling the child into slavery.

"What do you want for him?"

"You, sir, or rather the gentry, just find me another young driver in his place. Then while the boy is away, there'll always be someone of the same age who'll be able to do the work instead of him."

The teacher's heart sank. "That's impossible, old chap."

"Otherwise there's no sale... The gentry take away our money, they take our land, they even take the air and now—do they want to take the best of our children too? Because anyone who isn't good won't do for you. They only pick out the very best... Well, if you want to increase the ranks of the gentry, then pay the price."

And the teacher could not wrestle with this crystal-clear reasoning.

1933

SULLEN HORSE

A LEGEND OF THE HORTOBÁGY

1

Dawn is breaking.

The thirty-thousand acre back of the Hortobágy gives a great shudder. There are gentle creaking sounds, as when a horse yawns and the bones crack in its face. Soft wisps of mist float upwards and disperse in all directions.

The horses in the herd raise their heads from the ground and neigh towards the fading stars.

The young horseherds had all collapsed on the ground where they lay like clods of mud, one here, another there; they had dropped to the ground after the horses and now, tucked up in their sheepskin coats, they are snoring gently. They had been grazing the horses all night long and did not notice the dawn.

One human figure stands there immobile, an old man on the verge of senility, the oldest head herdsman, András Erszény.

The Sullen Horse.

That is what they call him on the pusztas. His two hands are clasped round a long straight stick. He leans on this, while his richly-ornamented whip, thrown round his neck and draped over his shoulders, is a decoration.

He stares towards the east; his eyes, screwed up, gaze into infinity.

For thirty-four years, since he has been here on the puszta, not a morning has passed without him staring the sun in the face. On 4 April the herd is driven outside, at the end of October it is dispersed. While the herd is in the open he stands guard over it night after night. Not once has he slept through the night and the dawn.

When they disperse the herds and drive them towards the Town, he still stays out on the puszta.

He is not attracted to his birthplace, he does not want to see his house and his wife there. He has no wish to see his wife. He is a hard man.

And he has been for thirty-four years.

2

Behind the sheep-pen the young herdsman is working away at something in the gradually brightening morning light. Just look! It is a bicycle. It has a bent pedal, and he is repairing it. He has turned out the contents of his tool-box on to the grass—a hundred varieties of odds and ends neatly laid out as in a workshop. He picks out a small pair of pincers and works with them, then hammers away with gentle tappings. He is so absorbed in his work, listening to the drumming noise, that he fails to notice that his father, the head horseherd Sárkány, is there behind him on his horse.

"And what the devil's this?"

The boy starts up in fright. He had wanted to repair it yesterday, but he had been sent off to help the watchman and there had been a lot of spring-cleaning work to do, he had not got down to it. By the time the evening meal was ready darkness had fallen. He could scarcely wait for morning to come and got up, turned out of the tool-shed and cautiously set to work.

Now he gives his father a scared look. He stands up like a mother hen protecting her chickens with her body. He had even put the radio out on the grass with all its parts neatly set out in order. He wanted to repair this too; it only required a little time, but a young herdsman has no time to spare for his own affairs on the puszta.

"Damn you!" Sárkány the head horseherd shouts haughtily and neatly spins him round, and his face turns red. "Haven't I told you?"

He had told him. The boy knows all too well that he had told him that if ever he dared touch that infernal bicycle again he would smash it to bits. But he did not believe that his father would do that, whatever he had said.

But herdsman Sárkány was suddenly seized with a fit of

blind rage. He dashed at the bicycle on his horse and trampled on it, out of his mind.

"Devil take you! Would you try to pull a fast one on me?"

The boy trembles as he watches the horse's great shoes pounding to pieces the delicate network of spokes in the bicycle-wheel and kicking the tools and odds and ends in all directions. And that was the end of the radio; it is crushed to pieces in the dawn beneath the horseshoes.

"Either you're a horseherd or a double-dyed idiot!" roars the old man, seizing his son and shaking him. Then he tosses him away like an old rag among the bits and pieces.

"I'm not having you make a filthy mess of the Hortobágy!" he pants and puffs, then leaves his son there.

The boy just stands there. His face flames; he's no longer such a little boy to swallow such insults, he is sixteen.

The watchman crawls out from beside the reeds surrounding the sheep-pen. He is an old man, unmarried and somewhat weak in the head. He looks with horror at what has happened. He crawls on his belly and picks up one of the tools that has been kicked away, then weaves his way to the bicycle, bends over it and pats it as if it were a girl who has had a beating. He pats it, fondles it and blinks at the boy,

"Rock-a-bye, rock-a-bye..."

In the distance the father's voice can be heard,

"Hey, you..."

The boy gives a start. He holds his head in his two hands. He waits, not having any desire to move. He waits for the shout to be repeated two or three times, then sets off in a rage, his head hung down and his big hat pulled over his eyes, towards the voice as if he is going to meet a murderer.

The idiot remains there and gives the poor dead bicycle-frame a stream of kisses.

3

The village comes awake too. Now the tiny houses stand there in the white light of dawn.

The horses are let out. They run between the houses,

their numbers gradually growing, without a single human being to accompany them; they all know their own route. They are off to the puszta.

Children watch them go. And even from the windows it is only the children who watch them. The adults go off to harvest, and the village is left to the children.

By morning the puszta is a miraculous world, morning belongs to the animals. Cows move over the flat ground singly and in groups, then merge into immense herds. Lambs come along, so do sheep, suddenly raising their heads on the bank of the little ditch and bleating to the sky.

A cow on the top of a six-foot high mound looks as if it is about to take off into the heavens.

Hungarian ewes surge forward; their horns are sharp and their long woolly fleece droops low. They cannot find space for themselves on the vast puszta and nudge and bump into each other.

Geese fly off cackling and cover the pasture.

Pigs grunt. They dig at the soil.

The puszta comes to life.

Herdsman Sárkány nods to his son who lets out his long whip and cracks it. The herd of horses circles round at a gallop, rejoicing in its freedom. The boy once again pulls his hat down over his eyes.

"You've got what it takes to be a horseherd!" his father rebukes him. "You've got Sárkány blood in you. Your father's a Sárkány, your grandfather was a Sárkány and all your ancestors were Sárkánys... They're ploughing up the Hortobágy and there are fewer horseherds... Their glory's coming to an end. But there'll always be a place for a Sárkány on the Hortobágy..."

The boy stares grimly straight ahead.

The other young herdsman, Pista, a round-faced, oafish lad, comes into sight.

"Am I to leave the herd to him? See, lad... It's yours. To Pista Czibere?... When I've got you here?... He's no horseherd, just a swineherd among horses..."

But the boy refuses to be consoled. In his heart there is no relief. A kind of wild and bitter anger seethes in him.

Father and son stand side by side, like two statues.

Around them grazes the herd of horses. The herd makes a sudden move, and they jump on horseback. They round them up from their horses. The puszta glitters and the clouds sparkle with sharp specks of purple and gold light.

They meet once again on their horses. The father swerves to join his son and says to him,

"Jancsi, lad, doesn't your heart leap with joy? You're my own beloved son... I'll find a husband for Juliska. I've had my eye on Péter Bundi's son for her. I'll make a farmer's wife out of her... I'll only keep you alongside me to enjoy the glory of the horseherd's life. Come on, lad, don't pull such a long face or I'll crack this whip about your neck..."

The boy refuses to calm down. His eyes flash, but he turns away so that his father cannot see.

"And all you want's a bicycle, you miserable little worm! It isn't even dawn and there he rides off on his bicycle... I told you so; but you wouldn't leave me in peace..."

The boy gallops away. Round the herd of horses.

All of a sudden he appears beside his father again.

"Today's the day of the Bridge Fair. Today your mother's coming out. They're bringing out the food... And farmer Bundi'll be there too; we'll get the girl's engagement settled... Then there'll be just the two of us, my boy... We're of horseherd stock... Hold your head up!"

A horse interrupts him with a yawn. It yawns like a human, opening its mouth wide and long.

Once more the father on his horse catches up with his son.

"Listen! Don't you dare play me up! Or I'll talk to you as I do to a foal. I'll take you to the Sullen Horse; he'll take you in hand... There you'll soon learn what's what..."

4

Morning has fully arrived.

Herds of cattle get to their feet. Cows stretch themselves. At the well the shepherd wakes and begins to draw water.

The sun shines on the well, its rays breaking on the sweep. The shepherd drinks water from the bucket.

The village is empty now. All the animals have gone out, except for a little calf still at home. And a three-year-old boy. The child has a long whip in his hand. He frightens the calf, which jumps and frightens the child, who runs off barefoot and dressed only in a shirt, dropping the whip.

Sárkány leaves the herd of horses to the care of the young herdsmen. He nods to his son and they gallop together over the empty plain.

They leave herds of sheep and cattle behind them. And pigs. They reach the Sullen Horse.

They greet each other without dismounting. They shake hands.

"Father, I've brought my boy to you."

The Sullen Horse nods. He gazes at the boy.

He in turn looks down. He is not going to parley with him.

"He's gone to the bad... He wants to go around on a bicycle. He's not ashamed of himself... Though he's the son of a herdsman. I'd like you to take him on and cure him of it for me... he's no respect for his father."

The Sullen Horse nods.

A young herdsman gallops up.

"Sir, the sorrel's dropping her foal."

The Sullen Horse nods towards the boy.

"Take him along with you." With these words they set off and arrive at a gallop where the mare is giving birth.

Shepherds are already on the scene helping.

The little foal is now lying on the grass. The puszta produces its own fruits. The new life begins to stir beneath the sun.

The horseherd releases the feet of the newborn foal from the caul. A horse looks over at the mare as she gives birth. The mare lies panting on the grass.

Sárkány calls to his son,

"Herdsman, show what you're made of!"

Another lad gallops up.

"Another one's just had a foal."

They gallop over in that direction.

The second mare has herself completed nature's divine work. She is lying on the grass with the little foal beside her just like a corpse in the caul, like a fish in a net.

The little foal makes a movement and tears open the caul.

The mare looks after her offspring.

Two horses come and sniff at the foal.

Such is the life of the puszta.

5

Peasant carts are crossing the puszta, with horses tied alongside them. They are off to the Bridge Fair.

A horseherd gallops along with horses; he too is off to the fair.

Here comes the cart with food on it. Sitting there are the wife and her daughter.

Jancsi rests with the young horseherds lying on their cloaks.

He is as sullen as a young bullock.

A young horseherd arrives at a gallop, jumps from his horse and strides over to them.

"It's a great day."

If anyone utters a word, it is like the tolling of a bell. On the puszta people do not speak. Here they only keep silent. Words are rare.

"What's the matter?"

"The woman is coming!"

"Which woman?"

"Mrs András Erszény... The Sullen Horse's wife..."

They are all struck dumb. It is incredible.

"She's coming?"

"Yes."

"She's not been out here for thirty years."

"Thirty-four... She's coming now... She's near to death, and says she wants to make her peace with her husband."

"Make her peace?"

"Because they had a terrible quarrel then."

Even Jancsi pricks up his ears.

"What about?"

"The Sullen Horse was still young in those days, and he owned his own herd... He married a herd-owner's daughter. She was dreadfully ugly but dreadfully rich. And at the wedding-feast he had them play:

> For it wasn't her beauty I loved,
> Poor lad that I was, but her wealth.

Then the young wife turned up her nose and the next moment deceived her husband."

They laugh. Beneath the open sky they laugh as if they were in the bottomless depths. The clouds echo their laughter.

"That was what made the old man so angry... He came out to the puszta... And for thirty-four years he hasn't set foot in Debrecen."

They laugh again. The ground reverberates with laughter.

"And she's coming today?"

"Yes."

Jancsi does not laugh. He pulls a face as long as a fiddle. They have a dig at him.

"What's the matter with him?"

They try to put the newly-arrived lad in the picture.

"He's crying over his bicycle."

Jancsi:

"I'm not going to be a horseherd."

"Then what are you going to be?"

"A chauffeur."

Silence. Everyone is silent. A shadow falls across them. The shadow races right across the puszta. Something makes the horses go wild and they begin to gallop. There is a great noise of galloping feet on the puszta. The young herdsmen leap on their horses and chase them, then get in front of them and turn them towards the big well, where they draw water. The long troughs fill with water. The horses crowd up to the troughs and drink. The buckets come up, the water in the troughs rises and falls, and the horses are like schoolchildren—good schoolchildren.

"Where's Jancsi?"

They look around, trying to find him. Jancsi has disappeared.

"After him! The Sullen Horse will kill him."

The puszta is full of dashing figures. Everything moves and gallops.

Now the children are going to school on the puszta. Even the school is in the open air, with the desks set out beneath the sky. There is a teacher at work there, a skinny teacher. He makes them sing.

Jancsi arrives there.

"Sir!"

"What do you want, lad?"

"I want to be a chauffeur."

"A chauffeur?"

The teacher looks at the son of the puszta in astonishment.

"That's a fine decision."

The young horseherd hangs his head.

"My father will beat me to death."

"He'll be glad about it."

"No. He's smashed my bicycle to pieces—and there wasn't anything wrong with it except that its pedal had been twisted... And my radio was almost finished too. The mechanic's son gave me one of those little crystal sets..."

And he goes into an explanation. And he astonishes the teacher with the technical terms he uses.

6

Wives on the puszta.

In the sacred days of old, women were forbidden to go out to the Hortobágy. All thirty thousand acres of pasture were owned by some hundred men who lived on it. A hundred hard-bitten herdsmen. They went their rounds there, living side by side, their lands measured by eye. There was not even a tree or a mound thrown up to divide the pusztas of Máta and Zám from each other. Only the shepherd knew where Pentezug was, yet for centuries there was hardly a quarrel; he recognized his own land by the place where the thyme grew best.

Today, however, it is the wives who bring out the food in carts. They get on to their cart in Debrecen or Nádudvar or Újváros, and there in the bottom of it is enough food for a month. They come out for a single day with the two horses sent for the purpose by the owner and they do not sleep there; when the sun goes down they have to return. Or at the very latest when Orion comes up... Well, up to that time, round about midnight, they may flirt as they like out there, but then they must go... The puszta may not be disturbed by women's skirts. For the wind on the puszta is dangerous too, but all the same a turmoil greater than any storm can be stirred up by the starched underskirts of womenfolk.

And that is scarcely visible fluttering above their boots. But all the same...

Why, even little Juliska causes a great stir in the hard hearts of the young horseherds. Pista, the chief of them, who stands by the flowing mane of the horses like a mobile grave-post from a tomb, utters not a word but just gazes at Juliska who stands beside him while he plaits his whip. The heavy ornamental whip made of thirty-two strips of hide. They smile at each other and Pista does not look up again; it is as if nothing has happened: his fingers work away and he has no other care in the world... Or perhaps it is as if everything were arranged, and the brown fingers can get on with their work; they smile once more at each other, and that is an end to all Sárkány's dreams. One or two little smiles seal Juliska's fate, and the decision has been made: her life is now bound to the stars of the puszta, for here there is nothing to bind anything to, even the rope of a tent.

Meanwhile their father listens in the hut to his wife's rapid talk and with a nod or two of his head decides that this must be done and so must that. This one affair of Juliska's will not be like this, but like that... But though Mr Bundi may have twenty-seven horses on the splendid puszta, all Juliska can see is the horseherd Pista smiling, whether she is awake or asleep. She would even go and pick flowers if there were any on the Hortobágy, on the parched grasslands, on St. Peter and Paul's day. There are thistlestalks, and since there is nothing else, Pista gives her one. Now they may chop her in two, to her this thistle is more beautiful than any cultivated garden-flower. She runs off now, carrying the flame of love in her heart, and only her mother will guess the secret of that little heart...

"Where's Jancsi, Dad?"

Sárkány's expression grows stern.

"There's something wrong with him."

"Something wrong? What?"

"He's been bewitched."

"How do you mean? He's still young. The rose of love hasn't opened for him yet."

"Love?... Not a bit of it! A bicycle—that's what he's in love with... He doesn't want to be horseherd."

The woman knows this well enough. She waits trembling to see what more problems are going to make life difficult.

"But I smashed it into pieces... You can see it, it's there behind the hut."

The mother runs over and looks at the wreckage of the miracle. She wrings her hands.

A young herdsman approaches at a gallop and shouts down from his horse,

"Has Jancsi come home?"

"What for?"

"He's escaped from the Sullen Horse... We don't know what's happened..."

The head horseherd snarls,

"I'll kill him!"

He hurls himself on to his horse and dashes off. The two riders leave a trail of dust on the puszta.

His mother clasps her hands and watches them go with a terrible fear. One brings up children, and look what happens...

Tears trickle from her maternal eyes.

She stumbles off to look for her daughter, and finds her beside the lad who is plaiting his whip. Terrified, she calls to her,

"Just come here, will you?"

The girl pulls herself together and darts over to her mother.

"Mother!" and she falls on her neck.

"Well, now, lass."

"Mother, I'll die for him."
"Has he spoken?"
"No, he hasn't but I'll die for him."
"Do you love him?"
"Yes, I do."
"Oh dear, your father will kill you."
"Never mind."

The mother is at a loss what to do.

"Is that why you wanted to come out to the Hortobágy?" she whispers in a reproachful voice.

"No, I didn't know then, mother."
"Then how did it happen? Tell me."
"I don't know. I only know that it did happen."

A stork circles round in the air. It settles on its mate. A stallion circles round a mare; their heads meet and they neigh together, biting at each other.

Love on the puszta is swift as lightning.

"Has it only just happened?"
"Yes, just now."

The mother looks dismayed. There is nothing she can do now. She knows that well from her own experience. A young horseherd has only to look once at the girl he wants to marry. It is very rare indeed if he has to look at her twice or three times before making up his mind... A young horseherd does not go courting. When the time comes, he gets married, and that is that.

7

The boy gallops along on horseback.

The puszta is not big enough to bear all his misery.

Suddenly he sees something that makes him stop. A car.

He looks up into the sky. Storm clouds are gathering. He looks down into the car. There is no sign of anyone near it.

"It's going to get soaked."

He dismounts and gazes at it. The car has soft leather upholstery. It would be a pity if it were to fill up with water. But he does not know what to do about it. He does not know how to put up the hood because he does not know how the mechanism works.

In the car he finds a book which describes how to handle the car. He looks at it.

"Damn it, it's in German."

He shakes his head, but looks at the diagrams and identifies the various pieces of the frame one by one.

The storm approaches with increasing speed, and he hurries more and more.

At last he sets to work, and one by one undoes the buckles, the struts, the gleaming nickel parts, and by the time the storm arrives the car is completely fixed up and he stands there beside it like a sentry. His horse takes fright at the storm and gallops away.

The gentlemen, the passengers in the car arrive as the rain is bucketing down. They are two gentlemen and are delighted to see that the car is all right.

They ask the young horseherd why he did not sit inside the car.

He does not understand German, but he knows what they are asking and pats the car lovingly.

"It won't do me any harm, but it would be a pity for *her* to be drenched with water."

"Do you want to be a chauffeur?" ask the gentlemen.

"A chauffeur? That's just what I want to be."

They seat him in the car and take him away with them.

The boy sits beside the gentleman who is driving, his eyes following his every movement.

8

Sárkány is once again with the Sullen Horse.

"Where's the lad?"

They look around. He is nowhere to be seen. A young horseherd reports that he has gone off.

"Where to?"

"That way, towards the west."

Sárkány the head herdsman goes in pursuit.

"Perhaps he's with the fuel-makers."

He rides that way. On the way he leaves behind the wild puszta and arrives at the young men who make Hortobágy fuel. They collect cow-dung from the puszta in carts and turn it over with forks. They make a fuel-store out of it, and stick it together to withstand rain and wind.

"Have you seen my boy?"

"He didn't come this way."

"Where can the villain be? I'll kill him, I'll kill him!"

"Perhaps he's with the sheep-shearers—the young shepherd is a good friend of his."

He rides off that way.

The sheep are rounded up into a pen, a great crowd of them. They are sent into the shearers and shorn of their fleece. The sheep, shorn thin, leap briskly from beneath the shears and run off nimbly as if they were newly-born.

"Is my son here?"

"No, he's not."

"Then where can he be?"

"Who can tell on the puszta if someone gets lost?"

In the distance a fire breaks out. They catch sight of the glow from it.

"Something's alight over there... Perhaps that's where the boy is. Children love to watch fires."

Sárkány continues his progress on horseback towards the fire.

It is a haystack that is burning. Shortly afterwards the little house nearby catches fire too. This is right on the edge of the Hortobágy, and they can see it in the village, and ring the bell madly. Firemen rush to the store and drag out the hoses. They go at a gallop out to the puszta. The straw is burning. The horses are restless in the summer stables. The little house is burning. The straw crackles as it flies from the roof. The wind stirs up the burning straw.

"Hey, is my son here?"

"We've not seen your boy."

A storm breaks. The fire draws the storm as if the one could not exist without the other. In the sky the clouds whirl past and the black herds of heaven thunder along. The swineherd, lying beside his pigs, gets up and gazes at the sky, shading his eyes with his hand. A black cloud moves across the sun. The swineherd hustles the pigs into a shed. Two horses gallop towards the village, having got loose from one of the herds. With the black clouds, the horses have gone wild and gallop in all directions over the puszta. A horseherd rides through the rain. A stud thunders past with the horseherds in pursuit. The cowherds pursue restless cattle with their big sticks.

Sárkány can be heard shouting now here, now there.

"Have you seen my son?"

"Nobody's seen him at all."

A herd of cattle dashes over the puszta. The huge beasts are like primeval wild animals in a flood.

A shepherd takes a walk with his dog in the rain.

Herdsman Sárkány gallops through the storm and arrives home. He comes across a horse struck dead by lightning.

The sky clears and the remaining clouds gleam bright. The earth is damp and the grass sparkles more gaily. But the horse has met its doom.

"Is the boy at home?"

The woman waits impatiently for her husband.

"Come along now, come in; lunch is ready."

The watchman is grilling fish on a stick. Sárkány has no appetite. He is gloomy.

Nevertheless his appetite comes with the fish, and he settles down to enjoy his food.

His wife speaks up,

"I've something to tell you."

"Well?"

"We've got a problem with that girl... I've got to tell you today, because I'm only out here with you for this one day."

Sárkány looks hard at his wife. What problem could there be? Is there nothing but trouble today?

"What are you making a fuss about?"

"She doesn't want to marry the herd-owner's son; that's the problem."

"I haven't asked her. It's nothing to do with her. That's my affair..."

"But that's not how it is."

"Then how is it? Are you against me too?"

"I'm not, but you can't give the girl orders. That's not the sort of world we're living in now... *She's* going to live with him..."

"She's going to live with him? Why, who does she intend to live with?"

The woman grasps her husband's hand and leads him out behind the hut and into the open air.

Pista the horseherd is standing there on the threshing-floor, tough and stern.

He has a pipe clenched between his teeth. He scrapes at the pipe with his finger and merely says to the girl,

"Are you listening?"

"Yes, Pista."

The lad works at his pipe unconcernedly.

"I'd like to marry you."

"Truly?"

"I would indeed..."

But by now the horseherd is upon him.

"You would indeed, if I'd brought up the girl for the sake of such a beggarly bastard as you."

The two men glare at each other. The woman wrings her hands.

The lad's eyes flash.

"How do you mean, sir?"

"How, you cur? Like this..."

And from the side of the hut he pulls out a stick and brings it down on the back of the lad's neck. He stands up to it.

He too bends down to the ground and picks up another stick.

"This'll do too."

With the two fall on each other. They do not watch to see where the end of the stick lands, but give each other a good beating.

Like two bulls in the meadow.

A bull grazes in the meadow, raises its head and gives a bellow.

The scuffle comes to an end.

The great sooty-necked bull goes on grazing.

These are men, they are ashamed of the weals they have received. They pant and regain their breath.

The woman whimpers.

"Perhaps the boy has gone to the fair."

The horseherd does not speak. He fetches out his horse and hoists himself on it. He goes off towards the fair. He gallops madly, then slows to a jog. He pulls his hat down over his eyes. His whole life and all his dreams have dissolved in smoke. His son wants to live on a bicycle; his daughter does not want to be a herd-owner's wife. And that means the end of life on the puszta... And he had already made plans for his daughter to go into the village... He would have made a big herd-owner's wife out of her... Ah well...

They are driving cattle towards the fair. Horses are being led along in fives and tens.

They are driving a herd of cows over the stone bridge. The Hortobágy Inn comes into sight.

The fair is a huge whirl. Cymbals, accordions, barrel-organs and all kinds of noise in confusion.

9

After the storm the Sullen Horse is busy settling his stud when they come and tell him that he is wanted back home in the hut because a woman is looking for him.

The aged man is astounded. A woman? For him?

For thirty-four years no woman has ever looked for him.

He does not move. He stands there and gazes into the distance.

The puszta wind brings music to his ears. He can clearly hear the band at the wedding-feast. He closes his eyes. His grey, tanned skin quivers. His face twitches.

As if in a dream he sees the wedding-dance where he ordered them to play

> No, it wasn't her beauty I loved,
> Poor lad that I was, but her wealth...

He sees his little wife as she suddenly stiffens and draws herself up. She is not beautiful, but she is young and his own...

He opens his eyes. There is nothing here but the bleak puszta.

"Can she come here?" asks the young horseherd.

"Who?"

"The old woman."

"As far as I'm concerned she can come."

He does not look at him. He just stands and waits, like a stone statue.

The old woman approaches slowly, giddily, with her head-scarf pulled down over her eyes.

When she arrives, she stops and says simply, humbly, with the grief of old age,

"András."

"Who's that?"

"It's me... Me... If it's true..."

He looks at her. And a great flame leaps in his eyes. It is his wife....

"Eszti?"

The woman just nods and weeps. She wipes the streaming tears with the corner of her kerchief.

"It's me, András."

"I don't know you."

"I'm your wife."

"I haven't got a wife."

"I'm still alive... for a while yet... And you're alive too."

"I've not been alive for a long time."

But the woman just stands there. Now that she has come out here, she is not going to leave him.

"András!"

"What do you want? Whoring mare! You deceived me!"

"No, that wasn't true... That's all I want to explain, while I'm alive... It wasn't true... I only did it to frighten you... I've put up with it for thirty-four years. But now I'm old and I can't bear it... I can't die, András, with the knowledge that you believe it to be true...."

The man suddenly relents.

"It wasn't true?"

"No."

"You say that before God?"

"In God's presence, András."

"Because He sees us here... With His own eyes, Eszti... He's up there in heaven... He'll strike you with his thunderbolt if you're lying..."

"I'm not lying... Thirty-four years have been enough for me... Have you heard anything about me during that time?"

András Erszény, head horseherd, thinks hard. No, indeed he has not heard anything—nor, for that matter, has he asked about her. But bad news travels fast... and no news of any kind about the woman had ever reached the puszta.

Suppose this were possible? That his sternness for all these thirty-four years had been in vain? Oh what an accursed life... accursed honour...

"I'm going to die, András... I've not got much time left..."

"Then what did it?"

"A song... It was that song, the one you had played at the wedding-feast."

Both of them shut their eyes. Both of them can hear once again that old song—

Poor lad that I was... I sought wealth...

"I wanted to show you that... it wasn't just for wealth. So that you'd come to your senses... and there'd be someone who loves me too. But that's a long time ago. Perhaps that wasn't true either..."

A wind blows the woman's black skirt... A wind flutters the wings of the horseherd's shabby ancient sheepskin coat. The Hortobágy wind plays with them, laughing at these children who have grown old.

The man stretches out his hand:

"I believe you, Eszti... Go and sin no more..."

The woman stoops over his hand and kisses it, firm as it is.

The man pulls it away, feeling the tears on the back of his hand. He looks at his hand.

"That's all right then... Well, Eszti... My dear little Eszti... Now we're going to the fair..."

He lays his hand on the little woman's shoulder and his eyes gaze into the distance. Into the clouds, and he seeks the truth, the distant light of something impossible... The Sullen Horse...

The Bridge Fair is a mad whirl.

A roundabout. Wooden horses, young horseherds riding on them. Brass instruments.

Fair-goers bargain with each other and come to terms. The sheep that have been sold are branded.

Shepherds with shabby boots bargain with buyers in good boots.

The horns of the cattle are branded. Smoke rises from the horns.

Children whirl round on the roundabout.

A flock of sheep is driven over the stone bridge.

A brass band.

A peasant cart with horses tied to it.

A trumpeter blows as if to burst his lungs.

They drive cows across the bridge.

Cymbals clash.

Carts and horses are driven across the bridge. The bridge is the central point in the incomprehensible infinity of the Hortobágy.

A big drum and a drummer.

They drive vast numbers of cattle over the bridge.

One trumpeter, two trumpeters, a brass band. Carts and horses.

A car; in the seat the boy Jancsi puts on the chauffeur's coat. He has been left to guard the car. He puts on the chauffeur's cap. He is proud.

Sárkány is at the bar in the barn, drinking. Drinking fearsomely.

Around him there is a swirl of herdsmen and buyers. Now everything in him is ringing loud in his ears.

He drinks and sings. He sits with some herdsmen and drinks and sings in a horrible voice.

He goes out and looks round... By chance he comes alongside the car, and his son is terrified. He curls up as he approaches and suddenly recognizes him.

He recognizes him, his only son in the chauffeur's fur coat and cap.

He gives him a long look. His eyes grow cloudy. Beads

of moisture cover his eyes and bubble out in huge drops from beneath his eyelashes.

"You're off then?"

"Yes."

He is no longer angry. He shrugs his shoulders and turns away.

The boy calls,

"Dad!"

He looks back. The boy leans out of the car.

"They're good people. Gentlemen. I'm going to be a chauffeur."

He opens his arms wide... He embraces his son, who leans out of the car and kisses his father's cheek.

Then he pushes him back into the seat.

"Just look after yourself... There too they can make a man of you... So long as you don't forget the honour of a horseherd..."

He stumbles back to the bar.

"Play up, damn you!" he yells at the gipsy.

He begins to dance. The little lad and the idiot watchman join him. He does not know how this one managed to slip out after him.

And he dances. He dances with a fearful splendour. He slaps the side of his boots.

The grazing herd comes to view. The grazing cattle. The sheep on the pasture. The storks in flight.

He tries to mount his horse. That lad, Pista. He slips off the horse.

At this he begins dancing again.

Beside him there dance an old couple. András Erszény and his wife. The Sullen Horse...

Everyone stands round them watching.

And he begins to dance once more. He threatens the world with his fist. But he is in a very good mood. His face is a mixture of tears and laughter. He is revenging himself on the whole world.

The Sullen Horse dances majestically. The little old woman stumbles. He takes her in his arms and leads her to a bench.

Then the two of them dance by themselves.

Sárkány the herdsman whose life has come to an end today, and the Sullen Horse whose life has come to new birth today.

The Hortobágy laughs as dusk falls.

The Hortobágy laughs with the delight of a thousand, a million years, at the frailty of the human race.

1934

CELESTIAL BIRD

The massed flowers of the lilacs burst through the iron railings. Inside there are cheerful groups of spring trees with their abundant foliage. The warden would like the town almshouses to be like a paradise on earth.

The old folk settle down slowly, sitting about on the wooden seats. The town has rounded up its beggars so as not to shame the living citizens. It gives them a good house, a beautiful garden and food. And the old-aged sit and keep silent, brood over their past lives, and then they keep silent and sit.

A sister who looks like a nun passes through their ranks, the embodiment of providence.

She has a word for each of them, something boringly gentle and indifferently kind.

"Well now, Uncle Illyés, and how are we today?"

The old man looks up at her, startled. His moist eyes begin to blaze from their depths. Passion and stifled anger.

"Why aren't I allowed to go out of here?"

Desire and hatred flash out of him.

"Now, now, not so loud!"

"I'm not a condemned man! I'm not a prisoner!"

All the broken old folk in the courtyard look at him with terror. His plaintive outburst makes them all tremble.

"It's good for you to be here..."

"How dare you say that? I'm locked in like a man sentenced for life... Tell me that I'm in prison..."

He puffs and pants. His lungs whistle like a decrepit accordion. He is shaken by wild passion.

"Why won't you let me out? I want to walk on God's good earth."

"You're tired, old dear. The flower-garden is quite

enough for you. Don't you see? That's life... What would you do outside? Have a good rest and calm down."

"Give me the long open road to the stars. I don't want to get dizzy going round and round in this prison of yours. I want the highroad and the poplars along it, under the open skies."

"You'd only get wet and cold out there. And you'd go begging at every house."

"What's it to do with you if I do get wet and cold? People give me alms."

"Uncle Illyés... You'd die in a ditch. Here you've got a nice clean bed, hot food and comfort and peace for your old age."

"I've not killed anyone, I've not committed murder. I've committed no crime against anyone. You've taken advantage of my old age. You guard me here with police bayonets. Why aren't I allowed to go out of here? I'm rotting away here."

"Stop torturing yourself!"

"Have you shut me up for eternal life? Taken away my freedom? Thrown me in here behind those railings? I don't want to waste away here. I want to live."

"You want to drink, Illyés, old chap. You want some brandy."

"Yes, I want brandy! That's my right as a human being... I want what I like... I want to walk along the road. To rest among the beautiful violets. I want to go walking along the highroad and sing the wanderer's song. Like the birds... But you've caught me and taken away my freedom. You've made a living corpse out of me. Murderers! Hangmen! I don't want life if there's no freedom."

The old folk tremble as they look at him. All their wrinkled, purple hands quiver, their weary eyes blink. The wind of life blows fresh through them all. Chilled, they watch bleakly. They nod and watch. Dreamily they tremble at their ancient comrade who still has a spark of life in him. They are resigned to their fate now. They are human. Now all they need is a meal at midday, a bite in the evening and a quiet bed. The calm of the musty house where there are no cares or woes. Nothing, nothing at all but just being alive.

"I'm a celestial bird... I want to fly. I'm a son of God; open the door!"

He tears his clothes and tortures himself. The blood throbs in his bursting eyes.

"I have an immortal soul. The great wide world is mine... But life has assaulted me and trodden me down... Let the celestial bird go free!"

He stretches out his arms, his withered, star-snatching hands towards Immortality.

From the prison of the human body his cry goes out into the vastness of the Universe.

The prison of Life is narrow. Desire clutches at the bold and incomprehensible Cosmos. What narrow bounds! What an unhappy existence it is here! Out, out of the bonds of the body to the broad meadows of the Universe.

Oh wretched celestial bird that I am on this earth!

1935

DIARY OF THE ELECTION AT SZEGHALOM

8 p.m., 30 March

The whole landscape is covered in snow. Snow and cold. The driver is wearing his fur-lined winter coat. He is a smallholder. He says, "All this, this snow, is because of the mess politics are in."

We stop outside the manse. The Calvinist minister, Zoltán Tildy, who is already well-known in the political world and the national vice-president of the Independent Smallholders' Party, is a candidate. He is an old friend of mine. I have come to see the last open election on the spot.

The lady of the house gives me a warm welcome. "My husband had a word with the lord-lieutenant and told him you were coming. He asked him whether there would be any restrictions on your movements." That astonishes me; I had not even given it a thought. "And what did the lord-lieutenant say?" "That of course there wouldn't be any. He was very amiable and spoke in a gentlemanly way."

The candidate himself is not at home. He is still going the rounds of the constituency. I feel at home in the enormous manse. These large parishes on the Great Plain took good care of their ministers in times gone by.

At eight o'clock precisely the phone rings. The local magistrate is on the line, and the minister's wife answers, astonished. The chief magistrate informs her that tomorrow from morning till evening Zsigmond Móricz may not move outside the door of his lodgings; if he does, he will be compelled to put him under arrest and keep him under guard at the police-station until the election is over.

9 p.m.

Tildy has arrived. He is very downcast at the latest news and adds that in three parishes the stewards who were to supervise his voters at the election were accepted only if they could produce a public notary's attestation of the verification of the signatures of the proposers. He has just been chasing round after this and has succeeded in obtaining the public notary's official stamp. He declares that this provision is something new in the history of elections. He merely knows the kind of things that they usually dream up, but he was not prepared for this. He is undoubtedly an expert; he has already lost two elections, but he has never yet come across this requirement.

10 p.m.

He still has to go over to Vésztő to the party group there. Since for today I am not interned, I ask him to take me with him.

It is a black night in the Sárrét. There is no moon and a cold wind is blowing. On the outskirts of Vésztő we have a breakdown. The bolts on the left back wheel have fallen out and the wheel has come off. If the driver had not slowed down to take the corner, we should have been shot out neatly at 70 kilometres per hour.

We continue on foot into the village which is several kilometres long.

The party group meets in the back room of a small village house. It is full of people who are happy and, flushed with success, they show us some letters. The letters are addressed to various party leaders in the name of the prospective candidate and with his signature. Each letter has been couched in an indignant tone and contains the statement that Tildy withdraws his confidence in them because they have betrayed him. Every letter makes the anger of the candidate seem probable because individual items are mentioned. The signature is an exact forgery of his own.

The Hungarians laugh at it. Nobody has been deceived by it; everyone who has received such a letter has brought it into the party office.

Apart from this they show us a bundle of filthy election ballads in which the candidate's name is well and truly dragged in the mud.

The smallholders are exceptionally intelligent folk with excellent brains. It is a joy to be with them.

After an hour and a half's work they and the driver have managed to repair the car. They arrive to tell us that the accident was the result of a criminal act; someone had removed the nuts to make the car overturn.

7.30 a.m., 31 March

The morning of the election.

I look out of the window. Every moment a car goes past in the street.

The sexton comes and says that the opposition party has twenty-eight cars. He declares proudly that they have not got a single peasant-cart, not even for hire. On the other hand "we" have been offered transport by seventy farmers.

Tildy waits anxiously for his driver who went home for the night to the neighbouring village with the ailing car. He ought to be here by now. It emerges that the car has been taken out of service.

There is exemplary discipline in the street. The electors walk in absolute calm along the long, broad street as far as the eye can see. They are on their way to the school, where the polling-station is situated.

8.30 a.m.

The car has arrived. There was good reason for the delay.

The candidate goes off to Füzesgyarmat, the next village.

We talk to his family. The minister's wife, well-educated and an excellent speaker, tells of the excitements of the past fortnight.

The telephone rings continually. Sometimes it is Budapest on the line, sometimes nearby offices. Everywhere there is exemplary discipline. The smallholders are as calm as they should be.

9 a.m.

The candidate has arrived back again. In Füzesgyarmat the police patrol would not allow him to get out of the car and turned him back.

Phone call to the chief magistrate. The police-captain is very kind and polite, and promises to telephone around immediately to prevent such a thing happening again.

Tildy goes off to Vésztő.

The family is in a state of agitation.

10 a.m.

Party officials come in and have very odd tales to tell. The main tobacconist's in the village has belonged to a retired army captain for fourteen years. One Friday the captain added his signature to Tildy's nomination form; next morning at eight o'clock local treasury representatives turned up and transferred the shop to treasury control. The tobacconist's wife rushed off to the other candidate, who said it would be possible to restore the status quo if he removed his name from Tildy's list and signed up for him. The wife declares in astonishment that her husband was an army officer and would not do this. "Then, madam," said the other candidate, "bring me fifty new signatures and I'll let your husband off the hook." The army officer refused to do this too, so the main tobacconist's is still under treasury control.

The estate bailiffs told the day-labourers on the farms, "Anyone who votes for Tildy need not turn up for work on Monday." In Füzesgyarmat the notary said the same: "Anyone who votes for Tildy will not be given any public work."

There is no end to these stories.

The people go off towards the polling-station in close lines.

A liaison official turns up and announces that the voting is going very slowly. In two hours only fifty people have cast their votes.

Discipline is excellent.

10.30 a.m.

The candidate arrives. He was stopped by the police in Vésztő as well. They would not allow him to enter the village. Nor could he get into Körösladány.

Voting continues to be exceptionally slow.

12 o'clock

Tildy went out to the polling-station. The police warned him to stay in his home. One of the presiding officials sent him a message: "Don't wander about. Stay at home."

Phone to the magistrate and to Budapest. Nothing is any use. From this time onwards the candidate has to stay at home.

We have lunch.

Polling continues to be orderly.

2 p.m.

More and more people turn up and worries increase. They declare that they have arranged the polling so that when the other party has an elector he can cast his vote immediately. The ballot is arranged according to the number of voters for the government candidate. Now they are only taking them five at a time, and one such group may take half an hour while they confirm the identity of "our" supporters.

"A man comes to vote. Our representative says, 'Number 417.' The presiding officer says, 'That's for me to determine,' and reads the entire list of names from 1 to 417."

The government candidate's cars blow their horns continuously and rush about. Nobody goes in them.

In one of them there was an old lady in a head-scarf. She had never been in a car before. She was so overcome that she even put her hands together as in church.

From the window I see a man rushing along, beside himself with rage.

"They've announced the closure-time," he pants, "for three o'clock."

"Never mind. Are the folk all at the assembly-point?"

"Yes, they are. It's terribly cold, but everyone's holding out. The men let the women and the infirm old folk go first."

"Don't let anyone go away. Anyone who is inside the officially designated assembly-point is legally entitled to vote, even if the polling takes till midnight. Nobody's to go home, even to have lunch. Tomorrow they may. The main thing is for the polling to be orderly."

3.10 p.m.

A sudden commotion in the street.

"They've broken up the crowds."

All of a sudden a great black crowd streams along the pavement by the corner of the church. They stand there undecided. The police, with fixed bayonets, stand there and move them on.

"They've sent away six hundred of our voters," announces a man.

The people in the street are reluctant to disperse. They walk. And not even as a group. So that no one can say that they are an 'organized group'. They go in pairs, accompanied by policemen. There is no reason to interfere. They are going for a walk.

Tildy is a broken man. He cannot understand this audacity. The presiding officials said that anyone who was inside the polling station might vote, while the rest were to go away.

"Sitkey suddenly rose from the president's chair a few minutes after three and said, 'That's the end of polling.' He went to the door and locked it with a key. He put the key in his pocket. Outside the door in the two corridors and the two schoolrooms crowds of people were standing about waiting their turn. Sitkey said, 'There are no more voters left. It's only a few children standing there.'"

The candidate is not allowed to go outside the house.

"Keep calm, keep calm! Explain to the folk that they are not to raise their voices, so that the police may have no cause to interfere."

Discipline is perfect.

4 p.m.

People in the street. The stewards arrive. They compiled a list of those present. They have entered a protest against the official record and have refused to sign it.

Men impassioned and despairing. Some of them weep. Almost everyone has tears in his eyes.

Telephone here, there and everywhere.

Phone messages arrive from the other parishes. It is the same story everywhere. At two o'clock they announced the end of voting and at three sent the voters packing.

6 p.m.

Now it is dark. People in the street. Order and calm.

The constituency returning officer is furious. He declares that Muzsnay and Sitkey were responsible for it all.

A delegation of stewards goes to see him. He takes up their complaints, receives the list of names they compiled and only after that signs the official record. The returning officer is a first-rate man.

7 p.m.

The folk from Vésztő arrive. So do those from Körösladány, Füzesgyarmat and Köröstarcsa. Everywhere the same complaints and despair.

They all say,

"It was only the women and old folks who voted in our district."

Another says,

"Those of us who had served at the front and if necessary will serve could not vote. The taxpayers could not vote."

Among the people from Körösladány there are some women; they have brought the flowers they intended to give to their member of parliament.

8 p.m.

The electoral rolls are brought in. They count up the final total of votes cast.

Only sixty per cent of the electorate have been able to exercise right to vote. 5549 of them were unable to vote. Of the known supporters of Tildy, 900 did not vote at Szeghalom, 77 at Vésztő, 200 at Füzesgyarmat, 1000 at Körösladány, 366 at Köröstarcsa, 250 at Bucsatelep—a total of 2793.

The excitement is tremendous. The folk threaten fearful things.

8.15 p.m.

There is a radio announcement. Deep and deathly silence.

The radio announces that at Szeghalom Imre Temesváry obtained 5301 votes, Zoltán Tildy 4553. The elected member for Szeghalom is Imre Temesváry.

Magyarország, *2 April 1935*

CHICKEN

In his desperation that life was so abominable that the grey-haired were being laid off at the factory and sent to the devil while their places were filled by red-cheeked youngsters, father refused to eat the cold potatoes that were for supper on Saturday night and declared they would go to the Blind Cat.

Even mother did not demur. If the final catastrophe had arrived anyway, nothing mattered any longer. They took little Icu with them, because she yelled until they did, and they also took Chicken, the girl who lodged with them, but mother told her in advance that each of them would have to pay for what they ate. This meant that since Chicken—that was what they called her, though her real name was Rózsika—had not earned a penny for the last three months, whatever she ate would be noted down all too fully in the account-book.

Chicken did not mind; it was all the same to her. There was so much in that notebook already against her account that a little more or less made no difference.

And they did have a good dinner. The four of them ate two portions of goulash and with it they drank two litres of wine—except that this went to father alone. By midnight he was half seas over. In his desperation he held forth at length about the tragedy of the grey-haired. He was young, he said, because he had a twelve-year-old daughter. The company at the inn enjoyed his harangue immensely and thought he was quite right.

At midnight Chicken found an admirer, a man who looked like a carter and sent sweets and flowers to the table. Mother put the sweets in her pocket, and as for the flowers, Chicken swept them off the table. In order to free herself from the carter's unwelcome attentions, she took little Icu home, but mother told her to come back and deal with the bill. Mother had never been so exasperated with Chicken; even though she made her call her 'mum' and her husband 'dad,' at the moment she had no maternal feelings in her at all and manifestly demanded that she find someone to pay the bill. How she was to do this and who it was to be she left to her, but her instructions were very ominous indeed.

Closing-time was approaching, and father was so weak that he had to be taken home. Even then mother forbade Chicken to help. Partly so that father should not embrace the young girl on the way, making drunkenness his excuse, and partly because if she were alone she would find it easier to deal with the bill.

So Chicken stayed there, left alone with her sorrows. She thought she would stay there for a little while and then just go home. She sat at the table and Adolf, the long thin waiter, came up and pretending to talk to her poured all the remaining wine into one glass—the women had not drunk theirs—and drank it all up in secret. He had to be careful, because landlords do not like waiters who drink.

Chicken was chilly, tired and sleepy. It was cold in the restaurant and she was wearing a low-cut dress, her only dress, which she herself had made and had cost eight pengős seventy fillérs in all. She had not wanted to wear the old loden coat because mother had worn it threadbare and had sold it to her in that state for a good price—and had noted down the good price in the account-book. The halo of poverty shone wanly above little Chicken's head; a solitary young girl keeping vigil all night as at some funeral. Fortunately the carter had been thrown out by the time she arrived back, because he had become drunk and truculent, so nobody took any notice of her.

At this moment a stranger came into the inn, a young man. The young man was a total stranger; at first glance it was obvious that he did not belong to these surroundings. Customers were still seated at all the tables; they were in the process of paying their bills. The young man looked round and without a word sat at Chicken's table, because there was most room there. Everyone stared at him, and the women envied the girl for having such a nice young man sit by her.

Chicken, however, wanted to get up and go away, because she thought if she was to behave respectably it would be a good thing to make herself scarce. But she was so weary at this late hour of the night that she merely thought of it and continued to sit there.

"Three decis of mulled wine," said the young man and looked across at the girl who was sitting at the other side of the table and was so far away that in this unaccustomed situation he had not even asked her permission when he sat down. He did not want to make her acquaintance. He had not come in search of adventure. He had escaped from the Gellért Hotel because he happened to be fed up with the company there. He wanted to go on the spree, and devil take the world. He thought he would have to be rude if he wanted to stand on his own feet here. But now he looked across at the girl and their glances met. He was taken by surprise. In the girl's eyes he saw that this frequenter of a down-town pub was afraid that he would accost her. Quite simply there was fear in her eyes and in her bearing, and at that he addressed her.

"Will you allow me to have the table cleared?"

Chicken pouted and looked at him. Her glance was not an offended one; it was rather timid and dignified. "What have I to do with you?" said her eyes, "and how dare you take notice of me?"

"Of course, damn your eyes, if that's how you'd like it!" she said.

The lad began to laugh, but only with his eyes. He kept on looking at the girl. "Damn your eyes"—what was this? And who was she?

He beckoned to the waiter who sidled up as fast as he could on his tottering legs. He caught the scent of money, and became as considerate as a diplomat representing his country.

The young man secretly passed him a five-pengő piece, which almost caused Adolf to take fright. He cleared the table rapidly. He stuck his fingers in the wine-glasses, and slipped out but whispered,

"They're mulling it now."

The young man signed to him to go away, then watched the girl with a sullen face.

He would gladly have parted with any amount of money to anyone who would tell him who this petulant little creature was. Why was she sitting here wearing practically nothing at this time of night? What was she waiting for? Anyone at all? Had she landed here from somewhere in the country? Because her tone when she said "Damn your eyes" was so direct and sweet. Had she been tipped out of the nest in some village and was she now trying to find a new one at the beginning of winter?

"Do you come from the country?"

The girl, in a superior tone:

"Whatever makes you think that? I'm from Pest."

So that was that. A girl from Pest. So much the worse. He sensed his fate. The inn began to spin round. Perspiration broke out on his forehead. One should not step outside the magic circle in which fate has set one, like a tree. What would happen if the plane tree were to pull its roots out of the soil and set out to try its luck? Only bad luck could come of it.

He pulled out his watch and looked at it.

The girl watched the movement out of the corner of her eye.

"Fuchs?" she asked.

The boy, shocked:

"What?"

The girl raised her bare arm—what beautiful arms she has!—stretched over and touched the watch with her little unmanicured fingers.

"Fuchs," she said with conviction.

"What do you mean 'fuchs'?"

"Gold. Don't you know Hungarian?"

The young man looked astonished at the watch and then at the girl. This was thieves' slang. In other words she was a moll. Her lovers were thieves, housebreakers, prison-fodder. That's what he had landed. Better watch out. The girl would steal his watch and his wallet. Right then, let her go on and steal them.

But how young she was, perhaps not yet twenty. Some kind of cheap scent came from her direction, as if the wind were carrying the perfume of violets or lilac. That smell too was reminiscent of the village. So much reaches the periphery of the city from the distant woods. From the agrarian world. Cheap perfume is more innocent than the marvellous and exotic distillations of the city centre.

The lanky waiter brought the mulled wine in a small earthenware jug decorated with flowers and with his dropping arm sneaked it on to the table together with a little glass.

"Another glass, please."

"Sure."

The young man's eyes now rested quite impudently on the girl. He filled the glass and put it in front of her.

"May I?... Will you have a glass of mulled wine?"

"I'm not used to that sort of thing... It's got a kick, damn your eyes."

The young man began to laugh quite openly. He began to feel the thrill of excitement. How was it possible for a Pest girl to have such a homely, countrified air? Or was it an air of innocence? And how was it that a gangster's moll did not drink wine?

He pondered. He could not decide what this extraordinary girl was doing here at all. She was like a young nun. What odd things the Pest night produces!

He took out his cigarette packet. A little blue box, blue as a forget-me-not. Till now he had never noticed that the state packs of cigarettes reminded one of forget-me-nots: that was odd.

The room emptied slowly. In the inner room the waiter was already turning out the lights. The light was dimmer, colder.

"Do you smoke?"

"Certainly not! That's all I need!"

Every word commands attention. The tone, the words, the manner—all are unexpected. Primitive, individual, special.

The girl thaws somewhat. She considers it her duty to say something. She cannot be so rude as to repulse his approaches.

"I once smoked a cigarette. Ugh! It made me cough so."

She laughs, but shivers. She puts her two little hands on her two bare arms. A draught comes from somewhere. Slowly she feels her way down her goose-pimpled arms.

"Are you cold?"

The girl gives a smile, but it fades away.

"Just a little," she says quietly. "I didn't bring a coat with me."

And she glances towards the pegs where there are no other coats hanging except her own, the rainsoaked, ragged, worn-out loden. And she quickly glances away, realizing that she has betrayed herself. But the young man's suspicions are not aroused.

"Why didn't you?" he asks sympathetically, to make her speak.

"It's not nice. It's worn out."

The young man smiles. The girl's voice is as gentle and fresh as the tinkling of the lily of the valley. She pleases him more and more. Her naivety too, the way she comes out with the secret of the worn coat.

He suddenly makes up his mind. This is the Blind Cat. The code of manners is different here from that of the Gellért. He moves to the seat in the middle and lays his right hand on the girl's bare arm.

After a few moments he speaks.

"You're frozen."

The girl makes no attempt to move, nor does her voice alter. She says simply,

"It's nice and warm... your hand."

The boy lets his hand rest on the girl's arm.

They sit like that for some minutes. Then the girl says,

"We're sitting here like we're in school."

"Have you been to school?"

"Of course. Whatever do you think?"

"How long for?"

"I did four years in secondary school and three at training-college."

The young man is thunderstruck. Flabbergasted, he takes his hand from the girl's arm.

"You're an educated girl, then? It's terrible."

"What is?"

"That a girl with all that education... has to be sitting here... at one o'clock in the morning."

"You're sitting here too. And you don't have to either."

"And you have to?"

"Do you think I'm here for fun?"

The young man draws back a little. Yes, one accepts that there are things like this and like that; everything is as it is, and what is is natural: that's how things have to be... All the same... If life wrecks something that it planned to be beautiful but let drop from its hands with patrician indifference into the mud—well, one is afraid of it, reluctant and loath to take it into one's hands, it is as if one were admiring it in a window... There's something suspicious about it too. She's a lying bitch. Little bitch. She can't help it, that's her life, that's her armoury.

"And... which training-college did you go to? Nightingale Street?"

The girl gives a laugh.

"Nightingale..." she laughs again. "Nightingale—that's a lark, isn't it?"

The lad knows now that she has never been to college. And yet what a sweet, intelligent little face she has.

"What's your papa?"

"He's dead. I was five when he died."

"What was he?"

The girl says something. Incomprehensible. It sounds as if she said 'forest superintendent'.

"Where's there a forest in Pest?"

"What forest?"

"Where he was superintendent."

"Damn your eyes, he was a police superintendent."

"And your mama?"

"She's dead too. I was twelve when she died. She was a teacher."

The restaurant is completely empty now. There is not a single customer. The waiter stacks the chairs on the tables.

The lad makes up his mind resignedly.

"Where can I go with you?"

"What for?"

"You know better than I do."

So saying he covers the girl with half of his cloak, whose ample folds enwrap her completely. The girl snuggles into it. She longs for warmth. She thinks of nothing else but how good it is to get warm. She observes that the young man is in evening dress.

"Are you a waiter?"

"Can't you see that I've got a white tie?"

"It's not folks' necks that I'm curious about."

"What then?"

"This..." and she taps the starched shirt-front on the left-hand side.

The lad feels a voluptuous thrill, a spiritual thrill. Such a simple girl, and how delicately she gets out of it.

"Aren't you afraid of the police?" he asks the little girl who snuggles against his breast like a shivering little bird.

"Why should I be afraid of the police? They'll not do me any harm."

"Don't say so, you little liar. Impudent little liar. Lying little monkey."

The girl looks up at him.

"What makes you think I lied to you? I've never lied yet... I often tell fibs, but then I blush."

"I didn't see you blushing when you said you'd been to training college."

"Well, where else?"

The lad feels he has been caught again. Yes indeed, where else?

"What did you study there? Pedagogy?"

"Damn your eyes..." and she laughs a little and snuggles deeper into the warmth. "What things you ask."

"All right then. You did go there. What did you study?"

"History."

"Bravo. And what did you learn in history?"

"Joe the first, Joe the second, Maria Theresa, the hatted king. When we learnt that I almost died of laughing. He always went around in a hat and never wanted to wear a crown."

The lad laughs. There is an inexpressible sweetness in this girl from the Blind Cat.

"Who was Joe the first?"

"Maria Theresa's son."

"No, that was Joe the second."

"Yes. Joe the first was his father."

"No, that was Charlie the third."

"Go on with you. There wasn't such a person. He was Charles. Stop talking. You're making fun of me."

"Do you know where you went? To the kindergarten."

"To hell."

"What's that?"

"I can see now you'd like to send me there."

The young man laughs. His heart is warmed through and through. The girl may have gaps in her education, but her voice, her manner, her eyes, her boldness, her mouth...

The girl extricates herself from the cloak.

"I've got to go home now. Mother will say, 'Where's that pig staying out so late?'"

"So you've got a mother?"

"I only call her that. Where I live."

"Is she a relative?"

"Yes."

"Or just an acquaintance?"

"Just an acquaintance."

"Why, don't you usually stay out at night?"

"Only very rarely."

The boy's face falls. This hurts.

"All the same, you do stay out occasionally?"

"Yes, so that mama won't think I don't want to earn some money. Then when I get home she asks me, 'Have you brought some money?' Nobody ever wanted to take me."

The boy does not know what to think. Now he is totally confused. Innocence? A pearl in the mud before swine? Or exceeding great cunning? It's fearful to think what may threaten him. In a choking voice he asks,

"If someone were to take you, would you go with him?"

The little girl says nothing. Then she looks at him. She examines him closely. Her eyes are clouded.

"How many times have you been already?"

"Where?"

'In a hotel with a man, you shameless hussy!"

The girl, her eyes large with astonishment, says,
"I've not been yet."

The lad hugs her warmly. But the devil gets to work.
"Then what do you live on?"

"I'm just getting a job—as a seamstress in the state clothing store."

The lad, grim and brooding, watches his own progress. Choking, but in a dry, soft voice he asks,

"Tell me, are you ill?"

"Ill? Why should I be? And what sort of illness?"

"That sort of ill."

"What's that?"

"Well..."

The girl stares straight ahead. A great many things come into her mind.

"I've heard something of the sort... I'm sure if my life were a very busy one, I might catch that too..." It occurs to her that the driver who made advances to her had a nasty disease, so they said, and she gives a laugh. "Come off it! Don't make me laugh!"

The lad whispers breathlessly,

"Where shall we go now?"

The girl does not stir. She is silent. The lad watches, on tenterhooks.

"Where to?"

"Damn your eyes, I'm off home. And you?"

That's good. It couldn't be better... But true, what about the burglars? She's a moll... Perhaps she daren't go because of her lover...

"Home? To your lover?"

"What sort of lover?"

"How should I know? Some burglar or other."

"Damn your eyes."

And there is such astonishment in those innocent eyes that he has to believe her.

"I live here in Lágymányos. 77 Rodostó Street, second floor, No. 7."

The lad breathes again with relief. Rodostó Street. He has not the slightest idea where it is. In a soft, calm voice he says with conviction,

"Now I'll take you back home, where you live... then some other time... by day... I'll come along and we'll have a look at things. Shall I find you at home?"

The girl says nothing. What is she likely to say?

"I'm always at home. I'm not one who wanders around. Why should I? It only wears out your shoes."

The young man stands up. He waits politely and bows as the girl comes out from behind the table.

"Damn your eyes, mother left this behind too. Look, this belongs to mother, this tattered old loden."

The young man takes it down from the peg and puts it round the girl's shoulders. He could not have handed her the most expensive ermine coat with more devotion and courtesy.

Then they go out into the night. Both of them with bodies afire. In confused fire and numb flames. Both of them think with terror of the unexpected which hurled them together for a moment. How good it would be to carry through the great marvel this instant. But they say nothing. Not even touching each other they walk in silence through the cold, muddy slum of the Pest night. Into the mist, into the unknown.

The Blind Cat, the inn-sign on the white wall, purrs and winks after them.

1936

LODGERS

Between numbers 23 and 77 Rodostó Street the houses have not yet been built. This means that the street itself is so muddy that when the girls come from work in the evening they cannot look anywhere except at their shoes. True, there is no point in looking around. What is there to see in Lágymányos in those plots of land for sale that produce maize and potatoes?

Well Rózsika was not really looking anywhere. She was more inclined to consider that if by some means, by the aid of some divine miracle—for God is good and comes to the aid of orphans—she could pay the back rent she owed, then she would never walk again along Rodostó Street.

At last she arrived home at number 77. She had looked after her shoes quite well and what little mud there was on them she rubbed off on the side of the marble staircase, and walked elegantly up the main stairs to the fifth floor, right by the lift.

Mother opened the door; the warm steamy smell of the kitchen wafted out. She did not return her greeting but turned her back and retreated further into the kitchen, where she continued her dispute with Icu. The twelve-year-old girl withdrew sullenly and Rózsika left them to it and went into the room.

Well, as she goes in, she almost falls headlong. A stranger, a big man is sitting on her little white bed. The room was dark; the only light in it came from the lamp in the yard outside.

Scared, she gazed at the man, who was dirty and thin and a mass of mud. Nor did he greet her but just looked at her, wondering who she was.

"Mama, mama!" she returned to the kitchen, "Whoever's this?"

Mother was silent for a moment, then began to shout.

"It's nothing to do with you! I've rented the bed to a lodger. He's paying one pengő fifty a day. You can go on the sofa; that's where your bed's made up."

For a minute the girl just stood in silence. She could not make up her mind which was more unpleasant, to stay with mama in the kitchen or be in the same room as the lodger.

In the end she decided she was angry with mama, and for the moment merely hated the lodger. So she went back to the unheated room and said,

"Good evening."

"Good evening," growled the man. He did not even give her a look but simply stared in front of him.

Rózsika went over to the sofa and examined it. Yes, they were her bedclothes that were on it. Well, here was a fine thing. She had never liked sleeping on a sofa; it was a rather second-rate business.

She began to take off her outdoor clothes and arrange her belongings as she usually did. The lodger wanted to behave discreetly and went out. Very properly, devil take him!

But she was fearfully angry. What was she to do now? The little child, the baby, was already asleep in its mother's bed. The whole room was just like a lumber-room, nothing but beds made up, and it was cold too. The stove had not yet been brought down from the attic, even though it was November. Now what was she to do? Ask for supper, and have 80 fillérs entered in the account-book? She decided to retaliate by not having supper. She got undressed in a rage, turned her back to the room, lay down and shut her eyes tightly so as to go to sleep immediately.

Yes, but that was easier said than done. She was hungry. Hungry and tearful. It was not enough for them to have worked her to death, now she could go to bed hungry as well.

She was still awake to hear father arrive and a lot of talking outside in the kitchen, but then she really did drop off. Her weary body was glad to be able to stretch out for a while. Oh what a lot of water she had had to carry today! She had been employed in cleaning a new flat. If only she had had enough sense to get something to eat.

She had no idea how long she was asleep; she had hardly slept at all when she woke up because she was very intrigued to know what kept them talking out there for so long. And she was terribly angry with that tramp who had occupied her bed and wanted to know who he was.

She poked her feet out of the coverlet, got up, dressed quickly and went out.

Mother gave her a long look and immediately began to take her belongings off her chair—for she had her own chair in the kitchen; that was where she usually sat and was least in anyone else's way. The lodger was sitting opposite in another chair. She greeted father, who laughed as he looked at her. He had already finished his supper and was picking his teeth.

"Don't you want any supper?"

"No."

Mother looked surprised, became annoyed and once again turned her back.

The strange man, the new lodger, sat there at the other side of the kitchen a good way from her. He was just like a big sheepdog who only needed one claw to deal with a little puss like her. But she was not scared of him; indeed with the utmost audacity she provoked him:

"Who on earth are you?"

Father and mother both looked at her quite scared. What did she intend and how dare she interfere with this lean and lanky stranger?

The man, however, raised his head at the unexpectedly fresh young voice. He looked towards the young girl.

"I work at the Bemberger factory, miss."

But the girl had already seen that this man was not at work anywhere. He was tired and drunk and fairly reeked with the stench of wine.

"Where do you say you're working?" she retorted.

"At the Bemberger factory, and tomorrow I'm getting twenty pengős."

"In the middle of the week?"

The man winced. The young girl saw clearly that he was becoming confused, and father looked on in surprise.

"Yes, miss. It's some back pay, and I'm getting it tomorrow."

"Then where did you get the money to go drinking?"

Father laughed. It was plain that father too found mother's lodger very suspicious. He was pleased that Chicken was putting him through it.

"Oh, my friends paid for that."

"You mean to say you've got friends who actually pay for you? Aren't they colleagues? Aren't you a pickpocket?"

The man glanced up. He looked at the girl whose voice tinkled like a silver spoon in a tumbler. She had some very harsh things to say, but somehow they came out in such a way that you could only laugh at them.

"No."

Mother turned round and spoke sharply to the girl,

"Chicken, Chicken, aren't you ashamed of yourself?"

The girl riposted,

"Certainly not! I know who I'm talking to."

The stranger said surprisingly softly,

"Oh young lady... such a beautiful young lady and she says such ugly things."

"Don't pay me compliments. It's too late for that."

The unshaven man looked at the girl for some time. He said, rather annoyed,

"Look, miss. I'm an educated man. Maybe I was at school longer than you were. I've got a school-leaving certificate."

"You've got a school-leaving certificate? Who was Attila?"

Now father began to laugh loudly. Why, this Chicken is an angry little viper; see how she's taking it out on him! He roared with laughter so much that it sounded as if he were gargling.

But the man waved his hand: he became wrathful and impatient.

"Don't remind me of him. He lived a long while ago."

"An ancestor of yours?"

Father once again begins to roar with laughter, and little Icu in the corner too. But mother turns round again to put the girl in her place.

"Be quiet! Why don't you have some supper?"

"Because I don't want you to bring out that pencil!" Chicken answered back, emboldened by the fact that the giant of a stranger dare not reply to her.

Papa laughs at this too, while mama does not know what to do. The stranger says,

"You're a very beautiful woman, miss. Watch out, because I'm a brute of a man!"

"There you are, you see. At last you've come out with the truth. How dare you occupy my bed? And now admit that you're not working."

Well, the pale giant begins to blush. He turns as red as a lobster.

"Chicken, will you be quiet!" Mother scolds her.

"Of course I shan't be quiet when you've put him in my bed, mother! Surely I've a right to be curious about who's sleeping in my bed?"

"You mean I'm sleeping in your bed, miss?"

"Indeed you are. You should be ashamed of yourself! Even my shoes are different from yours... Well, go away and lie down. Have a good sleep on my nice bed."

"Leave me alone... I'm not going yet, I've got plenty of time."

"Anyone who is going to work at six in the morning needs to sleep! But you're not going to work. Tomorrow morning you'll sleep till nine o'clock, because you haven't got any work; I'm telling you so."

The man said nothing for a long time, and father kept on laughing. Then the man said in a dark, sullen voice,

"See here, miss. I'm down on my luck."

"Do you often play cards?"

The man stamped his foot impatiently, clenched his fists and forced out the words,

"I'm only trying to get a job. I've been everywhere in the country."

"On foot?"

"No... by train."

"Have you got all that money? Where have you left your winter coat? And where did your shoes get so muddy? Maybe you've just come up from Szeged on the express?"

"I've come from the Bemberger factory: that's where I was working."

"Aha, so you were working... With the emphasis on the past... That's just how workers look! Just show me your hands! There you are, there's not a sign of work on them. Well, how are you going to pay mother for the bed?"

Mother was tearing her hair now, and screamed at Chicken,

"Don't confuse him! You can see he isn't feeling well."

"Yes, because he's full of wine. Which inn did you drink in?"

"The Transylvania Tavern."

"Where's that? Is it some thieves' den? Is that where your accomplices are?"

But mother could not restrain herself any longer.

"How dare you insult somebody like that?"

"I'm not insulting him! He's well used to it. Look, mother, it's staring you in the face that he's a tramp."

"You're dreadful."

"Why did you give him my bed, mother?"

The man blazed up. He drew up his big body. He swallowed hard, then again hunched himself up. Then his voice could be heard, dull and flat as the evening bell in the autumn mist,

"Please don't hurt the young lady..."

He pulled out a scruffy cigarette, looked at it for a long time, and then put it back in his pocket. Everyone was scared to look at him; the man was awe-inspiring. Now father had stopped laughing; instead he was gauging which of them was the stronger, in case they came to blows.

The stranger looked round with furiously blazing eyes and in a voice roused to sudden anger shouted,

"The young lady is right in all she says... I'm a man of thirty-two, and I've never managed to do anything in life... So just let the young lady curse me."

"I shan't have much time to curse you, because tomorrow in any case you'll just slip away, because you haven't any money on you except that one pengő you gave mama."

The man hung his head and said nothing. The girl also

felt that she must not keep up the tension for too long. She ended,

"All right, don't let's argue the point any more. Have a good sleep in my nice white bed."

"How beautiful you are, miss! You couldn't insult me. Yet there's no chastisement of God that I don't deserve... How do you know my life and my character so well, miss? That's not all I deserve, but rather that I should be run through with a red-hot pitchfork."

"Don't worry. You'll get all that too, though that's not my affair, but the devil's."

"That's nothing!" and the man broke into a kind of scream. "Hell and the devil, that's nothing... But it is something that such a beautiful little girl can turn such a searchlight on me."

The girl, astonished, said nothing. She looked for a while at the weeping man and then said,

"Don't play the innocent with me. A thirty-two-year-old man? Shame on you! You drink and go on the spree. Haven't you got a mother? Haven't you got a soul?"

The man stood up. He looked round dizzily. Without a word he went into the room. He brought out his hat and his decrepit little bag.

"Madam," he said in a choking voice, the bag in his hand, "you have a very beautiful and very clever little daughter."

"She's no daughter of mine... She's a lodger, like you."

"Lodger? Are you poor too, like me? Well, miss, you've given me a fine dressing-down... But it wasn't very nice, you know, to push a girl out of her bed and let it..." and he looked round with bloodshot eyes.

Chicken was scared now that this wild animal would turn on mother.

"That's nothing to do with you."

The giant looked round sluggishly, giving each of them a long stare, and said,

"Good night."

With that he opened the kitchen door, went out and closed it behind him. He disappeared.

They all stayed there in total bewilderment. The whole affair was as unexpected as if a corner of the ceiling had broken off without warning and the dust had got into their eyes.

Little Icu was the first to recover.

"She's got rid of the lodger."

But the adults were silent. Then father got up and shouted angrily,

"You should be grateful for that. He's a wild, murderous villain. A dyed-in-the-wool tramp. And that's the sort of folk you want! That's the sort you pick for your bed!"

There was silence. Chicken said nothing. She was scared and stared straight ahead, pondering gravely.

"He's down on his luck," she said, and her whole body trembled.

"He's a tramp," shouted papa, and he too was as worked up as if he had had an accident.

"Yes, a tramp down on his luck," said Chicken and burst into tears.

Then she went and sat in her place again.

"Give me some supper, please... Charge the usual to my account... I'm hungry too."

1936

THE DOCTOR

The doctor was on a bicycle, dashing along the main road. The bicycle was nothing special, but the road was quite appalling.

The doctor, however, was not bothered by it; he propelled himself calmly along and thought how this life of his was a peculiar thing. When he settled in the country he thought it was only a temporary state of affairs and he would soon find a place in a town, and then he could get back to Budapest, from which he had been compelled to come out to a village because he had to marry a girl. He had to marry the girl because the girl thought that he was going to marry her. Nor had he any objection to her. The woman was medically fit and had a reassuring spiritual life. Nor did it cause any social problems: she was the daughter of a widow who worked as a clerk and had left the country for Budapest, and he hoped that things would turn out well for her in the village.

Now for the first time it became crystal clear to him that they could not do so. She was very fond of dancing. And in a village there is nowhere to dance. Truth to tell, this desire to dance is a totally innocent thing: she likes rhythmical movement. Yes, but in the village the primitive concept of dancing is still valid; here it is impossible to practise dancing to a gramophone in a room at home, and even less so in a public place. A dance in a village is a very important ritual. How easy it is in Pest; after the theatre or dinner one goes out to a dance-hall, orders coffee, and one's wife dances to her heart's delight and calms her nerves. In a village this requires an organized dance. A ball or a wedding-feast. Or an amateur entertainment. And partners have to be found. It requires planning in advance: who are going to be there, who are the ones she can dance with—and they must be certain to attend—and there has to be a sufficient supply of partners so that no nasty rumours get around that she danced with one too often... Here this counts as organized crime...

The doctor was very much out of sorts as he cycled along the main road, because his wife was getting more and more irritable and depressed.

He had to visit an old peasant who was in bed with a touch of influenza. As he examined the old man he was surprised to observe his irregular pulse. There was some irregularity here in the functioning of the heart, some myocardiac strain.

"Don't you have trouble with your heart?"

"Maybe that's so... A long time ago... From the time when I was first married... My wife put me to a very stiff test at that time."

He asked him a stream of questions.

"I don't know, sir; I never noticed when she was still a girl that my wife was going to become such a great dancer, but after she was married she lived for nothing else. And it nearly killed me too."

"That's no tragedy," said the doctor against his better judgement. "Young women like dancing."

"It's not as simple as that, doctor. A young wife, who loves dancing so much and never invites her husband to dance! That's what I came to realize at the time. I said to her, 'Damn those ankles of yours! If you like dancing so much, I'll whistle to your tune and come dancing with you...' But that's not what she wanted. All the same, she nearly went mad over dancing. She was ready to get up and dance with anyone, anywhere... For heaven's sake, I said, this is no good, why does this woman dance so much? Well, do you know why? She needed to dance. She was full of blood. And desire. She had to have every man in the whole world! For dancing it didn't matter whether he was big or little, thin or fat, a gentleman or a drover, just so long as he danced with her. She didn't want to dance with her husband. Why dance with him when she can have her fill of him without dancing anyway? Dancing, sir, isn't respectable for a wife. It's lust, sir, that's what it is."

"And does your wife still dance now?"

"The wife? She doesn't dance, sir. She hasn't danced for thirty years, since we got married... I won't allow her to dance."

The doctor looked at him in astonishment.

"Then that's what's the matter with your heart... You've had to put up with so much excitement these thirty years that your heart's gone to ruin with it."

"Maybe. But if I'd let her dance, doctor, then my domestic happiness would have gone to ruin. Doctor, marriage is eternal warfare; I've showed her that I've won. So long as I'm alive, my wife isn't going to dance with anyone else... And that's that. Let her be satisfied with me..."

The doctor pondered for a long time on whether he was capable of such a draconian sentence. He thought the old peasant was right, but he merely shook his head; for that a man must be made of sterner stuff. And the woman too, obviously. Not a prescription for modern folk at all.

1937

THE RAM

There were always suitors hanging around the house nowadays, and the little boy watched all this with great suspicion and hostility. Aunt Zsuzsika was a particular enemy. The moment he caught sight of her shuffling along outside the fence, his whole body grew hot and he almost shook with unknown rage. His elder sister Juliska, so it appeared to him, must be in danger; strange men had their eyes on her — he did not know what their intentions were with her, but there was no good in it all. And the general confusion upset him. When they were living such a nice peaceful life here on the isolated farm, father, mother, Juliska and he and the servants. The whole farm is in good shape, when along comes Aunt Zsuzsika and wants to turn their comfortable life upside down. And the most outrageous thing in the whole business is that neither father nor mother will send Aunt Zsuzsika packing, the old witch, and even Juliska just laughs... Why does she laugh? She ducks her head and laughs and giggles at nothing. Doesn't she know what nasty things they want to do to her?

The little boy was playing with Matyi the ram when Aunt Zsuzsika came across the farmyard towards the fence.

"Go for her!" he said to the ram.

But the ram did not understand, and the little boy just stood and watched the old lady with hatred as she came on like a storm in her black merino dress that was fading to green.

By the time she had reached the inner yard, he had recovered himself and ran into the store where his father was ridding the peas of weevils.

"Dad, dad! She's here again!"

His father's big shaggy moustache shook with laughter.

Then he gave his little boy a playful cuff on the head and went out; he saw it was Aunt Zsuzsika approaching.

"She's allowed to come," he said. "She's Mrs Antal Nagy, née Zsuzsika Bodolay. Isn't that so, Zsuzsika?"

Aunt Zsuzsika just blinked at him, then bowed and said,

"There you are, sir; look, I've put on gloves to come." And she smoothed one gloved hand with the other to show that she wasn't going to bring shame on her relatives. She was always careful not to compromise the family. It did not put her out in the least that she was wearing a woman's glove on one hand and a man's on the other.

The little boy just looked at her with all the more hostility as he saw his father laughing heartily at Aunt Zsuzsika.

And she, entering into the spirit of it all, continued to show herself off.

"Just look! I've come in clean clothes too!" And she busied herself with turning up her skirt to show how pure and white her underskirt still was.

"All right, Zsuzsika," said father, whose greying moustache was actually tickling the tip of his nose. Then he called cheerfully to his wife, and Aunt Zsuzsika went into the house, while father went back to the peas.

The little boy went on playing with the ram.

He came across his father's pipe which was lying on the block. He picked it up and knocked it on his palm as his father did. The ram poked its nose into it, and for a joke he offered it the heap of tobacco in his little hand. And the ram ate it all up.

He was very surprised at this and ran in to tell his father. And father said, "And it'll do him good too."

From now on the little boy gave his whole attention to feeding the ram with such delicacies. He just happened to catch Aunt Zsuzsika promising a rich young man called Tassonyi. He also heard her say that if they preferred she would bring along Pista, the son of someone called Andrási, and he had even been on a vine-dresser's course. In the little boy's view, you were able to tell the one they preferred by the way in which all three of them laughed more heartily at him. So he already knew that it was Pista Andrási that Aunt Zsuzsika had in tow when about a week later she turned up again with a great hulk of a lad.

It so happened that he was by the stalls when they came, and they did not notice him loitering there. So he heard Aunt Zsuzsika pull up the lad and explain to him how to behave so as not to show that he was a peasant.

"Rub the dust off your boots," she said to him, "and beat it out of those nice black trousers. Have you still got that fat cigar? It's not broken? Put your gloves on—both hands. Have that nice meerschaum cigar-holder ready, then when we get there spread your legs wide apart when you sit down and light the cigar in the holder so that they can see what a great man you are. After that you can ask the young lady whether she would like to be your wife."

The little boy just listened to all this. He did not say anything, but he would dearly have liked to do something.

"Go for him, go for him!" he said to the ram.

But the ram did not understand him.

The little boy did not go towards the house. He had a vague feeling that they were now giving Juliska away to the rich peasant. He did not know what was disturbing him, but simply galloped around with the ram following him. They were so used to each other's company that the ram would not leave his side for one instant.

They had a good run in the stubble. They chased the guinea-fowl, which descended like iron being beaten on the corn-stooks. The little boy grasped the ram's greasy fleece and shook that instead of the peasant lad with his cigar. Now he surely must be spreading his legs wide apart on the green sofa in the sitting-room, smoking the smelly cigar. He did not even want to go home so long as Pista Andrási was there, but all of a sudden he got tired of running and he was seized by a painful curiosity: was Juliska still alive, or had they chopped her up by now?

Well, that Andrási was still there with them, but they were seeing him to the door, and he heard his father saying in a pleasant, jolly tone to the young man, "We'll see; there's nothing we can say at the moment."

The little boy frowned and looked at the strange lad

with hatred. Now he was pulling his pipe out of the pocket of his tight trousers and knocking it into his hand.

The ram began to take notice at this, then strolled over to the lad's boots and looked up at him, at the hand that was tapping against the pipe. It bleated once or twice too, but the lad did not understand that it was asking for the dottle; he just went on playing with his pipe, tapping it even more against his palm. Then he scattered the tobacco ash and stuck the pipe between his teeth.

At this the ram began to retreat. The little boy could see what it wanted to do and held his breath as he waited to see whether it would do it.

Well, when the big ram was a good distance away, it suddenly got down to business, made a dead set at the lad and butted him with all its might, catching him off guard so that he toppled forward on his nose.

"What the devil's the matter with that ram?" shouted father and went to help the young man as he struggled to his feet.

But the ram would not give up. Once again it retreated and once again made straight for the lad, who was not expecting a second attack and went down on his knees again. Right in front of Juliska, and trying to hide the shame of being tossed by a ram, he said, "Hey, young lady, will you be my wife?"

But Juliska laughed so much she could not answer.

"Whatever does that ram want?" said father, giving it a kick.

"He didn't give him the tobacco, that's why," exulted the little boy.

1937

GEESE

Once again the doctor had not come home to dinner.

The doctor's wife fretted and fumed irritably. She paced up and down and the cold made her shiver for her husband. All alone in that big house. In the end she got a coat and put on a head-scarf and hurried off to the other end of the village, to the notary's. She was certain she would find him there. As she struggled through the sea of mud, the big dogs in the notary's yard almost pulled her over and nobody was willing to come out and help her until she shouted loudly.

"Is the doctor here?"

Nobody seemed to know. The servants grumbled and muttered.

But of course he was there; they were playing cards.

The notary came jovially to meet the doctor's wife and began to embrace her, then poured wine for her.

"No! No! I don't drink wine," said the doctor's wife. She never drank anyway, but certainly she wasn't going to now, when her heart was full of grief.

"Give her some brandy," shouted the jolly notary's wife merrily, and the notary immediately picked up a big flask of brandy.

"Nor brandy either!" protested the doctor's wife, who was hurt only by the fact that her husband went on playing cards as if she were not there and did not bother even to give her a glance.

"But you're not going home from here sober!" joked the notary.

"Maybe so, Mr Notary, but in any case I'm just a *nobody*," she said loudly and with emphasis, "and *I* certainly haven't got the sort of character that lets other people make me tipsy. I know how to take care of myself."

The notary and the notary's wife quietly resumed their seats at the card table and left the doctor's wife to stay there on the dining-room couch and do whatever she pleased.

The game went on with great keenness and there was no talking during it; the doctor's wife saw that her husband's face was growing redder and redder and the big moustache under his big nose was quivering like a banner in the wind. It was the wind of his soul that shook his moustache and that made his nostrils throb. And that was how they went on for all of an hour, two hours. The doctor's wife simply sat there on the couch like a forgotten date in the calendar, but she certainly could not go off to sleep because she was wondering how much her husband was losing to these rogues through their low cunning. As for herself, she just works at home, rears poultry, wrestles with pigs and keeps cows; and what she makes on sales at the market is all brought here to these greedy folk by her husband—ah yes, she had a lot to think about. The horrors of village life. These few families who are dependent on each other and these spiders who tempt in the fly and slowly suck its blood...

By now she was unable to imagine what the time was; she only noticed that her husband was not sitting at the card table in the other room. He had gone out. Well, if he had gone out, he would come back again; it was not good manners to start trying to find out where he had gone immediately. That was obvious.

Yes, but time passed and he still did not return. The others just went on playing, three of them, including the teacher. All of a sudden she grew tired of it all and went in to them.

"Can you tell me, madam, where my husband has got to?"

"He's gone out."

"Yes, but where to? It's a long time since he went out. Where can he be?"

The deceitful creatures were not in the least concerned with him; they simply pretended that it was of no account.

They were playing cards and they buried themselves in their game.

"Well, wherever he's gone, I'm going to find him," said the doctor's wife.

"As you please," and with that they continued their game.

The doctor's wife went in search of her husband. The servants were just as bad as their mistress, and not one of them had any idea of what had become of the doctor.

"I think my husband isn't in the house; he must have gone home," said the doctor's wife, anxiously wondering what could have happened to the poor man. They've cleaned him out and now he's gone away, goodness knows where to.

Of course nobody showed her to the door, nobody stood up; they simply left her to go, if that was what she wanted. The doctor's wife felt she was not one of them. "I can't drink with them, carouse with them, I can't play cards, I only know how to work and that's a disgrace. These folk don't regard me as a lady, they want my husband to abandon me, they want to stir up trouble between me and my husband and then they'll somehow get hold of all the money..."

Thus she muttered to herself all the way home in the deep mud, and the mud fairly spattered in all directions. The further she went, the faster she walked until in the end she was running at the midnight hour.

At last she arrived home. She opened the door and went into the hall. Why, there were her husband's hat and coat on the peg. She went into the bedroom, and there lay her husband in bed, sleeping as if he had been struck dead. All the wine, the drinks, the passion for cards and the weariness of losing could be seen in his face, and he did not stir when his wife got into the bed beside him and tossed and turned, weeping and tormented, until she went off to sleep.

Next morning as usual she got up early because the animals had to be attended to. Of course the doctor could sleep on as long as he liked; there was nothing urgent for him to do. But when she was getting breakfast ready to take in she heard the gander cackle loudly in the yard.

She ran out. There was the bailiff from the council offices rounding up her beautiful big Emden geese with a cane.

"What are you doing here? What are you doing with my geese?"

"Well, the doctor has sold the geese to the notary's wife, and the notary ordered me to drive them there."

"My geese? To the notary's wife? Are you all mad? You're certainly not going to drive them away."

And she began to shout through the window to her husband to come out.

The doctor put on his dressing-gown and came out, his eyes heavy with sleep.

"Have you sold my geese to the notary's wife?"

"Yes."

"My geese? The ones I hatched out and reared from when they were tiny? My beautiful Emden geese that know how to take cabbage-leaves from the kitchen-table, my joy and delight? Haven't you left a single one for me?"

"No."

The doctor's wife felt that her heart would fail. Her soul was full of inexpressible pain. It was dreadful if they were spreading their net wider in the village and killing off its life. The morals of the village are open violence. Here they cut the dog's tail piece by piece and ants devour one morsel by morsel. She was helpless against the village.

She went into the house crying and threw herself down in front of the couch. She knelt there and stopped her ears and wept until the geese had been taken away.

"You're not going to take away my joy in life!" she shouted and leapt up. "I'll show you that you can't rob me of my husband. You may take away my money to the last penny, but not my husband."

She worked on stoically, continuing with her daily tasks.

Two days later there was a great commotion. Apparently the notary's wife had let the geese out and they had flown out of her yard and all come home. There they flapped and cackled happily at their mistress's feet. The doctor's wife knelt down in front of them and fondled their long necks.

"They're not going to make a feast of you!" she shouted. "Swindlers! They're not going to eat that lovely flesh of yours!"

She went into the kitchen, brought out the big knife and slit the necks of the geese in turn.

The geese lay there as neatly as pillows put outside to air.

"Look, here are the geese," she shouted in to her husband. You're going to eat them. But not fattened. You can chew them, but I'll show you that the notary's wife isn't going to stuff them and fatten them for her own stomach's sake or for the market..."

The doctor looked at the slaughter in amazement.

But he said nothing; there was nothing he could say. He turned and went back into his study and went on writing.

But for lunch he was given goose-giblets. He ate them in silence. When he put down his fork he said,

"The notary will have you locked up for this."

"Well, let him, if he wants to! If that's what you all want, just have me put in prison! Do whatever you like with me, it's all over with me anyway, I'm nothing, a nobody, to you."

Then with a sudden flash of enthusiasm she burst out,

"But they'll shut you up with me too, because you've eaten some of it!"

And she suddenly laughed quietly.

"I hope they'll shut us in the same cell... And then you can't go out in the evening to play cards with the lovely notary's wife and you'll learn that your wife isn't some withered old hag either... Because I don't know what you've done with your eyes. I've always been as much of a woman to you as the notary's wife—and perhaps just a little more useful too."

1938

LITTLE ORPHAN ANNIE

The little girl was playing by herself somewhere outside. She was such an odd little girl; she liked to be by herself and could while away the time with anything.

"Annie!"

Her older sister Eszti was standing in the doorway, calling over and over again, "Annie!"

At last the little girl heard her and instead of replying ran towards the house.

"Where the devil have you been? Come straight in. Mother's going to lock you in, because we're going to the cemetery."

The little girl did not understand. Why lock the door on her? After all, she was going to the cemetery too.

There were lots of flowers in the kitchen, autumn flowers with a nice smell. Annie was very fond of their smell and was ready to take a good armful of them to put on the grandparents' grave in the cemetery. She went over to them and tried to put her arms round as big a bunch as she could manage. But her two sisters got hold of her by the arm and dragged her away from the tub in which the flowers were standing.

"No-o!" she said plaintively.

"You're not coming," said Sári.

Sári too, as well as Eszter? Annie just stared. What were they up to?

"I'm coming too."

"You're not!" shouted all the children.

Annie thought they didn't want to take her along because she was too little. But now she saw that Peter, who was much smaller than she was, was being given flowers to take.

"Me too!" she whimpered and began to stamp impatiently.

"You're not coming. I've told you so already," bellowed Sári.

Perhaps Peter was going because he was a boy, but now she noticed that little Zsuzsi, who was only two and a half and even smaller than Peter, was being given flowers to hold in her little hand and she too was dressed up and she too was going.

Now she really did not understand what she was supposed to do. She became angry and slunk behind them with a sullen face, and before anyone had noticed her she slid a single candle out of the basket and hid it behind her back. She was going too, whatever they did, and she was going to light the candle like last year. It was very beautiful out there in the cemetery; nowhere in the world were there so many flowers, and on each grave there was quite a little garden. And the candles burn everywhere and the wind blows their tiny flames. She remembers she was out there for the first time last year, and the enormous delight of it all was stamped indelibly on her memory. Never had she felt so happy in the family as then. At Christmas they usually shut her out when they decorate the Christmas tree, and she has to stand outside the door in the cold. They only let her in later on when they are singing and praying in front of the tree, and by then she hardly has the strength to enjoy it all because she always gets so cold out there, and they never give her any presents, which is difficult to understand, and they say, "You're naughty!"

Mama was not dressed up yet, because mama always has so much to do that you have to wait for her. Mama was going to and fro in her big skirt, bad-temperedly finishing her incomprehensible work.

"It's true, isn't it, mama? Annie isn't coming? Mama, Annie isn't allowed to come with us, is she? Mama, Annie's going to stay at home, isn't she, and she's going to be locked in?"

All the children kept saying things like this and Annie just stood there and did not understand what she was expected to do.

"I *am* coming, so there, even if you burst!" she shouted with all the boldness of a five-year-old.

"You're not, so there! You're not, so there! You're not, so there!"

"Why not? What do you think?"

"Because we're the only ones going."

"Why should you be the only ones to go? Why can't I go, if you are? They're just as much my grandad and grandma as yours!"

At this all the children burst into loud laughter.

"Ha, ha! Do you hear that, mama? They're just as much her grandad and grandma! Ha, ha! Oh, you are a silly! Of course he's not your grandad, it's only our grandad and grandma in that grave!"

The mischievous brothers and sisters pranced and danced and kicked up an increasing row.

Annie was terribly astonished at this untruth. She could not say anything, but just stood there in fearful amazement that her brothers and sisters could dare to take away her very own grandad and grandma.

"I'm not giving them up!" she wailed. "Grandad's mine and grandma's mine too."

At this the children shrieked all the more and laughed and pulled at their mother's skirt.

"Can you hear the lies she's telling, mama? Can you hear? She's lying that our grandad and our grandma are her grandad and grandma too!"

On the ground that she had as much right as the others, Annie now set about mama and whimpered,

"Mama, mama!"

"She's not your mama! Don't call her mama!"

At his Annie was silenced. She had never heard anything so shamelessly impudent. How dare they say that mama was not her mama? She did not know what to do, but just stood there; her nose began to run as she stood there, and her eyes wept and her mouth laughed. Mama not mama, indeed!

"It's true, isn't it, mama! You're not Annie's mama!"

"Stop screaming at me! You'll make me deaf!" shouted mama at the top of her voice, but this time the children refused to be quiet; they kept on pressing her to declare that she was not Annie's mother.

"All right, so I'm not!" she screamed and turned away quickly, as if she were reluctant to look Annie in the face.

At this there was a huge burst of laughter and the children danced round the little girl who stood silent, her mouth drooping in amazement, her security gone.

"Then who is my mama?" she shouted scornfully, recovering herself; now she had won the battle.

"Nobody. You haven't got a mama. And that's that. You've no mama at all; there it is at last. Now you know. You're a nobody. You're not one of us. We just keep you for money, but they pay so little that we're going to kick you out."

Annie felt as though the heavens were being torn asunder and the house was collapsing and this was the end of the world. Dizzy and half-fainting, she heard her say this and tried to catch mama's eye, but she would not look at her.

"Mama?" she whimpered, "Mama!"

"Shut up now, you little beast," shouted mama, whereupon all the children shouted 'Little beast.'

"Mama!" cried little Annie in desperation. "Mama! Help!"

But help was nowhere in sight.

"Then who is my mama?" the five-year-old child agonized.

Now mama broke her silence and spoke in the coarse voice she always used to Annie,

"Your mama? A fine person she must be, devil take her, wherever she is! She's never looked you up once. She's never put her face round the door to see her infant. She's worse than a beast. Someone else has all the trouble of coping with her puppy. For eight pengős a month. All I get is eight pengős, but now that you're five years old, the League will reduce that. You're not going to call me mama for four pengős, that's for certain."

The little girl simply listened to this awful talk and seemed to swoon away to the depths of the world. She stood there with her mouth wide open and kept silent. She was bright enough to understand it and she immediately realized quite clearly what would follow.

"Then who's my papa?"

"Your papa... I'll tell you who your papa is! Whenever you go out into the street, greet every man you meet, because you don't know which of them is your papa. Your papa is the unknown soldier."

The little girl stood there dumb, with streams of tears and phlegm running down her chin. As for the other children, they had at last won their point: this was why they had never liked the stranger. They too had only just found out today, when their mother was so angry, that Annie had no connection with them. If they had known earlier, they would not have kept it secret until now.

Annie said nothing more, but shrank back into the corner from which she looked from time to time with hostility at the rabble; most of the time, however, she kept her thumb in her mouth almost stretching its corners apart.

At last the family was all ready. They went off and mama did indeed lock the door on little orphan Annie.

When she was left to herself in the darkening room she threw herself on the floor and began to sob her heart out.

It was no use. Nobody answered, nobody heard her, and she felt that nobody was ever going to hear her again.

She lay there on the cold floor for a very long time, and even sobbed herself to sleep. When she woke up, it was quite dark.

She stumbled to her feet, shivering with cold and her teeth chattering; her two legs and her whole body trembled.

All the same, she had not forgotten that mama was not her mother, and the children were not her brothers and sisters. She was all alone now and somewhere unknown to her her mother was alive—or dead. Her papa was an unknown soldier and perhaps he was dead as well. At this thought she began to cry again, and began to feel a terrible longing for her parents, her real parents, whether they were alive or dead.

Suddenly a thought came to her.

She looked for the matches and in the end discovered them. Then she looked for the little candle, but no, she could not find that. She must have lost it or one of the children had taken it from her and gone off with it to the proper grave.

She crouched down in the corner by the stove and crept under a chair; there she lit a single match.

She held it until it burnt her finger, and sighed,

"Father!"

Then she lit another match and sighed,

"Mother!"

And she went on and on like this until every match had burnt away. Then she leaned her head against the chair-leg and began to pray,

"Our Father, unknown soldier, thy kingdom come..."

1939

THE BREATH OF SPRING ON THE HORTOBÁGY

One is always making history. As I stroll along the dike, I am wondering how many years it is since I came here when they happened to be building this very dike on the flat puszta. The shepherds smiled at it. They were draining the old marshes, while here they wanted to make a new lake. They surrounded three hundred acres with dikes in order to contain the water.

That was hardly ten years ago, and today it is the most splendid marshland.

In winter they did not even cut the reeds, and the dry leaves of reed, bulrushes and grasses flutter and wither away on the edge of the water on the islands. But that is good. Good for the birds. They will find it all the easier to build their nests and lay their eggs.

Now the great sheet of water opens out. Hundreds of black wild ducks appear. They sit placidly on the water and whatever they are thinking or not they all wail 'yarp, yarp'. Not one puts its head into the water; none of them searches for food or thinks about its stomach. It will soon be dusk: any of them who have not had a good feast from the rich lake by now will never do so. Other things are occupying their minds: 'yarp, yarp!'

There is a smell of spring in the air and the air is wonderfully mild. It is 28 March.

Even humans fill their lungs and breathe again, and this is even more true of the lake and all its inhabitants. On the right in the distance is the endless puszta. Nowhere else in the country today is there such an immense tract of land. Here too there are tiny little round copses on the horizon. The flood of the mirage now lifts them up so that their transparent, fan-like crowns—for after all the buds have not yet burst in them—spread out and wave in the wind as if they were a bunch of flowers put into a glass.

"Arp, arp, shee, shee, vee, vee," the birds scream without a pause, never ceasing. But why do they set up such a wailing? Is the primeval sound the sound of pain? Does the newly-born fledgling already know how to cry? Is this all the knowledge of the ancestors of existence? There is no point in your wailing; I know there is nothing the matter with you, and if there is, it is the agony of the arrival of spring and the approach of happiness, and a voice must be given to all this. There are coots in the reeds, screaming coots, and on the leaves of the reeds there are tiny buntings. How cleverly they hide, but even they do not twitter, but wail, shriek and pipe.

It is a love-factory that screeches here. Perhaps it is not pain at all. As I listen, the mass of wailing rises up into a chorus of victory.

The sound of tens, of hundreds of thousands of birds merges into one, and what a concert that is! Stand there quietly—quietly in order to be able to listen perfectly to the unceasing noise, the roar of the pianissimo, the wail of jubilation, the joyful throb of wailing.

Here is the rice-field. To the right under the dike. The brand-new tiled roof of the waterworks is like a poppy left over from the winter and still surviving.

In Hungary the paddy-field is a marvel. Who produces rice here? We are a wheat-producing people.

The wise and sacred wheat is a Hungarian plant, which is so beautiful when it sends out rich shoots and waves densely to the sky, and even more beautiful when it offers its burden of gold, fluttering golden-yellow in the breeze. Of course it is most beautiful of all in the sack. The face of Mary on each tip of grain. But rice, that is still a new arrival. I wonder what it has to say, particularly here on the Hortobágy where trees are born moss-grown and by the age of ten have grown old on the alkaline soil. They live no longer than a sheepdog. Last night the old ancestral sheepdog died at the inn. Yesterday his tangled, matted coat drooped to the ground and he stood around, wasted away and peaceful, in the middle of the yard like his own statue. He was fifteen years old and the ancestor of fourteen offspring; that is quite enough for him in the service of perpetuating the race of sheepdogs.

I break off the top of a bulrush. It has already disintegrated. Its soft down is ready to travel, so that every silken thread may carry off a seed on the spring breeze. Oh, how many tiny seeds! A hundred thousand of them. Where do they expect to exist? If the hundred thousand bulrushes were all to find room in their hundred thousand seeds in nature's garden, in a few years the globe would be too small for the world of bulrushes. And every year the bed of bulrushes remains the same size! Perhaps it depends for propagation not on seeds but on new growth from stock in the struggle for existence. Then why those millions and myriads of seeds of which—wise nature must know in advance—not even ten come to fruition?

But how white the black earth of the paddy-field is: it appears to have been sprinkled with salt. The saltpetre in the alkaline soil is surfacing in the clods. Now the field is still covered with huge crumbling clods of earth. They would divide it into regular plots. Twenty paces wide and fifty paces long, like ridge-cultivation in horticulture.

Rice demands labour, a great deal of labour and a lot of water... It is an aquatic plant. From birth to death it must be kept under water, but the water must be shallow, not too much and not too little. How will the wheat-cultivating Hungarians learn how to cope with this? Who sow the wheat in autumn and take not a bit of notice of it until harvest—and what an ideal thing that is! Well, rice is much more demanding. The bailiff declares that the weather this season is ideal. There are winds to dry out the soil, and sowing can begin this week... They will let the water on to it, just enough to cover the surface to a depth of two or three centimetres, and then they will sow the seed.

What happiness success brings. Everyone who is concerned with the rice is proud and happy, and does not regret the toil and trouble. Not even the losses; in future things will be better. Here on this alkaline soil 30 quintals of rice are produced per *hold*[1]; in Burma 9. Why should one not be happy that after thousands of years when the Hortobágy went on producing nothing but dreary sheep's fennel, which is no good even for making hay, now it throws up thirty quintals of rice? Even the meadows rejoice at it. The spring breeze whispers anecdotes in my ears.

In the sky flights of verse take wing and sing.
Skeins of wild geese fly past.
In spring the Hortobágy is the world's largest pasture for geese. They fly down from the north pole. They are vagrants in the sky. They come for the hunters of the Hortobágy to fire at them. Those who do not know do not even dream that the arrival of the geese in spring is paradise for the hunters. They are capable of spending half a day in the holes dug for them, come rain, snow or wind, in order to lie in wait for the geese, take them by surprise and shoot them. I am no hunter; it grieves my heart to fire at an animal of the wild—I would sooner it shot at me. But the inn is full of well-heeled would-be hunters in such a spring as this, men who shoot geese in a way that makes each one cost more than if they were to buy Emden geese from the most expensive breeding establishment.

I am left with the song written in the sky.
As they float in the blue and white milky sea and call down from time to time in fresh, ecstatic tones, completely forgetting themselves. The sun shines brightly, the wind blows gently and now they begin to break away in pairs...
Here is the spring, here is love, marriage, the loneliness of creation...
It is the slogans of love that they are writing in the sky, in lapidary style on the velvet of the air.

What is there here in the Hortobágy to provide material for a film?
How long would it take to collect together enough

---

[1] 1 *hold* = 1.42 acres

events on a hundred thousand acres to hold the attention for two hours?

Now obviously is not the time. There is nothing here at all except great expectancy; everyone is waiting for the summer. The animals have not been driven outside yet. In an area seventy kilometres long some hundred folk are living.

Now it is those capitalistic ducks that are alive. Three of them hurl themselves into the air with wails of fright, but they can hardly manage to lift their fat bottoms.

And the water-beetle flies up with a thin, delicate droning like a tiny motor, to fly from one reed-bed to the next... Why does it fly? Why, if not in search of a mate? Is it fastidious? Does it like to choose? Has it not yet found the choice of its heart? The little water-beetle with its long moustache scents the air and God knows how far away— kilometres—it senses the true love born just to be its mate... A man in the train will look back dizzily into the crowd for a young woman with an alto voice; the water-beetle also scents something, something very sweet, very delicate and very overpowering.

And as the sun sinks slowly down and clouds come and go, sometimes casting shadows on the world of the water, sometimes making it gleam like a dish of gold, the tempest of birds continually sounds the alarm. Fortissimo, fortissimo. The music fills the depths of the water. What a concerto! Who could note down the score? Who will create the music of the primeval world? All this is the din of the birds. The amorous flood of little feathered creatures. It is not interrupted by four-legged animals. Four-legged animals are nowhere to be seen. There are only the shots of the hunters and even they fade and scatter in the distance—and false notes are appropriate too in the music of nature. Black-headed gulls by the thousand on the water. Now on a new stretch of water there sparkles the whirling, gambolling calm of white dots. What a whimpering the gulls make as they swarm like mayflies.

Now the rooks are going off to the wood at Ohat for the night. That is where their colony is.

What sensible creatures rooks are, how well brought up!

The sun is still in the sky, and the poplars still gaze up longingly at it, but they set off to sleep. They know already that evening is here and their slow-flying wings have to carry them twenty or twenty-five kilometres to their nests. For them that means an hour's journey. How creditable that they are already on their slow peregrination homewards from the lake! Great black rooks, imperturbable yet united, they are social creatures; with loud cawings they relate to each other the day's events. How tersely they can express themselves, yet one can sense that their pronouncements are weightier than those of the gossiping reed-buntings.

More and more birds appear in the sky. The storks with their necks and legs outstretched lie in the air like steel arrows; their great wings flap black once or twice, then come to rest, then sway and nod once again as if to cast a veiled pointer towards their prey in the lakes.

The herons fly with their necks curled back, the egret twists its long neck into a hoop and the purple heron throws back its crest, and they float dreamily and slowly over the puszta.

The spoonbill is really a kind of stork; it too plies its path through infinity with neck outstretched after the white storks. I wonder whether their morals are alike?

At Cserepes there are two storks' nests in two old trees. One of them contains two females and one male, the other two males and one female on her eggs. In the nest with the two females life is ideal, calm and happy. Where there are two males and one female there is nothing but squabbling. The males chase each other from morning till night and scarcely have time to settle on the nest. And when one comes down, seemingly letting itself drop on a thread, the other dashes from the far distance and assaults it, tearing, beating and attacking it till the blood runs. The idea of a harem gives cause for thought. There are examples, and thousands of them at that, of males keeping a mass of women under lock and key for themselves, but even among storks it must be quite rare for one female to retain two males or a hundred for herself. Even a stork, if it is masculine, takes to the knife, the dagger, the gun for the sake of a woman and steeps its rival in blood... Just go on singing, you songsters; one thing is certain—that the singers are not females... The song is a contest between males, a miracle that creates a tingling desire to conquer a female...

The whole reed-bed murmurs, rustles, clamours, thunders. It is a male chorus in all its clangour.

I have just relapsed into silence to listen to the chorus in the reed-bed, that orchestral fortissimo, when I witness an eternal miracle.

In an instant all the tempest of song is stilled.

In an instant there is utter silence on the lake.

I suddenly thought I had gone deaf and jerked up my head in terror. But the silence, that silence remains.

What is this? Has the conductor signalled it to stop? And have the singers and musicians laid down their scores?

For several minutes I remain silent, waiting expectantly for it to begin again.

In my confusion I look at the time:

It is five minutes past six.

Is my watch fast? I regard six o'clock as closing-time, exactly. I should like to know whether it was the same time yesterday and whether it will be the same tomorrow. Does the reed-bed clock keep exact time? Is it neither fast nor slow? Does the Lord God adjust it?

It is incredible. The orchestral music does not begin again. In one instant a hundred thousand birds have ceased their song. Is it perhaps knocking-off time as well? The end of the day's labours? Are they not allowed to continue their work of hunting and fishing, or does the evening meal happen to be on its way now? The evening session in the coffee-house?

The reed-bed nods its great greyish-brown heads in the gentle breeze; they are the only things left to tell ethereal tales. Have all the millions of birds in the whole wide world grown dumb at this moment? Except that here to the left two drakes engage in some tardy quarrel with singular lack of decorum. Were they not part of the great ensemble, or are they shouting at me to go to the devil and stop disturbing the beautiful, heart-enchanting silence?

Now the owls begin to flap their way over the puszta. Now it is their time. They are miners and carry off into the night their great miner's lamps of eyes.

The grass on the puszta still carpets the endless plain with russet and red-brown shades. Only where there are patches of water does the tip of the blade of grass begin to pierce it through with green.

Little crested birds settle on the tasty morsel and peck at it. From time to time they fly up a little way and then settle down once again. They are not afraid, they do not fly high into the air at the approach of footsteps; they are not scared like the geese who keep inscribing their cuneiform script incomprehensibly high in the skies.

Look, a little skylark! It is like a grey clod of earth and so close that I hardly notice it. One does not observe things that are nearby on the puszta, but becomes a viewer of the distant scene. One looks over and beyond everything because one is straining to see something. The lark rises with a whir and, as if its own whirring set off some gramophone turntable inside it, begins to twitter and does not cease until it has pierced its way into the sky. Then it stays there and totally forgetting all that scared it down below continues to chirp and twitter its song enthusiastically. It sounds as if it has bought a bird-imitating whistle in a shop and is playing it unceasingly. I watch it through a spyglass; it quivers in the western light of the sky as if it were the ray of a star. It is a little black quivering rag, moving neither up nor down; the lens has fixed it beneath a star— but no! Now it begins to descend; what more does it want, I wonder, of the earth? See, down and down it comes, and there is no variation in its twittering song, lower and lower. János Arany? There's a mistake somewhere, infallible poet—was it not you who wrote "It's silent in descent"?[2] My skylark flies right down to the ground and only ceases singing when it is a few inches from the earth. Then it loses its head and hurtles down and alights, making a smooth landing at its destined landing-ground.

---

[2] The reference is to Arany's poem *Télben* (In Winter), v. 6.

Now a second skylark strikes up, then a third, a tenth. Now the puszta suddenly fills with twittering music.

And they make as much of a row as incorrigible children. The cricket does not yet interrupt the song, while the croaking of frogs from the fishponds is still a very faint, gentle and experimental cello-sound in the early spring. Everything belongs to the skylarks. At this hour it is they who occupy the stage. Sound-duels, twittering ambuscades and feints and sallies scream towards the night. And again after night is over, just before dawn. And then in May before the sun raises his head thousands and thousands of skylarks sing in joyful chorus, as if to weave the sky full of pearls.

On the right the flatland stream of the Hortobágy winds its way along. In the course of one kilometre it makes a bend like a duck's intestines. Above the water a peewit wails, but only because a stranger, a human, is around. A rook calls down. What does it call? It is having an easy time of it now; it does not say to everything 'Ca-ake, ca-ake!' Now it is cawing 'pyaa, pyaa, I don't want it...'

The black-headed gulls have already donned their summer plumage; they are wearing black fur hats. In winter their heads are white in the snow. Now they look coquettishly at the declining sun and at me.

There in the west the sun sinks into the mirage, which is now a bluish river of mist, a hand-breadth deep. The bottom half of it is quickly dispersed, the upper half curves itself into a sickle like the moon. But this is horizontal, a glinting, gleaming golden croissant turning to purple and lilac. Who is going to snatch it in its jaws, the earth or the sky?

A gigantic world-event, and it plays itself out so delicately—the sun, light and life have ceased to be.

But we know that it is only for one night, and we are reassured.

While I search for the vanished sun, a black patch of cloud takes its place, as if smoke were rising from an extinguished fire. It is neither smoke nor cloud, but a swarm of starlings. It breaks up, reassembles into a solid mass and scatters again.

How many can there be? A thousand. Many thousands. It is a disorderly mass of starlings that bury the sun.

On the nine-arched bridge a water-beetle falls on to my hand and stays there. Poor thing, it has lost its way; it intended to fall into the water in pursuit of the nocturnal scent it loves so much, but the unfortunate pilot made a poor landing...

The night is alive. The night too is full of life, of spring.

Go, little parachutist, go in pursuit of love... and quietly, so that my feet do not cause a stir, I let it down into the water of the river...

Híd, 21 April 1942

ON THE WILLOW-CLAD BANKS OF THE TISZA, WHERE I WAS A CHILD

My whole life has been exhilarated by the unalloyed joy of being born in a place so beautiful that it must have come out of a fairy tale.

I have always been ashamed to admit to my children that I was unable to ensure that they too had such a perfect, regular and bewitching birtplace. They were born here in Budapest. Budapest is the world's most beautiful city, and it was not a bad district where they were born—there were trees there by the Military Academy, and opposite us was the Botanical Garden; nearby was the People's Park. And however long the excursions we made, we could take them only to even more beautiful places like the Gellért Hill, the Sváb Hill, the Danube and Leányfalu...

But compared with this what a fairyland was Csécse, up there on the bank of the tawny River Tisza, that little village of sixty-two houses! It is so surrounded by orchards and plum trees that when you approach it by cart, the only thing to be seen from a distance is the forest of fruit trees; in the middle of them is the splendid wooden belfry, on the top of which is a spear with a button on it.

That village is truly clean and a veritable kindergarten.

I have never known why the adults stay there when they have grown up—but it is a paradise for children. Perhaps it is in fact for the children's sake that the parents settle there till they die, in that tiny little village with its six hundred acres...

Our house was at the end of the village. My father's family had a house at one end of the village, my mother's at the other. If they opened the gate, from both yards you could see right along the whole village to the church in the middle. And that was no great distance from either end;

you must not imagine they were large house-plots, they were rather small serf-plots, held in tenure. For there has been no new division or commassation of land there. The houses still stand as they did in 1807, when my grandfather's father went there to marry, and Lukács Ferentz Moritz took the noble Miss Mária Pap to be his wife. With her he acquired the plot of land at the Kóród end of the village which to this day is still situated at the other end of the village from that which clergyman Nyilass's daughter, Widow Pallagi (whose husband was also a clergyman) obtained. It was these two poles that intermarried. Destiny appeared to decree that these two broods at each end should bind the village together and bring into existence a family that only waited for me to experience the joys of childhood before it flew away from the little village when I was six to other bleaker, harsher climes, arriving finally in Budapest.

But for me it was an enormous gift from heaven that I was able to spend the first six years of my life in Csécse.

Since then sixty-three years have passed, but even now when the subject turns up I brighten up immediately and become carefree and full of song as a skylark.

My first great memory is of the flood.

I must have been four years old. One spring morning—it can only have been spring, because that is the only time there are floods—well, I remember the water coming into the veranda of the house. I know, I remember, that I stood up on the bottom beam and then I was above the water. The bottom beam is the one that runs along the side of the veranda and carries the wooden posts supporting the eaves. Well, that beam cannot have been thicker than the sort of tree house-builders consider suitable for such light work. Yet when I stood on it I could hug the post with dry feet and look out over the water in the yard and more particularly back there in the garden.

Since then I have always felt just about as high above the roaring waters flooding by. I stand on that beam at Csécse and watch the flood.

My father appeared from somewhere and caught me in his arms.

"There you are, lad; that's the flood!"

Laughing, he threw me up high and caught me again.

"The Tisza's come up."

Well, the Tisza to our village was the special, oriental chief god that had remained here since the age of idol-worship. The Tisza. The Tisza was everything. There it was impossible to talk for half an hour without the Tisza coming into the conversation. It was the Tisza that they loved and feared. It was the Tisza that carried off the miserable little things that existed, and which brought an enormous amount of joy and profit.

Without the Tisza it would have been impossible to live for a single day, because they drank its water. The girls went down to the Tisza with earthenware jugs and brought back the lovely tawny water. "Whosoever drinks of Tisza, his heart longs to return there," says the proverb. And it does too. And then they brought fish from the Tisza. We loved it. We were brought up to believe that fish was the king of foods. It's still true today. Meat I have not eaten for a long time, but fish is not meat. In our house eating fish was not just nourishment, it was a feat of valour. And we learnt to eat it—that tiny tench fried to a turn—so that its bones did not upset us. And every time Father, who later went to live in a fishless, waterless region, came home with a glowing face if he could bring fish or catch it, he always spoke his mind about the quality of it compared with the fish in the Tisza. And he told tales about fishing expeditions up there... So beside my father I experienced the mentality of mankind's first predatory age. Primeval man lived by plundering. He carried off what the earth produced, what the waters gave and everything he could take from his neighbours. At home, in my childhood I was left the impression that I was living amongst the ancestors of fishermen, predators and fowlers. Even today, when in a museum I see a coot's eggs, or wild birds' eggs, my heart misses a beat, as if I had discovered diamonds by the basket-load. Loach, tench, pike, pike-perch: these are all degrees of life's joys. Water-chestnuts, sloes, field pears and rose-hips; cornel cherries, plump plums, crab-apples— these were the poorest and most modest products of woodland and puszta; mushrooms, raspberries and honey—and finest of all, fresh honey in the comb, for which you had to smoke out a whole hive of bees, and even then a stray bee or two stings your tongue... These are the greatest marvels and delights.

And I cannot explain all this or make anyone believe, least of all my own children, what ethereal and celestial delights all these things can bring into being.

Why should they rejoice at such trivialities, when they are used to the shop-windows of Budapest, where all you need is money and all the marvels of nature are there for the having?

But I still shared in the feelings of primeval man. When spring came and violets bloomed on the Tisza embankment, it was an intoxicating and incredible delight; the only greater one was that next to the violets there was sorrel, and you could tear off those lovely smooth, tongue-shaped lengthy leaves, collect them into handfuls, and bite them... Obviously, when there were also sorrel stems bending fat and tasty towards the grass, that was sheer sensual pleasure...

The child of nature is used to unpretentious things that no town child can ever know. To this very day I like things only when they have reached a mature age. When the time has come. Even today I feel it wrong for sucking-pigs to be killed for the New Year. I feel it wrong for a product that has not reached maturity to be regarded as a greater delight than fruit and crops of the best and most respectable kind that have attained their proper age.

It is a tremendous enrichment for a man to make his way upwards in life from poverty to wealth. To go, one might say, right through the stages of cultural development.

I started from the flood. My father sat me in a boat and went out with me over the water and on to the Tisza itself, which in popular belief was bottomless. It certainly was for us, for both my grandfathers died in it. Yet I was happy and proud to be on the surface of this dangerous Tisza, which could do me no harm because Father was with me. This feeling produced a bond of friendship with the water such as only the children of seashore boatmen's families can experience.

Just as through personal friendship with wild fruit I came to know the primeval world of forest and meadow-dwellers, predators of shrubs, trees, nests and animals, so on the Tisza I absorbed the link between fishermen, sailors and people of the water and this most primitive element of nature. For the land is land—that is the positive. But water, all that great mass of water—that is something higher and more dangerous, the incomprehensible negative.

Only after all this came the higher regions: one autumn morning my father took me out of bed. It was dawn; the village rose at dawn, it was at dawn it began to live, and this was the real, the first impression, the first feeling, the first act of will, morning life.

Well, my father took me out behind the house, and there was a big herd there. My father had bought a whole herd of bullocks, and the young animals were bellowing and roaring loudly in the garden, from which everything that could be grabbed had already been dug up. He set me on the back of a bullock and I said "Gee up!"; and as my body made contact with that warm, animal body, a spark seemed to leap between us, and since then I have never been afraid of four-legged animals. All those large-eyed young cattle were so friendly to me, who was no bigger than the head of a cow, yet I sat there above them and lashed at them with a little whip, and they did not harm me; I sensed that a man can be master of greater—much greater—bodies and masses.

Autumn came. Csécse was surrounded by plum-orchards. The orchards were known as "plum-orchards" because plums were in the majority, but there were as many apples there and pears too, though fewer of these—apparently they were not good enough for the market. Oh, the plum-harvest! those downy blue plums can really make a child fall in love. There were so many plums that for a whole week the entire village busied itself with making plum jam. Indeed, for several weeks. People came to help each other. Those were the time of the best and finest stories and singing; and there is the happy memory of the fire alight all night long under the copper. They stirred the plum jam with long-bladed wooden spoons, and in the meantime all the inhabitants of the village went mad with delight and joy.

And there were the other marvels, the subject of so many songs: hemp-retting, swingling, maize-husking, feather-plucking—yes, and the harvest itself. There they still used sickles to reap every stalk, for they were afraid that scythes would flatten the heads and they would be lost in the small fields. Then there was bringing in the harvest: sitting there high up on the good stubbly sheaves of corn, up as high as a tower on the top of the waggon; and threshing, as they did the threshing with real flails, where horses trod the corn in the barns, the sheaves of corn on the threshing-floors...

And I was the happy boy whose father was the first to buy a threshing-machine.

When he already had a mill. Yes, there were mills on the Tisza, where they ground the good smooth red wheat into marvellous white flour, and the only mill in the village belonged to us. And so it was that I felt I was standing somewhere in the midst of life, and all around me, because of me, the process of preparing food for the whole world was proceeding apace...

What a great and splendid feeling this was! It is something I have continued to feel unceasingly throughout a long life.

And in this I rose to the heights. High above those who fetch wild birds' eggs from the reed-thickets. This world slowly shrank into insignificance for me, since even as a child I realized that it was something far greater, far more gigantic, to produce ever more delicious and valuable food in well-laden carts, enormous stacks of wheat and huge thundering machines.

The colour and warmth of those first childish impressions have not diminished, nor has that intimate sympathy with small creeping creatures and berries, but I swelled up into a mighty figure—that is the progression: to be master of the great masses!

And we too. At first I had only one brother, Pista. I cannot remember a time without Pista. Of course, he was scarcely two years younger than I was. This Pista was mine; he was in my power, that was his place, and I could do whatever I wanted with him... Then the younger ones came along, Dezső and Miklós... a veritable little army, and they swarmed everywhere, keeping up a continual noise of crying, singing, whimpering and laughing; they demanded, they quarrelled, and you could take whatever they had from them. I can say that I am glad to have lived so long because I am always conscious of the great happiness that was mine then, and what a sense of power I possessed.

For childhood nurtures all those abilities which complete adult life merely develops and perfects.

This complete and, one might say, geological development can only be given by a small village and in that village such a centrally-situated family as my parents' was.

The most primeval era of Hungarian life is represented by the willow-studded banks of the Tisza.

Even at the time of the arrival of the Hungarians it was settled in the same way as it still is. It escaped the devastations of Turks and Tatars, and the villages have remained on the same sites, at the same distances from each other and with the same relative populations as when the first records were made; in other words things are as they were in settlements a thousand or two thousand years ago, and it is the same race providing seed for future.

I came across a tax-assessment of the early sixteenth century, about the time of the Dózsa rebellion, in which Csécse bore the costs of one and a half plots. At the same period Milota, one of the two neighbouring villages and to the east, paid on six plots and Kóród, the other to the west, on nine. And today the population of Csécse is about 371, Milota 1030 and Kóród 1195. Is that not remarkable? The relative populations have not changed in the course of five hundred years.

And I still shared the traditions of five hundred, a thousand or three thousand years that those folk, my own family, had preserved in this region. But my children were unable to receive these traditions. Budapest is not Csécse.

1942

Printed in Hungary, 1988
Franklin Printing House, Budapest
CO 2690-h-8890